TO Annabelle, WITH Love

Can THIS BE Love TRILOGY

JULIANNE MACLEAN

Prologue

June 19,1892

> *Dear Annabelle,*
> *You did not reply to my previous letter, so I have taken the liberty of writing again to request an appointment with you regarding the painting.*
> *I implore you—please do not let the past dictate your decision in this matter. Come and meet me at the gallery before the exhibition. The painting deserves this recognition.*
>
> *—Magnus Wallis*

ANNABELLE LAWSON TIPPED HER HEAD back against the rough bark of the oak tree on the hill and laid a hand on her stomach. Her heart pounded uncontrollably. She'd always feared this day would come—that after all these years, Magnus would be bold enough to contact her.

She took a deep, slow breath, telling herself that at

least this way she'd been warned that he had returned to London. It would have been excruciating to meet him unexpectedly somewhere. Not that this wasn't excruciating enough on its own.

Meet me at the gallery.

Her stomach began to churn. He wanted to see her. But how could she see *him*? She had not forgiven him for what he'd done all those years ago. He'd ripped her heart to shreds and stomped on it. He'd treated her appallingly. Inexcusably. He was her brother's vengeful enemy and had no heart of his own.

No. She could not see him. It would be too painful and agonizing to revisit all those feelings.

A cool breeze fluttered the letter in her hand, and Annabelle gazed beyond her easel, down the grassy hillside toward her home. Or rather, her brother's home, which she had been struggling to capture on canvas.

She folded the letter and stuffed it into her pocket. Picking up her palette and brush, she took a step forward, but stopped and laid a hand on her stomach again, waiting for the churning sensation to pass.

She had not felt anything quite so intense in years, she realized suddenly. Eight, to be exact, because that was the last time she had dealt with Magnus—the day he left England for America. Permanently.

She had been so very relieved that day. Relieved that he would disappear and never bother her or Whitby again. Whitby had made sure of it. He paid Magnus handsomely to leave, with an allowance forthcoming as long as he remained in America. Magnus knew that if he ever returned, the payments would cease.

But he was here now, wasn't he? Here on English soil, opening old wounds and causing Annabelle to question whether he had ever really been gone. Because the scars he had left were still etched sorely on her heart.

Forcing herself not to let those thoughts distract her further, because she wanted this painting finished, she assessed and appraised her work. It was nearly complete but did not yet convey what she wished it to convey. Determined to get it right, she dipped her small flat bristle brush into the black paint and redefined the outline of the far side of the house. She tried to touch-up the other side as well, then used her painting knife to delineate the lines she'd just added.

Annabelle stepped back again to examine the subtle changes. She'd been working on this for what seemed like forever, and still she wasn't happy with it. It was dull. It evoked no emotion. Anyone could have painted it. Whitby would be just as well off with a photograph.

Letting out a frustrated sigh, she set her palette down upon her paint box and backed up against the tree once again. She continued to stare at the painting. What was wrong with it? What was missing?

The same thing that was missing from all her paintings, she supposed. Originality. Passion. Life. She didn't take chances with them and she was never happy with them. She was her own worst critic, and she would tinker with them forever if she could.

Another breeze blew by, gusting through the leaves overhead. Annabelle spent a few more minutes staring with dissatisfaction at the painting, wondering what she could do to fix it, then at last shook her head and decided to give up. The truth of the matter was—she hadn't the slightest idea how to make it better without taking the chance of spoiling it. Best not to risk it.

Consequently, she cleaned her palette and brushes, set all her supplies into the paint box and closed it.

Perhaps Whitby would think it was fine. He always disagreed with her about her paintings, after all, and fought to convince her they were marvelous, when she invariably thought they were catastrophes.

Lying back on the grass to give the paint time to dry, she laced her fingers together over her stomach—which thankfully had settled somewhat—and crossed her legs at the ankles. She squinted up at the leaves against the bright white sky, listened to the whispery sound they made in the wind, and thought again of the letter in her pocket.

The painting deserves this recognition.

She realized then that she had been so shaken by the thought of seeing Magnus again, she hadn't considered the larger picture. He wanted to show one of her paintings in an exhibition.

No, not just any painting. He wanted to show *The Fisherman*—which she had not seen in thirteen years. She could barely remember what it looked like and wasn't even sure she wanted to see it. She'd always regretted painting it and had wished it did not exist in the world. Many times. over the years, she had wished she could get it back and destroy it.

But *he* seemed to think it was praiseworthy.

Was it possible he was right, and this exhibition could be the key to her future as an artist? And if that were so, could she ignore this opportunity, because of her personal feelings toward Magnus?

Surely, she was stronger than that, wasn't she? She knew the truth about him now, and she was a woman, no longer the naive girl she had been so many years ago when she'd stepped onto the train....

The Train

Chapter 1

June 1879

"*T*HAT SHAWL IS ENTIRELY TOO young for her," Aunt Millicent said as she smoothed her skirts on the train seat. "She's turning seventy-five. The color is far too daring, and it's not even fashionable. Speaking of which, why in the world did you wear that hat? It is the worst thing I have ever seen. It looks like a purple haystack on your head."

As always, Annabelle ignored her aunt's narrow-minded taste in millinery, because she was not giving up the hat. It was satisfyingly unique.

"I suppose it suits our surroundings," Aunt Millicent added with a self-important, haughty tone. She glanced around the second-class carriage, while looking down her nose in repugnance at the merchants and tradesmen.

Annabelle ignored her aunt's snobbery as well, for they'd had no choice about the traveling accommodations. First class was full, and they couldn't possibly wait for another train, for, as it was, they were already late for Aunt Sadie's birthday party.

"The shawl is a very tasteful shade of blue, Auntie," Annabelle replied, trying to distract Millicent from her discontent. "It's like the sky. It will accentuate the vivid color of her eyes."

"Her eyes do not need to be noticed in that way. Not at her age."

Growing frustrated, for she knew Aunt Millicent wouldn't budge about the blue shawl, Annabelle turned her eyes toward the window. They were slowing down. The train was screeching to a halt to pick up passengers at Leicester Station.

Steam spurted and hissed from the engine as a crowd gathered on the platform. Annabelle looked out and smiled at a family—a young couple standing in the shade of the station overhang with their baby in a brand new pram. The woman, wearing a fashionable green plumed hat, raised a gloved hand and waved, and Annabelle waved cheerfully in return.

"Now *that* is a lovely hat," Aunt Millicent said, wagging a finger. "See how it fits in with all the others?"

Continuing to ignore her aunt's harangue and thinking they might be stopped for more than a few minutes, Annabelle reached into her bag for the book she'd packed. She was bent forward, quite distracted by the inconceivable mess inside the bag—why in the world had she put a cigar cutter in there?—when the door to their carriage suddenly swung open, startling her, for she was seated next to it. She jolted upright.

"I do beg your pardon," a man said, stepping inside behind an elderly lady and looking around the full carriage. He gestured to the seats facing Annabelle and Millicent. "These appear to be the last available seats. May I?"

Naturally, Annabelle left it to her chaperone to respond, but even if she had been the one required to reply, she wasn't sure she would have been able to speak, for her heart was racing in her chest and her mouth felt strangely tingly inside. Because the man standing before her, removing his black overcoat right in front of her eyes was, in a word, magnificent.

The elderly lady removed her coat, too, but Annabelle was only aware of the man—tall, broad-shouldered, and dark. His hair was shiny black, his eyes brown. He turned to face her again, and she had to struggle to keep her eyes downcast, though she did glance up briefly to observe the fine lines of his shoulders and back as he assisted the elderly lady by hanging her coat with his on a nearby hook. He was attentive to her, but they did not appear to be traveling together.

Then all at once he turned and glanced down at Annabelle's feet—his eyes lingering there for a moment.

For the first time in her life Annabelle was embarrassed by her boots. They were made for boys, and they were *not* the least bit fashionable, but they were so much more comfortable than ladies' boots, especially when she spent most of her time tramping around the countryside with her easel under her arm.

She quickly drew her feet under her skirts.

When the man finally took the seat facing her, he smiled politely, first at Aunt Millicent, who looked down her long, aristocratic nose suspiciously at him, then at Annabelle, who managed to smile casually in return.

She hoped she wasn't blushing. That would be mortifying.

Determined not to stare, she raised her book, opened it, and pretended to read. Yes, pretended, because she could hardly concentrate with such a handsome man sitting not three feet away from her, facing her squarely.

Trains could be decidedly awkward sometimes.

The train blew its whistle and they lurched forward, rocking back and forth as the locomotive began to slowly move away from the station. Annabelle looked out the window at the young family again and watched them through the spiraling coal dust until they disappeared from view.

Soon they were under way, the wheels clacking fast beneath them as they gained speed on the tracks.

Feeling the chugging sensation beneath the soles of her boots, Annabelle peered over the top of her book to steal another glance at the gentleman across from her. He gazed absently out the window, so she recalled her artist's mantra—*there is no substitute for close observation*—and studied his face meticulously.

It was pure perfection—a straight nose, a strong chiseled jaw, and high cheekbones. Yet, accompanying all those sharp, manly angles was a set of full, moist lips that looked quite agreeably soft. What she wouldn't give to paint him.

It was an odd thought, because she never painted people. She only did landscapes, preferably rugged ones, which was perhaps where this marked fascination with this man came from. He, too, was rugged, like the jagged English coastlines that captured her imagination more than any other place or thing.

She loved the sound of the sea, surging and crashing up against the rocks, and she loved to try to capture the unfathomable depths and distances that were an intrinsic part of the ocean and coastline.

She couldn't explain it, but strangely, this man made her body feel the same way. He made her blood quicken, made her mind tick like a clock wound tight. Just looking at him made her feel happy to be alive when there were so many beautiful, wondrous things to comprehend.

Though of course he was not a thing. He was a man.

Just then, he gazed directly at her, and she froze, caught in the embarrassing circumstance of ogling. She almost panicked and lifted her book to cover her face, but that would have been childish, and she was not a child. She was twenty-one.

Instead, she smiled politely and lowered her book to her lap, lowering her gaze along with it. It was at that instant she noticed she had been reading the same page for the past ten minutes.

"Are we all traveling to Edinburgh?" the elderly lady asked, causing Annabelle to look up again. The wrinkles on the lady's face were in happy places, at the outside of her eyes, suggesting a lifetime spent smiling.

The handsome gentleman replied, "I'm going past Edinburgh and on to Perth."

The lady leaned closer, raising a hand to her ear.

"Where?"

"Perth!"

The lady stared for a few seconds, as if trying to decipher what she'd heard, then nodded. "Oh, yes, yes! I once had an uncle in Perth."

The gentleman looked curiously at Annabelle and her aunt, waiting for them to respond to the question as well, but Aunt Millicent turned her face away, no doubt finding the exchange intrusive.

The elderly woman turned to the gentleman beside her and began a conversation about whom she was going to visit in Edinburgh—her daughter and children—and how long she would be there, but it was a rather awkward conversation, as the woman was almost completely deaf and had to hold her hand up to her ear every time the man spoke.

The two of them were shouting by the end of it, and when they finally stopped talking, Annabelle glanced up and found herself sharing an amused grin with the handsome man.

It was not a grin at the expense of the elderly lady; they were not making fun of her. On the contrary, Annabelle recognized a look of compassion in the gentleman's dark eyes. He, like she, was able to see the humor in life sometimes. *What a dear lady,* they both seemed to be saying to each other.

Afterward, Annabelle returned her attention to her book but the printed words on the page held little allure. For one thing, she was still on the same page as before, and for another, her dancing thoughts were making it difficult to make sense of the story in her brain.

This was going to be a very long trip indeed, she thought as she crossed her legs at the ankles and struggled not to look up again.

To be honest, she was afraid to, because—good heavens—she could sense that the intriguing man was now ogling *her*.

About an hour into the journey the train chugged along at full speed across the rolling English countryside, the sun was beaming in through the windows, and Aunt Millicent's head was beginning to nod.

Millicent resisted sleep as best she could, jerking her head up every time it fell forward, but it wasn't long before her eyes dropped closed and her mouth fell open. She tipped her head back on the upholstered seat and began to snore.

Annabelle had just become absorbed in her book again when she was interrupted by an unexpected question. "Suspenseful?" the man across from her asked.

She lifted her gaze. "I beg your pardon?"

He pointed at her book.

Glancing at the elderly lady, who didn't seem to be aware of their conversation, Annabelle paused uncertainly for a moment before replying. The man was a stranger, after all.

"Apologies," he said after a few seconds, apparently realizing that he'd made her uncomfortable. He went back to his own book.

Annabelle immediately regretted her hesitation. She hadn't meant to be rude. "No apologies necessary." The man's gaze met hers again, making her feel strangely giddy. "It's been very suspenseful. Have you read it?" She showed him the cover.

"I cannot say that I have. May I?"

Annabelle passed the book to him and he flipped through it—using his finger to keep her page—then handed it back. "I must pick that one up. I like a good mystery."

He certainly was exquisite to look at, she thought. A famous sculptor couldn't have created anything more beautiful. She'd never seen such magnetic eyes before. How old was he? Late twenties perhaps?

Annabelle glanced down at his hand and noted he wore no wedding ring. A deep feminine element of her being rejoiced. She noted also that his hands were large and rough-looking. He was no idle gentleman, that was certain, and the idea of his male strength and ruggedness thrilled her beyond all.

"Are you on your way somewhere, or returning home?" he asked, his voice deep, yet soft at the same time.

"We are going to my great aunt's seventy-fifth birthday party," Annabelle replied. "She lives near Newcastle. And you?"

"Business." His eyes roamed over her face from the top of her head down to her chin, and it felt like a sensuous caress.

She couldn't deny she secretly enjoyed it, which felt rather wicked and exciting.

A short time later, Aunt Millicent was snoring like a dairy farmer, and Annabelle had relaxed significantly regarding her conversation with the man seated across from her, even though she didn't know him at all and they had not been properly introduced and he was very handsome and she was.... Well...she was young and unmarried and painfully aware of his attractiveness.

"What kind of business are you in?" she boldly asked.

"I'm a clerk in a bank."

"You live in London, I presume?"

Another bold question. Annabelle glanced prudently at her aunt. Still dead to the world, thank heavens.

"Yes. My mother currently resides with me, and it's just the two of us. My father passed away a number of years ago."

"That is very good of you to care for your mother. She is a lucky woman, to have you for a son."

"As is your mother, to have such a lovely daughter." He glanced at Aunt Millicent, whose mouth still hung open. She twitched and slapped herself on the cheek.

Annabelle grinned. "She's my aunt, actually."

"Ah."

"I never knew my mother," Annabelle blurted out, realizing too late that such a personal admission was even bolder than her earlier questions. She didn't even know this man's name. Yet something made her continue. Perhaps it was the transitory nature of the circumstances. She would probably never see him again after today.

"I'm sorry to hear that," he said.

"She died when I was not quite a year old," Annabelle continued, "and my father passed away a year later. So, I was adopted and raised by my mother's closest friend, who had married the Earl of Whitby. They'd known each other since childhood."

He remained silent but inclined his head.

"My adoptive parents are gone now," Annabelle continued, "but I still have my older brother—*adoptive* brother, that is—to care for me, and of course, Aunt Millicent, who has been living with us since I debuted in society."

"You were raised by the *Earl* of Whitby?" the man asked.

"Yes."

He stared at her for a long moment, appearing utterly staggered. Then his voice softened with an odd hint of resignation. "Well. It seems I am in esteemed company this morning."

He was looking at her differently. The fire in his eyes had gone out.

Perhaps he thought she did not wish to speak to him because she had been raised in an aristocratic household while he was a bank clerk. She wanted more than anything to assure him that was not the case.

"I am hardly that," she explained. "My parents were simple country people."

"It matters little what your parents were. I can see you are a charming, intelligent woman all on your own."

Annabelle's cheeks felt hot all of a sudden.

"I've embarrassed you," he said, with an almost melancholy tone. "Please forgive me. My only excuse is that I couldn't help myself. I was bewitched by your friendly, open manner."

She raised an eyebrow. "Who's being charming now?"

He quietly laughed and Annabelle laughed, too.

A moment later she leaned back against the seat and eyed him lightheartedly. "So, tell me, sir, what do you do when you're not banking? I see you like to read."

For a brief moment he looked as if he weren't sure he should continue conversing with her, then he seemed to let go of his reservations and laid his hand on top of the closed book. "Reading is an enjoyable pastime, but what I really like to do is fish."

"Fish?"

"Yes. Nothing can compare to the experience of rowing a boat across a calm lake at dawn, when the air is crisp and your nose is chilled, and vapor rises from the water. Then you cast your line and hear the sound of it slicing through the air, and the hook hits the water with a quiet splash. Everything is so peaceful in the mornings, and the sky has a certain glow."

Annabelle imagined what he had described. She could see herself sitting in his boat. It was a lovely thought.

"You make it sound wonderful," she said. "I've never been fishing before."

"No?" His eyes were warm and his smile calm, almost soothing. "Perhaps one day someone will take you."

Annabelle recognized the romance in his voice. He was telling her in no uncertain terms that he wished *he* could be the one to take her.

An unfamiliar longing coursed through her as she

imagined seeing this man again in such a private setting, being alone with him in a rowboat, sharing such a moment. There was something about him, something that stirred her blood and excited her in a way she hadn't experienced before. It was the way he looked at her—as if he found her the most beautiful creature in the world.

"I would like that," she replied breathlessly.

His eyes traveled from her face down the front of her bodice to her knees, then back up again before he slowly leaned forward. "Please allow me this impropriety," he whispered, glancing briefly at Aunt Millicent, who was still snoring. "But may I ask your name?"

Annabelle experienced a surge of both apprehension and excitement. The whole tone of their exchange was highly improper. She would never be speaking to him this way if Aunt Millicent were awake, or if the elderly lady beside him could hear what they were saying. Thankfully, she had barely looked up from her lap.

Annabelle shifted nervously in her seat, then whispered in return, "It's Annabelle. Annabelle Lawson."

He continued to stare at her face, almost entranced, as if he didn't know what to make of her or what to say next.

"And what is your name, sir, if I may be so bold?" The fact that she had also whispered the question gave the whole conversation an air of secrecy and subterfuge. It was without a doubt the single most exciting conversation of her life.

He leaned forward even more. "John Edwards."

A long, lingering, and delightfully sensuous gaze passed between them. Their faces were scandalously close.

"Tell me, Miss Lawson, what do *you* like to do when you're not talking to strangers on trains?"

Annabelle smirked at him. "I paint."

"Do you indeed? You're an artist. I should have guessed."

"How would you guess such a thing?"

"Don't all artists have deeply tortured souls?"

Annabelle laughed out loud, and Aunt Millicent stirred beside her. Both Annabelle and Mr. Edwards quickly sat back as Millicent opened her eyes, stared dazedly up at the ceiling, then closed them again and drifted back to sleep.

Mr. Edwards swiped a hand over his brow, as if to say, *That was close.*

Annabelle shook her head with mock disapproval, then leaned forward again. Mr. Edwards did the same.

"Let me assure you," she said, "I am not tortured."

"Are you certain?" he asked with a teasing glint in his eyes. "You don't feel wretchedly miserable or trapped? As if the life you are supposed to lead is beyond your reach and nothing has meaning?"

He was toying with her, of course, but she could not deny her astonishment that he had hit the mark exactly, because yes, sometimes she did feel trapped. Especially when her aunt dressed her up like all the other London girls and paraded her around at balls— because she was not like other girls.

She hated the Season, she had no interest in fancy gowns and heeled shoes, she had a strange fascination with Egyptian mummies, and she had a ferret for a pet.

To be honest, there were times when she was truly screaming inside her head, trying to fit into this polished, aristocratic world, and not be a disappointment to her family, who had taken her in and loved her like one of their own. She felt she owed so much to them.

But she could not possibly express such an unconventional sentiment to Mr. Edwards.

"I paint landscapes," she told him. "And I would describe my experience of painting in the same way you describe fishing. Nothing compares to the bliss of standing before a view of an autumn forest, setting up my easel and contemplating the first brushstroke. Though my favorite thing to paint is the coastline. Unfortunately, we don't live on the coast—though I wish desperately that we did—so I must content myself with the countryside most of the time."

He pointed a finger at her. "See? You are tortured after all. Frustrated by the geography of your existence."

"Yes, I suppose so. You win."

He watched her look out the window, and she could feel a glimmer of attraction in his gaze

Oh, how he flattered her, just by the way he looked at her. She didn't think she'd ever felt so beautiful before.

"I wish you could paint me fishing," he said. "I would hang the painting over my mantel, and every time I looked at it, I would feel content."

Content because it would make him think of fishing? Or because it would make him think of *her*? She supposed she would never know the answer to that question.

"I'd enjoy painting you," she said openly. "I've never painted a fisherman before."

"Perhaps one day we'll make it happen. We'll take your paints and a blank canvas out to my favorite fishing hole."

Annabelle gazed out the window, feeling dreamy. "Wouldn't that be splendid," she replied as she imagined such a wonderful day.

It wasn't long, however, before reality settled in and she had to accept that it would never happen. He was not the kind of man her aunt would approve of. He was a stranger on a train, and he worked as a bank clerk.

As she watched the trees fly by outside the window—so fast she could barely focus on them—she was distressed by the extent of her disappointment. She was not free to do as she wished, for she was a London *debutante*.

Oh, how she hated that word. If only her life were just a little different. She could only imagine all the things she would do.

Thinking such a thing made her feel guilty, however, for she had been blessed with so many privileges. She was grateful for her life. Truly she was. She had no right to feel frustrated.

Chapter 2

$\mathcal{M}$AGNUS WALLIS SAT ACROSS FROM Miss Annabelle Lawson on the fast steam train to Perth
and cursed the cards he had been dealt all his life—
today in particular.

He had not asked to meet her. If he had known
who she was, he most definitely would have waited
for the next train. But *bloody hell,* he had not known,
and he had been attracted to her the very first instant
he'd noticed her—with her lovely dark hair and that
eccentric purple hat.

He'd known immediately that she was one of a
kind, perhaps a bit of a rebel. Not just because of her
unconventional attire—not to mention those intriguing black boots—but because her eyes were so full of
life, as wild and green as the irrepressible sea.

And now he was in very deep, completely over his
head as a matter of fact. He was sitting forward, listening to her describe her art with passion and hunger,
gesturing with her hands as she spoke, her luscious
smile dazzling and intoxicating. All this, after he'd

lied to her and given her a false name.

Magnus shuddered inwardly. He shouldn't have done it. He'd known it was wrong, even as he was speaking the words, but he just couldn't stomach the possibility that she would recoil in horror, which she surely would if she knew who he was.

Her aunt would probably go into convulsions, for he was Magnus Wallis, Whitby's undesirable cousin, whom they all blamed for Whitby's brother's death. They thought he was a monster like his father, and all his life he'd been feared and loathed and shut out by the very people who had given Miss Lawson a home.

Lovely Miss Lawson....

All at once he found himself glancing down for a brief, appreciative moment at her extravagant bosom, which heaved enticingly as she took a deep breath to continue talking. He thought of their earlier conversation about going fishing together and imagined teaching her how to bait the hook and cast the line, then imagined her standing in front of her easel, dabbing paint on a fresh canvas.

In that moment, he wanted nothing more than to disembark from this train at the next stop and lead her out by the hand. To pretend they were two very different people. To continue talking like this—openly and passionately.

But no.... That could never be, because she was a member of that family. She had been raised within their walls, while he had been tossed over them, and she was under Whitby's protection. Magnus knew she was untouchable, as far as he was concerned. He should not even be speaking to her. Nothing could come of it but frustration.

Yet he was still drinking in her every word, wasn't he? Still eyeing her full, sumptuous mouth and stealing glances at her lavish breasts, which continued to rise and fall with her enchanting enthusiasm. She was a delicious young beauty, to be sure, and heaven help him, he was a hot-blooded man.

He was indeed in way over his head.

When Aunt Millicent woke, Annabelle checked her timepiece to discover it was closing in on noon. The elderly lady beside Mr. Edwards had fallen asleep some time ago, so he and Annabelle had been free to chat for over an hour about everything imaginable—art, politics, books, the theatre, the pleasures and trappings of society, trains and coaches, the view outside the window.

They shared many interests, and when they did not agree on something, they respected each other's opinion and expressed a general feeling of enlightenment at having never considered such a viewpoint before.

Overall, Annabelle found Mr. Edwards to be the most fascinating and intriguing man she had ever met, and she could quite decisively say that she was enraptured. She felt as if she had found the perfect companion for the journey—someone she could converse with about anything, even subject matters her aunt considered inappropriate for *genteel* conversation.

Perhaps this strange freedom she felt stemmed from the fact that Mr. Edwards lived outside her world. He was not bound by the same constraints as she. He was different. He made her feel alive and alert, and more consciously aware of the physicality of her being. Her heart raced with excitement over a certain word he spoke or a particular way he moved. She felt her skin tingling with arousal. She could hear her heart pound in her ears.

And she did not want this train ride to end.

So, it was with great disappointment that Annabelle watched her aunt awaken from her nap. Aunt Millicent smacked her lips a few times and gave a sleepy little whimper.

Without uttering a word, Mr. Edwards stopped talking, calmly reached for his book and opened it on his lap before Millicent had even realized she was awake.

"What is the time?" she asked.

"It's almost noon," Annabelle replied, trying not to reveal her disappointment.

Mr. Edwards did not even glance up. He behaved as if he hadn't heard the question.

Aunt Millicent nevertheless eyed him suspiciously when she noticed the other lady asleep. She glanced at him and Annabelle, looking concerned.

Perhaps her aunt did not want to admit she had been negligent regarding her duty, or perhaps she believed that Annabelle and Mr. Edwards had both been sitting in silence, reading the entire time.

Whatever she thought, thankfully, she asked no questions.

After the train made a brief stop in Sheffield, where everyone got off for lunch, they were soon chugging noisily down the tracks again. Aunt Millicent's knitting needles stabbed with impressive vigor, making it necessary for Annabelle and Mr. Edwards to ignore each other.

Having already lost interest in her book, Annabelle rested her forehead against the cool glass, gazing dreamily at the white sheep dotting the green countryside. The train rocked back and forth, smoothly at times, jerkily at others, and she might have fallen asleep herself if the elderly lady next to Mr. Edwards had not spoken up.

"What a lovely lunch," she said as she shifted in her seat. "Did you enjoy your meal as well?" she asked Aunt Millicent.

"Very much, thank you!" Millicent shouted in reply, nodding in an exaggerated fashion.

Mr. Edwards grinned at Annabelle, his heated gaze raking boldly downward. Her heart jolting with a wicked thrill that settled in the pit of her belly, Annabelle glanced quickly at her aunt, certain that if her conservative chaperone had seen the decadent spark in Mr. Edwards' eyes just now, she would pick up the elderly lady's cane and knock him over the head with it.

But Aunt Millicent was not looking at Mr. Edwards. She was absorbed in her knitting. Meanwhile, he appeared amused by the whole situation—the two of them sitting across from each other with a clear attraction neither of them could pretend didn't exist, yet unable to converse the way they would have liked. And they both knew Aunt Millicent was not about to encourage an introduction that could, heaven forbid, lead to an unwanted acquaintance.

Hence, the next two hours passed in almost complete silence, except for once or twice when the elderly lady asked a question, and everyone looked up from their books or knitting to contribute.

The train made a few stops along the way, and everyone got off to stretch their legs.

Late in the afternoon, Aunt Millicent's head began to nod again, and she went out like a wet candle.

Annabelle glanced across at the other lady, who had also fallen asleep. Then she found herself smiling eagerly at Mr. Edwards, who had just set his book down. He rested his elbows on his knees, clasping his large hands together in front of him.

With bated breath, Annabelle waited for him to say something, but he took his time before he raised a finger and gestured for her to come closer.

Annabelle leaned forward. She and Mr. Edwards swayed from side to side with the rocking of the train, their faces only inches apart. His eyes roamed from the top of her head to her nose and lips.

She studied his face, too—his strong cheekbones, the shadow of stubble along his jaw and chin, and the depths of his dark eyes. She gazed at him with more than an artist's appreciation for male beauty. She was just a woman now, and he was so impossibly handsome, it hurt just to look at him....

At last he spoke, in a low, husky voice, almost a whisper. Just the sound of it made Annabelle's skin tingle deliciously with gooseflesh.

"How daring are you?" he asked.

Annabelle swallowed, shocked by the spell he'd cast over her—there was no other word for it—and she couldn't believe her own blatant disregard for the concept of consequences. She felt as if she would blindly follow this man to the door and jump off the train into a slimy green swamp if he suggested it. If it meant she could be alone with him for just five minutes.

That scared her a little.

"What do you have in mind?" she asked nevertheless, curious, while at the same time struggling to hold tight to her common sense, murky as it was at present.

He hesitated before he began to explain in a quiet voice. "Miss Lawson, all day I've been dreading the moment when you will get off this train."

"So have I," she blurted out, before she had a chance to think rationally.

While the two ladies snored beside them, Mr. Edwards reached for Annabelle's gloved hand, turned it over, then slid his fingers up to the sensitive inside of her bare wrist. With the tip of his finger, he drew tiny feathery circles over the delicate blue veins....

Annabelle's body went weak from his touch. She had never been so quickly enamored with a man before, nor had she ever experienced the true, aching cadence of lust. She had not understood its power.

"I can't let you go," he whispered, "knowing I will never see you again. Meet me somewhere. Anywhere. Could you do that?"

Annabelle panicked as she considered it. What he was suggesting was beyond improper, yet she wanted it with urgent desperation.

"Do you mean alone? I'm not sure that would be...." She didn't know what to say next.

He hesitated, then bowed his head and shook it. "I'm sorry, Miss Lawson. I am tactless. Of course it is not possible to meet alone, and you should throw me off the train for even thinking such a thing." He looked up, his eyes apologetic. "Forgive me. Is there another way?"

Staring into his dark, passionate eyes, she found herself leaning suddenly toward caution. Attractive though he was, he was still a stranger, and she would be wise to be wary of believing in his integrity. Was he testing how far he could go with her? And when he'd sensed her reluctance—as a well-bred young lady—was that the only reason he retreated, and was behaving slightly more respectably?

Perhaps he made a habit of taking advantage of young women he met on trains. Perhaps he only wanted to steal her overstuffed reticule.

Aunt Millicent twitched and snorted.

Annabelle immediately pulled her hand from Mr. Edwards' grasp, as anxiety cooled her thoughts. She was being rushed to make a decision. Her aunt could awaken at any moment....

Which was why she answered so quickly, whispering, "Perhaps somewhere we could be properly introduced."

Though she didn't know why she should even bother with such a formality. Even if this man's intentions were honorable, her aunt would never encourage such a match. She was very ambitious. Aunt Millicent knew Annabelle would have a substantial dowry, thanks to her generous brother, Whitby, and so she searched among the aristocracy for a husband for

Annabelle. Even though Annabelle was not truly one of them.

"Where?" Mr. Edwards asked, staring intently at her. "A shop perhaps. But no, what would be the point? We'd only say hello and good-bye again."

Annabelle experienced a sudden flash of fear. Indeed, what *would* be the point in seeing him again, unless she intended to defy her family and run away with him and live the modest life of a bank clerk's wife?

Goodness. She was getting ahead of herself. She'd met a handsome man on a train. She'd known him only a few hours, and already she was plotting an elopement, despite the fact that she was slightly wary and had just wondered if he wanted to steal her reticule. She had best regain control of her senses.

"Perhaps it is not a good idea," she said. "I couldn't deceive my aunt that way."

His gaze fell upon Millicent for a long moment before he nodded, almost in defeat. He leaned back. "Of course. You're right. I shouldn't have suggested it."

She recognized the disappointment in his eyes. He was surrendering to the reality of their situation—that he was not a suitable acquaintance for her—and all Annabelle's suspicions about his integrity fell away, because she felt positively beastly over the direction this was heading. She had enjoyed their conversation so very much. He *was* the kind of man she would wish to know. He was intelligent, polite and interesting, not to forget handsome and exciting—so much more so than all the young lords she'd been dancing with of late. She did not wish him to think she considered him beneath her. She did not. But her family would certainly not support any—

Just then the steam whistle blew, and Aunt Millicent sat straight up, eyes wide. Annabelle sucked in a breath, while Mr. Edwards calmly turned his head toward the window.

"What is the time?" Millicent asked, looking around, confused.

"It's just past three," Annabelle replied.

"I must have dozed off."

"Did you?" Annabelle struggled to smile casually at her aunt. She and Mr. Edwards glanced briefly at each other.

"We should be arriving soon," Millicent said, running a hand over her hair, patting down some untucked strands. "Thank goodness. It was a rather tedious trip, don't you think?"

"Yes, Auntie," Annabelle lied.

In a matter of minutes, the train slowed down, but Annabelle's heart was racing faster and faster, for she was about to disembark and never see Mr. Edwards again. She had just rejected him, and surely, he was under the impression she did not wish to see him again, that she did not trust him, that she found him neither interesting nor appealing.

Though she did not know him well enough to trust him, she certainly *did* find him appealing, in every possible way.

With the slower lumbering of the locomotive and the noisy screech of the brakes, Annabelle felt more and more as if the walls of the train were closing in on her. She was running out of time, and soon she would have to say good-bye to Mr. Edwards for good.

If that happened, she knew she would always wonder what would have become of them if they'd had more time to get to know each other.

Aunt Millicent leaned forward and shouted at the older lady, "We're pulling into the station!"

The woman jumped and awakened. "Are we here?" She reached shakily for her cane.

Annabelle was breathing hard now. This was it. They would get off in a few short minutes.

She glanced across at Mr. Edwards who returned her steady gaze.

"Don't forget your book," Aunt Millicent said, picking it up off the seat and handing it to Annabelle.

"Does anyone see my pen?" the elderly lady asked, appearing flustered as she searched around her seat. "My grandson gave it to me. Did it fall on the floor?"

Everyone leaned forward to look. Then Annabelle was struck by a thought. Well, not so much a thought. It was more of an involuntary action. She reached into her own reticule for her pen and sketch pad, and while everyone was distracted by the older lady's panic, she scribbled something on a small corner of the pad and ripped it out.

The pen was soon located by Mr. Edwards, who had spotted it under Aunt Millicent's feet. Annabelle crumpled the note in her hand.

She knew she was doing something rash and imprudent, but she couldn't help herself. She could not get off this train and say good-bye to Mr. Edwards forever. She could not explain it. She simply had to see him again, even if it was only to discover he was an unscrupulous character. At least then she would know.

The train screeched to a halt at the station and they all stood.

"It was a pleasure traveling with you," the older lady said to Annabelle and Aunt Millicent.

"Likewise," Millicent replied.

One of the uniformed guards opened the door and helped the elderly lady down first, and as soon as Millicent took the first step down, Annabelle turned and discreetly slipped her crumpled note into Mr. Edwards' hand.

He glanced up, surprised at first, then his eyes filled instantly with a flirtatious spark of understanding that sent Annabelle's senses whirling. He held her for a moment in the pounding allure of his gaze.

That instant, she knew she *had* to see him again. She simply *had* to, and she prayed he would understand what she had written in the note and would not let her down.

Physically wrenching herself away, she turned for the door and seized that opportunity to steal just one more backward glance at him before she left the train.

Magnus watched Miss Lawson walk the length of the platform until she was gone from view, then immediately opened the tiny crumpled note and read it. He stuffed it into his breast pocket.

What had he done? What the devil was wrong with him?

Sitting forward, he dropped his head into his hands, raking his fingers through his hair. He could never have her. Never, never, never. She came from that *world*. She lived with—and loved—the very people he despised, the people who despised him equally in return.

He still could barely comprehend that she was one of them, because she was so undeniably different, and for most of the day while they talked, he had practically forgotten the connection. He supposed he'd been distracted by the lovely green of her eyes.

Magnus sat back again and gazed with weariness out the window at the mulling crowd on the platform. The uniformed guard blew his whistle, signaling that it was time to depart.

This was a wretched predicament indeed, he thought, recalling the pleasure of stroking her slender wrist and the displeasure of having to resist touching his lips to it.

His actions until then had been beyond reproach, to say the least, but he hadn't been able to stop himself in the end.

No, he should not see her again. He should not, for on top of everything, he had lied to her about who he was.

The best thing to do was put her from his mind. Forcefully. Permanently. He was a strong man. He could do it.

But as the train pulled away from the station, damned if he wasn't thinking about her luscious full lips again and feeling a rush of desire he could not overcome.

Chapter 3

1892

STRUGGLING TO BANISH THE PAINFUL memories of her unforgettable first love—her only love—Annabelle gazed up at the swaying branches of the oak tree and listened to the leaves fluttering in the wind. She covered her face with both hands.

A lump formed in her throat. She swallowed over it, fighting to suppress it, but couldn't, because it had been years since she had recalled, in such vivid detail, the day she had met Magnus for the first time on the train.

Yes, Magnus. That was his real name. It had not been John Edwards, as he'd led her to believe.

Generally, these days, she only remembered the unpleasant things about Magnus, because she had forced herself to forget the way he had made her feel when she first met him. Forced herself to forget how handsome he had been, how charming and polite with the elderly lady, and how her body had responded to him.

He had awakened every passion that existed inside her, when she had not even known she possessed such passions to begin with. She had never been in love before.

Nor since. It had been thirteen long years, and she was a woman now—an experienced, sensible woman—no longer the girl who had stepped on that train, believing in love and romance and the private mate of one's soul. Those naïve beliefs had been very dangerous and had set her up for a tremendously painful and damaging fall....

She dropped her hands to her sides and squeezed the cool, green grass between her fingers. It hurt to remember all this. Why was she doing it? Because now she knew she would see him again?

His letter angered her suddenly. Why was he back there, thinking he could write to her as if none of it had happened?

Well, it *had* happened.... All the lies and betrayals.

She rolled over onto her stomach and rested her chin on her hands. She watched a bee land in a patch of clover a few feet away. The bee collected some nectar—aware of what it was after—then buzzed away, free to search for more.

Annabelle inhaled the scents of the grass and earth, so close to her nose. She closed her eyes and again thought of the letter in her pocket. She also thought of the first one he had written a few weeks ago, when he first arrived in London. It was locked away in the cedar box inside the deep drawer of her desk, unanswered.

She could feel the key to the box, which she wore on a long chain around her neck, inside a locket, pressing uncomfortably between her breasts.

Annabelle sighed and rolled over onto her back again. She had started something today with these memories, and somehow, she knew that if she were to see him again, she would need to remember everything, especially how he had hurt her. She could not forget that. She would need to strengthen her guard, so she forced herself to go back to the two excruciating weeks that had followed that first day on the train, the weeks she had spent longing to see Mr. Edwards—*Magnus*—again. When she thought of nothing but his face and his hands and the sound of his voice. When she dreamed of being reunited with him, being held in his arms, and finally running away with him.

Oh, she had been so very young and innocent.

Paintings

Chapter 4

August 1879

The crumpled-up note Annabelle had placed in Mr. Edwards' hand had read:

National Gallery
Two weeks, 2 p.m.
Dupre

*T*HE DAY HAD FINALLY COME.
There she stood, pacing back and forth in front of Dupre's painting, while her brother Whitby was elsewhere in the gallery, moving along at his own pace.

Whitby and Annabelle had come there many times in the past, and thankfully he learned to give her time alone to admire the art. Which was why she had chosen this place.

Annabelle checked her timepiece, praying that Mr. Edwards had understood what her message meant and would be able to find her. Her heart began to pound when she noted the time. It was two o'clock. She nervously glanced around at the other patrons.

Oh, she hated this. She hated worrying that he would not come, or that he had met another young lady on another train and forgotten all about her, while she had spent the past two weeks dreaming of nothing but him.

She anxiously squeezed her reticule. The wretched truth was that what she felt for Mr. Edwards two weeks ago had proliferated into an ardent, sweeping desire—more powerful than anything she'd ever known. She constantly had butterflies in her belly and was either deliriously happy with the dream that he, too, was missing her, or she was inconsolably miserable, thinking she would never see him again.

The logical part of her brain realized she had begun to idealize him. She was probably romanticizing their conversations and overestimating the level of desire he felt for her in return.

Yet she could not stop herself from believing that she loved him, like no woman had ever loved before.

Annabelle chuckled rather bitterly, finding some humor in the fact that she was finally grasping what the poets had been going on about for centuries.

An older couple wandered into the room, and Annabelle made an effort to look as if she were just another gallery patron, admiring the paintings at her leisure. She stood before the Dupre, staring at it: *Willows, with a Man Fishing.*

It was not a large painting. It was not even twelve inches wide, but it was a good choice for today—

rather brilliant in its romanticism, she had to admit. It was a painting she wanted very much to show Mr. Edwards. She wanted to explain that the Barbizon style was very different from the way she painted, and if she were ever to paint him in his boat the way they had discussed on the train, she would approach the trees and the water very differently.

Though that took nothing away from how she felt about this painting. She had always admired it for its quietness and intimacy.

She turned away from the Dupre, glancing discreetly around the room, hearing only the echoed sounds of a woman's heels as she walked quickly through another room, and the whispers of the other patrons quietly discussing the works of art.

She glanced at the timepiece dangling from the Chatelaine attached to her waist.

It was ten minutes past two.

Annabelle dropped the watch and tapped her gloved hand upon her thigh. She was beginning to lose hope. He wasn't going to come.

No, she mustn't jump to conclusions. He was only ten minutes late. He could be dashing up the front steps of the gallery at that very moment, as eager to see her as she was to see him.

And so it was that two more hours passed, every minute painstakingly slow, and when a man finally entered the room where the Dupre was located and spoke Annabelle's name with affection, she was barely able to keep the tears from her eyes. Tears of disappointment, heartbreak, anger. For the man coming to fetch her and take her home was her brother, Lord

Whitby.

Over the next fortnight, Annabelle grew to despise
the Dupre painting, each day hating it more than the
last. She didn't want to think about it. She was irritated
on the days Cook served fish for dinner, and most of
all, she was angry with herself for becoming deeply
infatuated with a man who had evidently toyed with
her feelings and taken some perverse pleasure leading
her to believe there was something special between
them, when there was no such thing.

She had fallen victim to the charms of a thoughtless man, who no doubt flirted with every woman he
stumbled across and had probably ruined more than
his fair share of young innocents. He probably had a
whole host of illegitimate children, too. Maybe he
wasn't even a bank clerk. Maybe he was one of those
confidence men. Or worse—good heavens—a stage
actor.

She held firmly to the certain belief that he was a
rake of the worst kind, until on the fifteenth day there
was a surprise waiting for her in the formal gardens
at her country house in Bedfordshire—that surprise
being Mr. Edwards himself.

Annabelle had taken a walk to be alone, and lo and
behold, there he was, waiting for her beyond the tall
lilac hedge, leaning at his ease against one of the columns of the open rotunda.

Heart throbbing suddenly in her chest, she stopped
dead in her tracks, not quite ready to believe she was
seeing properly. But then he pushed away from the
column, removed his hat and held it at his side, and

she knew it was really him.

He was wearing the same black jacket and trousers he had worn on the train. He looked exactly the same, just how she remembered him, tall and handsome and so darkly appealing.

Annabelle struggled to comprehend what she was feeling. One part of her wanted to stick her nose in the air and storm off, for she was so angry with him for not being there to meet her that day in the gallery.

Another part of her was melting into a puddle of forgiveness because he had found her. He had come all the way to her brother's country house. He had not forgotten her. Perhaps he'd had a good reason not to visit the gallery that day. She had certainly considered that over the past two weeks, but in the end she found it easier and safer to presume otherwise, for she had not wished to continue pining away for a man she would most likely never see again.

But here he was.

Magnus held his hat in a firm grip, his breath ragged, his mind in turmoil. It had been a full month since he'd seen Miss Lawson, and part of him had hoped that when he came here today, her effect on him might have diminished.

But no, it had not. Seeing her now in her clumsy black boots and wildly knotted hair—her eyes as vivid and piercing as he remembered—sent him dangerously out of control with desire for her.

He knew then, with devastating certainty, that he had failed in his valiant struggle to forget her.

"Miss Lawson," he said in an apologetic tone,

because any fool could have seen she was angry with him. "Hello."

When she made no greeting in reply, he cut straight to the point. "I came to tell you that I'm sorry...for not meeting you at the gallery."

At least part of it was true. He *was* sorry. Sorry for disappointing her.

But the truth was—he *had* been there. Unfortunately, Whitby had been there, too, so Magnus had been forced to retreat in order to avoid a confrontation with his enemy.

Not that he feared confrontations with Whitby. He could handle himself, and there might even be a very serious confrontation about Annabelle sometime in the near future. In fact, over the past two weeks Magnus had begun to dream about it. He'd never been more determined to take what he wanted from his powerful, influential cousin who had always enjoyed keeping him in his place.

Because this time what Magnus wanted was Miss Lawson.

Blood quickening in his veins, he slowly, cautiously, approached her as if she were a deer that might bolt at any second.

Finally, she spoke, her expression cool and stern. "I waited for two hours."

He nodded, because he knew how long she had waited. "I swear to you, I wanted to be there. I thought of nothing else after we parted on the train. I was counting the days until I could see you again, but on my way to meet you, I...."

"You what?"

He narrowed his gaze, considering whether he should speak the truth and tell her his real name, after tearing himself apart about it for the past month.

I withdrew because my name is Magnus, and I am Whitby's cousin. The one he loathes. Why am I loathed, you ask? Because I am my father's son, and surely, you've heard the disturbing stories about my father's brutality....

He tried to imagine her response. She would probably be aghast. She would run back to the house and call out the dogs.

Just then he experienced a twinge in his stomach—that old familiar shame and agony from his childhood, when he had been rejected and spat upon in the streets by those who knew that he and his father were banished by an earl. He had been called a lunatic. A son of the devil.

No, he couldn't tell her. Not now, when he was standing on thin ice to begin with.

"I had concerns," he tried to explain, struggling to choose his words carefully, while pushing all thoughts of his childhood to the back of his mind. As she listened, he felt a spark of hope....

Suddenly he was aware of nothing but the need to conquer, to hasten forth into an overrun battlefield, swinging his sword at an oncoming charge of enemy soldiers. He would do anything to have her—to win her heart and take her for his own.

Swallowing hard, forcing his brain to formulate the right words so as not to scare her off, he continued what he had begun to say. "I had concerns about our situation. I am not someone your family would approve of."

That was the truth.

Annabelle stared uncertainly at him, her freckled cheeks flushing pink as she wet her full lips, until Magnus couldn't resist her anymore. He'd been having erotic dreams about this woman for a month, and here she was at last, standing before him in the flesh. She was a unique, beguiling beauty, a sweet, ripe maiden, and he wanted to touch her.

Moving closer, he raised her gloved hand to his lips and gently kissed each knuckle.

Somehow, she would belong to him. No matter what it took.

Annabelle did not pull her hand away. She stood motionless, watching the top of Mr. Edwards' head while he dropped leisurely kisses across the back of her hand. His lips were soft and tantalizing. She felt the moist heat of his breath through the thin fabric of her glove.

She had to scramble to keep her head, for her body was aching to be even closer to him, to step into his arms and feel his chest pressing against her breasts. She felt dizzy, intoxicated by something far more potent than wine.

Somehow, however, she managed to withstand the force of her desires. She could not give in to those feelings, not so easily when she was still hurt by his failure to meet her that day, and she still knew little about him.

A moment later he gazed intently into her eyes. "I wish you would speak, Miss Lawson."

"I don't know what to say. I was very disappointed when you did not come."

Something in his manner changed. His eyes glimmered with a sensual light and his voice softened, like a caress. "I wanted to see you, but there was another far more serious problem."

"What was that?" she asked.

"I wanted only to be alone with you, and I was plotting ways to steal you away and take you home with me—to my bed."

His bed…?

Annabelle should have been scandalized. He had said something very wicked, something no gentleman should ever say to a well-bred young lady like herself. But surprisingly, she was not scandalized. She was filled with a strange inner excitement that caused a passionate fluttering in her belly. If she understood him correctly, he had not met her that day because he had wanted her *too much* and had not trusted himself to resist her.

Forgiving him suddenly became very probable.

"Why did you wait until now to tell me this?" she asked, nevertheless. "I've spent the past two weeks thinking all kinds of hateful things—like how many ways there are to push a man like you out of a fishing boat."

He looked down at her hand in his and chuckled. "You had every right to be angry with me, and I probably deserve to swim with the fish." He continued in a quieter voice that was almost a whisper. "To be frank, Miss Lawson, I wasn't *ever* going to tell you. I was never going to see you again because I wanted to do the right thing. I do not wish to complicate your life. I am not from your world, remember."

It was true, and she had known it would be complicated. He was not the sort of man her brother or aunt would accept as a husband for her, despite the fact that her parents were who they were. Whitby considered her his sister, and he was an earl.

"We could have been friends," she said.

"Do you really think so? You and me?" He shook his head. "Even if we could be, I believe I would rather pound my head against a wall than spend every day trying to resist kissing you, then one day watch another man take you as his wife."

Annabelle shook inwardly. Was he really saying all this? They barely knew each other. No man had spoken so candidly to her before.

Mr. Edwards was either impossibly rakish and arrogant, or he was utterly and hopelessly in love with her.

She placed her hand over her heart. This did not seem real. She felt as if she were standing within the pages of a fairy tale. It was certainly magical enough. Except that he was, unfortunately, not a prince.

"I don't know what to make of you," she said, stepping onto the cement floor of the rotunda and walking to its center. "You say you want to do the right thing, yet here you are, skulking around in my garden, telling me you wanted to take me to your bed."

Still holding his hat in his hand, he followed her into the shade of the tiny sanctuary and leaned a shoulder against one of the columns. "You are wise to be cautious. I have behaved deplorably, but only because I've lost my head over you. And that, my dear, is the truth."

She turned to face him. He was gazing at her with blinding charismatic splendor, confidently amorous, as if he wanted to unbutton her bodice and thought she might be of a mind to let him do it.

Heavens above, he *was* arrogant, but it stirred her blood like nothing she'd ever experienced.

"Mr. Edwards," she said very primly, lifting her chin and squaring her shoulders, "will you not even *try* to disguise the fact that you are attempting to seduce me?"

She couldn't help it—her lips betrayed her with a hint of a smile. And she had been trying so hard to be proper and virtuous....

He grinned at her in return, and with a sharply honed, animal-like instinct, he seemed to perceive her willingness to flirt. Somehow, instinctively, he knew she was surrendering to him.

But she supposed he was surrendering to her, too, for even she, in all her innocence, could not have missed the unmistakable spark that flared between them from the first moment they made eye contact on the train. It had been blazing hotter every day since, hot enough to make him leave London for the countryside, just to see her again. In secret. She quivered with pleasure at the thought of it.

"Seduce you," he said, as if he were pondering such a suggestion for the very first time. "I suppose I am, but I cannot help myself. You are so very lovely." He took a step away from the column and sauntered toward her. "This is all very improper, isn't it? You are probably wishing you'd never met me."

"That's not what I'm wishing," she replied, revealing the truth without caring about the impropriety of it, or the consequences.

Then she strove to be sensible. She had never behaved like this in her life.

"You know.... I should return to the house, because this *is* indeed improper, and I should not be out here with you."

But she wasn't sure she could leave if she tried. Her feet seemed stuck to the ground.

"Don't go," he said.

They were both breathing quickly now. "But I feel nervous all of a sudden."

He moved forward, closing the last small distance between them, disarming her with his dazzling dark eyes. "Do you?"

She considered it a moment. "To be honest, I am not sure. Perhaps what I am feeling is not nervousness, but rather...." Oh, she didn't know what it was.

"Excitement?" he suggested.

She wet her trembling lips. "Possibly."

With a slow smile, he backed her up against the column and rested a forearm against it, just over her head. Her heart was pounding like a drum, so fast she thought it would bounce right out of her chest.

He brushed his forefinger across her temple and leaned in close, whispering in her ear, "Have you never been excited by a man before?"

She swallowed, finding it increasingly difficult to breathe. "Only once, by a man on a train."

He smiled at that, his face now barely an inch away. She could feel his breath on the tip of her nose.

"Are you flirting with me, Miss Lawson?" he asked in a husky voice that gave her shivers.

Her knees were going weak. They might as well be made of clotted cream. She closed her eyes. "I don't know. Am I?"

Yes, she was. To pretend otherwise would be futile, for her body was tingling with a thousand sensations she couldn't begin to understand.

Was this normal? Was it normal to feel so instantly enraptured by a man one barely knew? A man who was, by certain standards, completely unsuitable?

"I think you are," he said with a hint of amusement, his whisper a hot, moist breath on her lips.

She had been kissed only once before in her life—by a rather inept young man when she was sixteen. He had surprised her and stolen the kiss behind the stable, then ran away. His lips were cold from the winter air, and tightly puckered. That had been a swift, unexpected kiss that she had giggled about afterward.

This was nothing like that. Mr. Edwards was not trying to surprise her. He was preparing her, teasing her and patiently drawing out the intensity of the moment. She could feel the heat of his lips already, as he brushed the tip of his nose lightly like a feather over her cheeks.

He *was* going to kiss her. She knew it, and she wanted him to. No amount of propriety or common sense could keep her from letting him do it.

Quietly, he whispered, "Miss Lawson, since I met you, I have not been able to stop thinking of you, though I've certainly tried, and I anticipate this situation is going to become exceedingly complicated."

"Yes," she replied.

"If you are not completely certain of your feelings for me, tell me now and I will go. I'll walk away and never bother you again. But if you truly want this as much as I do, then you must be prepared for a difficult time."

She knew she should be contemplating the issue at hand and what the future would hold—but all she could feel was the bliss of his body so close to hers.

"I can't tell you to go," she said. "I know I should, but I can't. Not today."

For a moment he gazed into her eyes, as if *he* were still contemplating it as well, attempting to convince himself that he should leave, regardless of her response just now. Then he looked down at her lips and his mouth covered hers in a kiss that sent a powerful yearning straight to her core. It was soft and sensuous, and he groaned huskily at the pleasure of it, but it was all too brief. It left her wanting more.

"Now I'm done for," he whispered, caressing her cheek with a finger.

"So am I. What will we do?"

He rested his forehead upon hers. "I have no idea. Perhaps you should think further about this."

"I don't need to think. I just want to see you again."

"Your brother would never approve."

"Let me deal with that when the time comes. If it comes."

His body went still. "Do you think he would be reasonable?"

Annabelle recognized the doubt in his voice. She detected a hint of bitterness as well. He did not believe there was hope.

"My brother cares for me very deeply," she explained. "He wants me to be happy."

But in all honesty, she was not sure that Whitby would permit her to marry someone like Mr. Edwards. Whitby would surely think him a very shrewd fortune hunter who was greatly overstepping his bounds.

"Meet me at the lake tomorrow," Annabelle said. "There's a rowboat at the north end. We'll take it to the island and have lunch there."

"You can get away like that?" he asked, looking doubtful.

She began to worry that he would change his mind again and fail to appear, that he would leave her waiting like he had at the gallery. He seemed so very hesitant.

"I'll bring my paint box and a canvas," she replied, finding herself willing to take the risk. "No one will expect me back for hours."

He turned his back on her and walked to the other side of the rotunda, staring off into the distance, at the lush green hills and dense forests. "This is a beautiful place."

There was something melancholy in Mr. Edwards' voice, and Annabelle feared she would not see him again after today. But she couldn't let that happen. She crossed to stand beside him. "Yes, it is, but it doesn't mean everything to me."

"It should," he replied. "You are fortunate to have been raised here, to have had so much. Not everyone is so blessed."

She was more than aware of that, and felt guilty for

being disloyal to her brother, who had done so much for her. Yet she could not turn away from this.

Mr. Edwards shook his head. "This is madness. You know that, don't you?"

"Yes, I know it, but I don't care. I've only ever been frustrated with my life—as it is anyway."

He chuckled softly, almost bitterly. "I don't quite understand that, but I admire your spirit."

"Does that mean you will be there tomorrow?"

Placing his hat back on his head, he faced her. "What time?"

She breathed a sigh of relief. "Two o'clock. But you had best not keep me waiting. I won't forgive you a second time."

She started to back away, but he caught hold of her hand. "One more kiss."

Annabelle grinned mischievously. "Not until tomorrow."

"Is that your way of making sure I'll return?"

"Perhaps." She backed away. "Or perhaps I simply don't *want* to kiss you."

He smiled and placed his hand on his chest, as if she'd shot an arrow straight into his heart. "You'll be the death of me."

"We can't have that, now." Annabelle dashed forward, rose up on her toes and kissed him quickly on the cheek. "There. Now go. Sneak out of here before someone sees you."

He followed her to the edge of the rotunda and leaned against a column again, watching her leave. "Don't worry. I'll be very sneaky."

Not really understanding the hidden truths in that

statement, Annabelle darted excitedly back to the house.

Chapter 5

"*You* didn't keep me waiting this time," Annabelle said the following day as she emerged from the path through the woods and spotted Mr. Edwards already sitting in the rowboat, which was tied up at the dock. He looked as if he had been there for a while.

"You said you wouldn't forgive me a second time," he replied, "so I was careful not to be late." He rose, stepped onto the dock—causing the boat to rock rather violently—then approached and took the easel and paint box out of her hands. "You carried this all the way here on your own?"

Heart already aflutter from the nearness of him, Annabelle handed everything over. "I'm used to it. I carry these everywhere."

She also wore a lunch sack strapped across her shoulder, so while he placed her painting supplies in the boat, she lifted it over her head. "I brought sandwiches, and I even snuck a bottle of wine from the cellar."

"I hadn't taken you for an adventurer, Miss Lawson. Do you often take such risks?"

"To tell you the truth, I rarely get the chance."

As he took the lunch sack out of her hands, his voice was laced with teasing. "I find that hard to believe." After he set everything in the boat, he looked across the lake. "That's the island?"

"Yes. There's a good spot to drag the boat onto the beach on the other side."

"Right, then." He held out a hand and assisted her into the boat.

"You brought your fishing gear," she said, noticing the rod and creel as she sat down. "Can you show me how it's done?"

"Of course." Mr. Edwards untied the boat and stepped in with remarkable agility. Then he sat down, picked up the oars and started to row.

Annabelle sat quietly watching him steer the boat while she listened to the sounds of the water lapping against the hull and the oars creaking in the oarlocks. She felt the boat propelled forward with each strong, swift stroke.

"Did you come from London this morning?" she asked as they headed toward the middle of the lake where the water was deep.

He was rowing fast and hard, the muscles of his shoulders straining. "Yes. I caught the early train."

"And you'll take the train back this evening?"

He nodded. "I must be at my desk by nine tomorrow morning."

At his desk....

"I'm trying to imagine you at work," she said. "Do

you talk to many people? Do you arrange loans?"

He looked over his shoulder to see how much far-ther they had to go. "No, I work with numbers. I record figures, balance debits and credits, that sort of thing."

"Do you enjoy it?"

"Not really."

Annabelle's brow furrowed as she digested the flat-ness of his reply. She shook her head at him. "Why do you do something you don't enjoy? Why not try something else?"

He looked over his shoulder again. "I must earn an income," he said bluntly, seeming strangely distant.

"Yes, but you never considered being a fisherman, for instance?"

"I enjoy fishing too much," he said. "I wouldn't want to turn it into work."

They reached the deepest part of the lake and he stopped rowing. "This looks like a good spot, if you'd like to give it a go before lunch."

"Give what a go?" Annabelle asked.

He reached for his fishing pole, which was lying flat along the side of the boat. "I'm going to teach you how to fish. Hold this." He handed the rod to her, then reached past her to drop the anchor over the transom. "Will you mind baiting the hook?"

"Not at all. What will it entail?"

"Picking up a worm and putting an end to his life, I'm afraid."

Annabelle gazed uncertainly at him for a moment, and he nodded. "Maybe I'll handle that part."

He reached for a small tin box with a lid, opened

it and showed Annabelle what was inside—a mass of squirming worms in some dark earth. Annabelle passed him the rod.

"Watch out," he said, "the hook is quite sharp." Then he proceeded to harpoon a most unfortunate wiggly worm. Annabelle made a face, which Mr. Edwards seemed to find amusing as he wound the reel, then cast his line in an arc to send the hook and worm sailing through the air. They plopped onto the water's surface, and he passed the rod to her.

"Hold it right here. Both hands."

She wrapped her hands around the well-worn cork handle. Feeling rather silly, just sitting there holding the rod, she glanced wryly at him. "Now what do I do?"

"Reel it in slowly to drag the bait. Not too fast."

Annabelle followed his instructions.

"Look, there's a falcon," Mr. Edwards quietly said, pointing over the treetops on the far side of the lake.

They watched the bird fly above them, and Annabelle felt like she was floating, until Mr. Edwards touched the rod. "You can jiggle it every now and again, like this. That's right. Now reel it in a little more."

"How will I know if I've caught something?" she asked, focusing on the task at hand.

"You'll know. You'll feel it."

She continued to slowly bring the hook back to the boat, and when it came out of the water, there was no fish, nor was there a worm swinging on the hook.

"Where did he go?"

"He appears to have made his escape." Mr. Edwards

reached for the line and placed another worm on the hook. "Would you like to cast this time?"

"I'd love to."

"All right, let me see...."

The boat rocked as he leaned forward and reeled the hook all the way to the tip of the rod. Then his large, warm hands curled around hers. Annabelle felt a quivering sensation in her belly.

"Hold it right here," he said. "Then tip it back. That's it. Now swing the rod forward so that the hook goes as far as you can cast it."

She did as he instructed and listened to the whizzing sound of the reel spinning and the line slicing through the air, then the quiet splash of the hook and bait as it hit the water.

"Well done," he said softly. "Now bring it in as you did last time and—"

Just then, the rod tugged in Annabelle's hands, and a sprightly thrill zipped up her spine. "I think I've caught something." The rod was pulling and bending. "Upon my word! Mr. Edwards! What do I do?"

"Reel it in!" he said, laughing.

"Oh!" She panicked and began winding the reel at an alarmingly fast pace, and the rod continued to tug and pull in her hands. "Goodness! Maybe you should do it!"

Before she knew what she was about, she was trying to pass the rod back to Mr. Edwards, but he raised both hands in the air. "Steady on, Miss Lawson. You're doing fine. Just keep reeling."

Suddenly, the fish at the end of the line flew up out of the water and flopped around in the air. Annabelle swung the rod back and forth, laughing as the boat rocked beneath them. "Help!"

Mr. Edwards took hold of the rod. A second later, the fish was in the boat, flip-flopping at Annabelle's feet until Mr. Edwards grabbed hold of him…but he slipped out of his hands again.

"It's a perch—and a dodgy one at that!"

"I thought you said fishing was a relaxing affair!" Annabelle shouted, and they stared at each other for a few seconds before they both burst into fits of laughter.

They continued to laugh while Mr. Edwards caught the fish in his hands and freed it from the hook. Then he tossed it back into the lake with a splash.

"What are you doing?" Annabelle asked. "That was my first fish!"

Mr. Edwards could barely speak, for all his laughing. "I don't quite know how to break it to you, Miss Lawson, but he was too small. He'll be better off maturing a bit before he succumbs to the sad fate of becoming someone's dinner."

"I see."

Once they collected themselves, Mr. Edwards closed the bait box and set the rod back down in the boat.

"What are you doing?" Annabelle asked. "I thought we were just getting started."

"There's not much point casting again," he replied. "With all the noise we've been making, we've surely scared every fish within a ten-mile radius all the way to kingdom come."

He was still chuckling when he drew up the anchor,

set it in the boat and picked up the oars. "We'll have lunch—*quietly, please*—then try again later."

Annabelle wiped the tears from her eyes and watched Mr. Edwards steer the boat toward the island. "That was great fun."

"It's not usually as exciting as all that," he replied, "but at least you experienced the thrill of the nibble."

Annabelle managed to calm her laughter as the boat coasted along smoothly. "It's rather addictive."

She leaned over the side and let her fingers glide across the surface of the water.

"This boat rows like a dream," he said.

Annabelle admired the graceful movements of his muscular arms. "You're a strong oarsman."

"Plenty of practice." He winked at her, and another thrill zipped up Annabelle's spine, just as it had when she'd hooked the fish.

She had never met a man more exciting than Mr. Edwards, despite the fact that they were forced to sneak around like this and meet in secret. But perhaps that was part of the allure.

Within minutes he was dipping the oars into the shallow water, pushing on the gravel as the boat scraped onto the shore. He hopped out with a splash and pulled the heavy boat—with Annabelle in it— onto the beach.

Annabelle passed the lunch and her painting supplies to him, then stood up and put her hands on his shoulders. He grabbed hold of her waist, lifted her out of the boat, and deposited her effortlessly onto the dry shore.

"Thank you," she said, grinning up at him before

she turned to pick up the lunch sack. "Shall we head in that direction? There's a nice clearing where we can set down the blanket."

"Lead the way."

They crossed the beach to the path through the woods, and Annabelle marveled at how her body was drumming with sensation from the mere sound of his shoes on the footpath behind her.

They arrived at the grassy clearing. She retrieved the picnic blanket from the sack, along with the food and wine. "I didn't bring wineglasses because I feared they might break. The best I could do was a couple of tin coffee cups."

"I admire a practical woman."

He took the folded blanket from her and spread it out on the grass, where they sat down together and enjoyed a delicious lunch of sliced ham, cheese, and bread.

Afterward, Mr. Edwards stretched out on his side, leaning up on one elbow. "Tell me, did you bring your painting supplies as a mere ruse, or did you truly intend to be an artist today?"

"That depends," she replied, "on whether or not I feel inspired." She was feeling the effects of the wine, to be sure. She wondered if it was obvious to Mr. Edwards.

"Are you feeling inspired?"

She brought the cup to her lips and regarded him over the rim as she sipped. "Yes."

A simple answer. Direct, and probably scandalously delivered.

He sat up. "What do you wish to paint?"

"You."

"And how?"

Under the current tone of their exchange, she could easily have said, *Nude, here on the blanket.* But she'd already been daring enough as it was.

Besides, ever since she met him, she had been thinking of only one way to paint him....

"In the boat. I want to paint you fishing, like we talked about on the train."

He inclined his head at her. "I thought you wanted to experience the thrill of the nibble again."

"I do, but first I want to paint you experiencing it."

He smiled at her again. "You are lovely, Miss Lawson."

"Thank you, Mr. Edwards," she replied, enjoying how he flattered her.

He glanced at her easel, lying folded on the grass. "How long will it take you? Because I have a train to catch."

"Well, I will sketch you today, and perhaps have time to block in some of the color, but we'll have to come back another day if you want me to finish it."

He took a slow sip of wine. "I like the idea of you sketching me."

"You'll like the finished piece even more when it's hanging over your mantel."

His dark eyebrows lifted. "You intend to give it to me?"

"Of course."

"I'd have to pay you," he said.

"No, it would be a gift."

"And what did I do to deserve such a thing?"

Annabelle thought carefully about how she should answer that, then decided she would simply be honest.

"You have inspired me. I was bored before I met you."

He gazed at her for a long moment in the warm sunshine, looking almost puzzled. "How could you be bored? You have everything."

Annabelle gazed up at the treetops that circled the clearing and watched a blackbird flutter into the sky. "I don't mean to sound ungrateful. It's just that sometimes I feel like a bit of a misfit. Maybe it's because I wasn't born into this life. My parents weren't aristocrats, so I've never truly felt like I belonged, and I am not like other women my age. I don't like to gossip about people, nor do I like to shop—unless it's for paints or brushes—and I wear these dreadful boots." She lifted her foot to show him. "And I have a ferret for a pet, who often accompanies me when I go trekking over the countryside to paint."

He studied her with smiling eyes. "What's your ferret's name?"

"Helen of Troy. But I just call her Helen."

Mr. Edwards smiled.

Annabelle glanced at him. "You probably think I'm strange now, don't you? I'm sure my aunt thinks so. She calls me eccentric."

"No, I don't think you're strange," he replied with a chuckle, "because I often feel the same way—that I don't belong."

"Why? You seem very normal to me."

He shrugged, and she had the distinct feeling he was not telling her everything.

Not wanting to pry, she made a joke instead. "So here we are, a couple of misfits."

"A couple of misfits indeed. Maybe that's why we are friends."

Friends. But it was already so much more than that.

Annabelle and Mr. Edwards continued to sip the wine as they talked about everything from his work to her family life. Then it was time for her to pack up and start sketching.

They walked back to the beach, where Annabelle set up her easel. She looked around at the lake, up at the sun to see where it was and which way the shadows were falling, then pointed. "Can you row out there? Not too far. I want you close enough so I can see the details of you and the fishing pole."

He pushed the boat out a few feet, then hopped in, causing it to rock until he was settled. He picked up the oars and pushed off the gravel bottom as he turned the boat around.

"Aren't you worried I'll leave you here?" he asked with a sly grin. "How do you know you can trust me?"

"I suppose I'll find out."

He began to row hard in the direction she had suggested, while she unpacked her canvas and sketching pencils.

"That's far enough!" she shouted, hearing her voice echo across the lake. "Come back a little closer!"

He rowed in a circle and headed back toward her. "How's this?"

"Perfect! Now drop the anchor and catch some fish!"

While he hooked the bait and cast his line, she began sketching the lake and woods on the opposite side, capturing the rough lines of the background, then the shape and dimensions of the boat. She worked hardest on Mr. Edwards, the lines of his shoulders and arms, the position of his head, but he was difficult to capture because the boat was always changing direction.

He fished for about a half hour while Annabelle sketched him. He caught two trout, which he proudly presented when he rowed back to the island.

"Thank you for posing for me," Annabelle said, tucking the picture into her bag.

He hopped out of the rowboat and dragged it onto the beach. "I do beg your pardon, but aren't you going to show me your masterpiece?"

She grinned impishly. "Not yet. It's just a sketch."

"But I'm curious."

She packed away her pencils. "That's unfortunate, because you're not going to see it until it's finished."

"Finished?" He sauntered slowly toward her, and Annabelle found herself gazing at the full height of him—from his head down to his boots and back up again. He was so handsome he took her breath away.

"Just one peek," he said.

"No, I told you, not until it's finished."

He raised an eyebrow and lowered his chin, smirking.

Annabelle's stomach spun like a top as he drew closer, looking as if he intended to wrestle it out of her grasp. And win.

Clutching the bag to her chest, she backed up a few steps, knowing he was going to follow.

And oh, how she wanted him to.

Nevertheless, she wagged a finger at him teasingly. "No, Mr. Edwards."

He stopped before her, anticipation brimming in his dark eyes. Then she laughed and bolted. She managed only about ten strides before he caught her around the waist and scooped her up into his arms like a bride.

He dropped to his knees and set her down gently on the grass while she laughed. He had the bag in his hand within seconds, holding it high over his head where she couldn't reach it.

"Mr. Edwards!" she called out in mock effrontery, while he grinned down at her.

"I will give it back in exchange for a kiss."

She had wondered when he would ask for one. He had been a perfect gentleman all day, and she, quite frankly, had been waiting for him to behave other-wise. She'd been dreaming of it since the moment he'd left her on the rotunda the day before.

"You, sir, are a scoundrel."

"A cunning one, if I do say so myself."

She tried not to smile. She wanted to be cunning, too, but heaven help her, she was melting like butter beneath the heat of his gaze. Staring up at his hand-some face in the sunlight, she would have given him anything he asked.

"Just one," she replied, even though she wanted more than that, but if she let him take more, he could easily take everything. And she possessed enough common sense not to let that happen.

His expression went slowly from playful to serious as he set down the art case and repeated her words.

"Just one."

Annabelle wet her lips. He wet his, too, then kissed her softly, chastely, before drawing back and gazing down at her for what seemed a very long time.

"Perhaps one more?" she said breathlessly.

He kissed her again, and this time Annabelle cupped the back of his head in her hand, delighting in the heady sensation of his lips parting, his tongue sliding into her mouth and mingling with hers.

She let out a tiny whimper and slid her other hand around his waist and up under his jacket, where she stroked the firm, strong muscles of his back.

His breathing changed, and he rested a hand on her hip while he moved over her, his body pulsing gently.

Annabelle wanted to devour him completely—to wrap her arms and legs around him—but before she had a chance, he broke the kiss.

"May I remind you, Miss Lawson, that you are on a secluded island alone with me?"

"I am quite aware."

"And how do you know you can trust me?"

"That's the second time you've asked me that question."

His eyes clouded over suddenly. Gone was the desire she had seen in them only seconds ago.

Rolling off her, he sat up and rested an arm on his raised knee. "I must be raving mad."

Annabelle sat up, too. "Why?"

He shook his head, taking a long time to answer. "I've never been in a situation quite like this before. It's easy to forget who we are in a place such as this."

"I haven't forgotten who we are," Annabelle

insisted. "We're just people. And I am happier now than I was before I met you."

He glanced back at her with a hint of disdain that surprised her. "Because you were bored in your *palace*?"

Annabelle was taken aback. For a moment she wasn't sure where his anger was coming from, but then she understood—or thought she did—and inched closer to him. She put her hands on his shoulders. "I am not just amusing myself with you, if that's what you think."

"Then what are you doing? Because you know your family would never approve of me." He raked a hand through his hair and spoke harshly. "You shouldn't have come here with me today. You should have looked down your nose at me on the train, like your aunt did. Believe me, it would not have fazed me. I'm quite used to it."

She stared at him, bemused, while he waited for her to say something. When she did not—because she didn't know what to say—he shook his head and stood.

"Why *did* you come here with me today?" he asked. "What were you thinking? I am a stranger to you."

She gazed up at him uncertainly. "I don't understand why you're angry all of a sudden. Did I do something wrong?"

He glanced down at her briefly while he paced, then turned his back on her and looked across the lake. He rested his hands on his hips.

"Mr. Edwards?"

He faced her and spoke tersely. "I apologize. You

did nothing wrong. I am just struggling with the logic of what we are doing. By all rights, you are forbidden to me, Miss Lawson. Do you understand that?" He gestured down at her with a hand. "But you're so bloody hard to resist."

Growing increasingly uneasy, Annabelle tugged her skirts down to cover her ankles and boots. Perhaps he was right. Perhaps it *had* been extremely imprudent of her to row out to a private island, in secret, with a man she barely knew, a man her family would never approve of.

"We should go," he said flatly. "I don't want to miss my train." He offered his hand to her.

She gathered her skirts and he helped her rise. "Will I get to finish the painting?" she asked.

She didn't know why she was asking him that now. She supposed that despite the rising tension between them, she couldn't bear the thought that she would never see him again.

He considered it, and then, as if he could read her mind, answered the real question she was asking. "I enjoyed myself with you today, Miss Lawson. More than I should have. I suppose my dilemma lies in the fact that I do not wish to hand myself over to you, only to be casually tossed aside one day in the future because I am beneath you. And we both know I am."

Annabelle felt her brow furrow with umbrage. "I am not like that. I would never treat a person in such a cavalier manner. I do not *toss* people away."

He stared at her intently. "But your family might. It happens all the time."

She narrowed her eyes. "Did someone toss you

away once? A woman? Did you love her?"

She didn't know where that bold question had come from. All she knew was that she wanted to understand Mr. Edwards in the deepest possible way.

After a pause he shook his head. "No, there was no woman. At least no one I've ever...." He didn't finish.

Annabelle was surprised at how relieved she was to hear that he was not carrying a torch for someone. Perhaps she would be his first love.

He was certainly hers. She knew it already because she had never felt like this before. She hadn't even known such desires were possible.

"I want to finish the painting," she firmly said.

He wet his lips and didn't answer right away. His chest was heaving with indecision. Then at last he spoke in a quiet voice. "I want you to finish it, too."

Annabelle inhaled deeply with relief. "When?"

"Next Sunday? Same time?"

A whole week seemed too long to wait to see him again. She would go mad. But in the end, she agreed because there was no way around it. He had his clerkship in London.

She would simply have to accept that she would spend the next seven days dreaming of him, and fighting the insurmountable fear that he would leave her standing at the lake, waiting and waiting again, as he had at the gallery.

Chapter 6

*T*HE FOLLOWING SUNDAY, ANNABELLE ARRIVED at
the lake and was pleased to discover she would
not be kept waiting—for there in the boat, casually
lounging back, was Mr. Edwards.

And he was there waiting for her every Sunday
afternoon for the next six weeks.

It was the happiest, most romantic summer of Annabelle's life. Mr. Edwards always brought two fishing
poles, and he and Annabelle spent countless hours sitting in the small boat, bobbing up and down in the
waves, enjoying the summer heat and the peaceful
outdoors.

It wasn't *all* peaceful and relaxing, of course. One
particular afternoon they argued when Mr. Edwards
tried to show her how to gut a fish.

Annabelle proudly won the argument, drawing the
line at hooking a worm, which she had become quite
an expert at, she could not deny. And she never panicked, not even when a floppy trout landed with a
splat on her boots in the boat.

Though they spoke of nearly every subject under the sun that summer, they never mentioned the argument they'd had that first day, nor did they speak of the future. If Mr. Edwards talked about his work, it was only to relay an amusing story about a coworker or customer, never to draw attention to the differences in their social positions. Perhaps they simply wished to enjoy themselves and forget how their lives differed. Or perhaps they preferred to imagine that those lazy summer afternoons would never end.

Annabelle wished they wouldn't. She wished it most ardently when she and Mr. Edwards stretched out on the picnic blanket after their lunches, their heads together as they stared up at the sky, watching the puffy clouds drift by at a snail's pace. They would pick out shapes of things and watch the blackbirds soar freely against the blue.

And that was the time when he would kiss her, his lips warm and soft as they met hers, tasting like red wine. All he had to do was lean toward her and her entire body would purr with the passion-filled delight at his presence and the overpowering desire for more.

But despite her feverish longings, Mr. Edwards refused, unfailingly, to do anything more than just kiss, and never for more than a few minutes. Each time, he explained that he wanted her to have choices, in case she later changed her mind about him.

"I won't," she always said.

"You might," he always replied.

So their physical intimacies made little progress. And it was not until the summer's end that she fully understood why.

It was the last Sunday in August.

Magnus leaned a shoulder against the old English oak on the hill, which overlooked Century House, Annabelle's opulent home—an aristocratic mansion of unparalleled grandeur, set amidst terraced formal gardens and magnificent statuary and mazes and fountains.

He stood for a long time simply looking at it, while his emotions were tearing him apart inside—for the summer was at an end. The sunlight and shadows had changed, the air had turned crisp, and today....

Today was the day Annabelle would finish the painting.

He glanced down and kicked his booted toe against a large exposed tree root. He thought about what he had been doing all summer long—spending romantic afternoons with Annabelle, charming her into falling in love with him, never telling her who he really was.

He had suffered for that misrepresentation each and every day, constantly vowing that he would tell her the following week. But then she would arrive at the dock with her easel, all smiles and playful teasing, and he hadn't been able to say the words. He couldn't bear the thought of her reacting to him with revulsion.

Just one more day, he'd tell himself. If he could only make her love him a little bit more, it wouldn't matter when he told her. She would forgive him for keeping the truth from her and love him regardless.

But now, on this day, he found himself facing the reality of what their future would be, even if she did forgive him. He thought of the bed he rose from that morning—the coarse wool blanket and the mattress full of holes. He had dressed himself, then shoveled coal into the stove himself, but not until he'd tramped down the road at dawn to purchase a jug of milk from the worn-out dairymaid.

He thought of the breakfast he'd eaten—the same breakfast he ate every day of his life: bland porridge in a chipped bowl.

And his mother was run-down and depressed again, drinking too much as usual. The previous night, he had returned home to find her in a drunken swoon with her head on the kitchen table, a half-empty bottle of whiskey in front of her.

He quietly slid the bottle out of her loose grip and emptied it in the muddy yard, knowing he would never hear the end of it when she woke, but he followed through, nonetheless.

Magnus lifted his weary gaze and looked down the hill at Century House again, and imagined Annabelle waking between clean, white embroidered sheets, eating a breakfast prepared by a devoted kitchen staff. Her maid would have helped her dress and styled her hair, and another set of maids would have cleaned out the grate in her fireplace, swept her polished floor, and fluffed her feathery pillows.

Hers was a world very different from his.

He felt nauseous all of a sudden and slid down the side of the tree to sit on the ground. Resting his elbows on his knees, he raked both hands through his hair.

What did he think he was doing? How could he be so selfish, thinking he could take Annabelle away from the life she knew and alienate her from her family, then drag her down into the hell that was *his* life?

He supposed the problem was that he felt something for her that he had never felt for any other woman. He loved her laughter, her intelligence, her nonconformity. She inspired him with her artistic creativity, challenged him and made him think, and she made him feel at ease and at home—which was something he rarely felt with anyone. He had grown to care for her very deeply and devotedly. What concerned him most today was her welfare and well-being. Her future happiness.

But even with his feelings as profound and passionate as they were, he wasn't entirely certain he could be self-sacrificing enough to do the right thing—which was undoubtedly to give her up.

"Are you ready to see it?" Annabelle asked later that afternoon, meeting Mr. Edwards at the water's edge as he dragged the heavy boat onto the beach.

"I've been ready for six weeks," he replied.

She had noticed with some concern that he'd seemed downtrodden most of the day. He was not his usual flirtatious self. He had been very quiet.

During lunch she'd asked him if he was feeling unwell, and he'd assured her he was just tired after a long, busy week. She had accepted his explanation, hiding her fear that it might be something more.

"Well, come and see it, then," she said, holding out her arm. "But close your eyes." She took him by the hand and led him to the easel.

"All right. You can look now."

Mr. Edwards opened his eyes and stared at her painting for the longest time while she watched him apprehensively. His eyes moved over the details in the center of the canvas, then he studied every corner.

At last he looked at Annabelle, who warmed at the tenderness and wonderment in his expression.

"What do you think?" she asked hesitantly.

He slowly approached. "It's beautiful, Annabelle. Too beautiful to give to me. It should be in a gallery somewhere."

She shook her head. "I'm not famous enough to be in a gallery."

"You should be. You *will* be."

Annabelle smiled, dumbfounded by the astounding pride and elation that came from knowing someone truly appreciated her work.

No. He more than appreciated it. He was awestruck. Not just with the painting, but with her.

All at once she wanted to shout out loud across the lake and hear her voice echo back in return.

She was so happy to be with him, and so proud of this piece! It was beyond a doubt the best thing she'd ever done.

"Can I assume you like it?" she asked.

He came to her. "I more than like it. I love it. It has movement, yet stillness at the same time. And the reflections in the water...." He returned to stand before the painting and moved his hand over it as he spoke. "They look so real, yet when you study them, you are struck by the fact that you are seeing only the surface of the water, and there are deep, unknown depths beyond. It's the most incredible thing anyone's ever given me. I am not worthy of it."

"Of course you are."

He returned to her and cupped her cheek in his large, warm hand, stroking with his thumb. His touch gave her shivers.

Slowly he lowered his lips to hers and kissed her while he held her face in his hands. The kiss deepened, and Annabelle reveled in the flavor of his tongue and the heat of his mouth closing over hers. She let out a small whimper as she wrapped her arms around his broad shoulders, feeling all at once flooded with a rush of need so strong, she feared she would never be able to let him go.

She wanted more. She knew there was more. So much more....

He drew his lips away and whispered, "No, Annabelle."

But she refused to take no for an answer. She tried to resume the kiss. "Please, just this once."

She could see in his eyes that he was straining to resist, but soon he gave up the fight and kissed down the side of her neck.

Then Annabelle began to back up toward the trees, leading him by the hand. This time he relented. Eyes laden with desire, he followed willingly. As soon as she reached the shade of a tall oak tree where the scents of pine and chamomile were thick in the air, she sat down on her knees in the grass, still holding his hand as she looked up at him.

He hesitated, but only briefly before he knelt down before her and eased her onto her back. His body and mouth covered hers, and emotions welled up inside her.

She wanted to tell him that she loved him, but she was afraid, because she knew if she did, he would remember their impossible situation—that she was forbidden to him, just as he was to her—and he would put a stop to this.

Suddenly driven by a sense of urgency, she reached for his hand and held it firmly to her breast.

Their gazes locked and held.

Annabelle's body trembled with excitement and fear as she recognized the passion in his eyes and felt his physical strength as a man. He was heavy on top of her, powerful and aroused, looking as if he wanted to take her completely—and if he decided to, there would be nothing she could do to stop him.

But she did not want to stop him.

She could see, however, that he wished to stop himself. It was clear in his eyes, so she wrapped her legs around his hips to keep him close.

The height of his arousal became obvious as he pressed his body tight against hers, and she took in a deep, shuddering breath.

"This is very dangerous," he whispered, his voice strained.

"I know, but please don't stop."

She wiggled her hips, her body flooding with a willful desire for pleasures beyond anything she knew. She wanted to give herself to him completely and love him forever, and those emotions were so strong, her awareness of duty and responsibility to her family meant nothing.

Something about the way she moved must have

roused him further, because he covered her mouth again with a deep, rough kiss that was nothing like any of the other gentle, tender kisses on the picnic blanket. This was powerful and demanding and it was the start of something new.

Annabelle slid her hands down his broad back, lifted the back of his jacket and tugged his shirt from the waistband of his trousers. She massaged the strong muscles at his lower back, marveling at the smoothness of his skin and wanting to touch the rest of him, everywhere.

He groaned and rolled off her slightly to lean on one elbow while he quickly unbuttoned her bodice. Then Annabelle unhooked her corset in the front and felt a pleasurable freedom as it came loose. He slid a warm hand up under her chemise.

It was shocking—the feel of his hand on her bare flesh. No one had ever touched her there before, and when his mouth found hers again, she whimpered at the lust that was spreading through her body. It was incomprehensible, and the intimacy of his caress only made her love him more. She kissed him deeply and affectionately, wanting to show him with her body just how much she loved him.

"Annabelle," he said, resting his forehead on her chest, "I want you, but I can't take you. I can't."

"Yes, you can. Please don't stop."

He paused in silence for the longest time, his shoulders heaving as if he were out of breath from rowing the distance of the lake. A squirrel chirped somewhere in the distance.

For a moment Annabelle thought he was going to

stop, as he always had before, but instead, he tugged her skirts upward until he found the tapes that fastened her drawers and drew them loose.

Her heart began to pound with trepidation. This was happening so fast. Was he going to take her virginity? He could if he wanted to. She had told him to do it. But was she truly ready?

Before she had a chance to think anything through, he moved lower and began kissing her knees, then her thighs, then higher still until pleasure consumed her.

"What are you doing to me?" she asked breathlessly, all doubts and fears vanishing in an instant.

He gave no reply. He only reached a hand up to hold hers.

She squeezed it, and in the next few minutes, all she knew was the blinding heat of sensation and pleasure. Her body throbbed and she cried out, tears spilling from her eyes. He did not stop until she went limp. Then he covered her legs with her skirts and moved to lay beside her, leaning up on one elbow, looking at her.

Annabelle turned her head on the grass and met his gaze. "What did you do to me?"

He did not answer the question. He simply rested his hand on her belly, and for a long while they lay in silence, relaxing and listening to the ducks quacking on the lake, until Annabelle's breathing returned to normal.

Mr. Edwards gazed out across the water and said, "I think I deserve a medal."

"Why?" she asked.

"Because you're still a virgin."

A breeze blew through the trees behind them, and Annabelle's face grew serious. "It wouldn't matter if I wasn't."

And she meant it. She wanted him to be the one. Annabelle reached for the front of his trousers, but he quickly caught her wrist in his hand.

"No, Annabelle."

"Why not?"

"Because I'd lose my medal, and you'd lose something else more important than your virginity. You'd lose your freedom to make choices."

"Regarding a husband?" she asked.

"Yes, and I will not take that away from you."

Annabelle bristled. She wasn't entirely sure if he was doing this for *her,* or if it was a more selfish rationale. Perhaps he did not want to be obligated.

"Then what are we going to do," she asked in a desperate haze as she sat up and hugged her knees to her chest, "now that the painting is done? I don't want to say good-bye."

He sat up, too, resting his elbows on his knees and linking his hands together. She waited for him to answer the question, but he said nothing.

"You could come and pay a call," she suggested. "I could talk to my brother. I believe if he could come to know you, he would admire you as much as I do."

Mr. Edwards took a moment before he rose to his feet and walked to the edge of the woods, leaning a hand upon the rough bark of an elm. "No."

Annabelle was baffled by the firmness of his reply. "Why not? I would talk to him first."

Mr. Edwards shook his head and walked toward the

water, where he bent down, picked up a rock, and pitched it hard, as far as he could into the lake. "I remember the way your aunt looked at me on the train."

"I would talk to her, too," Annabelle argued. "I would make her understand."

He faced her. "Understand what? That you've been lying to her all summer? Sneaking off to meet a bank clerk alone on a secluded island? I'm sure she would be happy to hear it." He turned toward the lake again. "No, Annabelle, they'll never understand."

A sick feeling moved into the pit of her stomach. "You're not even willing to try?"

He looked over his shoulder at her, tilting his head as if he thought she was very foolish.

She had seen him look that way only once before— the first time they had come here—and today she sensed there was a side of him she did not know very well. A darker side.

It worried her. She wanted suddenly to see where he lived, to see his home and his mother. This summer had been nothing but a fantasy after all—because real life was not an endless string of leisurely Sunday afternoons.

"We should go," he said flatly, just like he had that first day, when they'd argued. "I can't miss my train."

"Why do you do that?" she asked pointedly. "You always want to leave when things get...." She didn't know what they were exactly, but she knew something was different.

He went to pack up her easel and paints, while she sat bewildered on the grass, watching him. What had just happened? A moment ago, he had looked at her with desire in his eyes. Now all he wanted to do was get away from her.

"I don't care what they think anyway," she blurted out, referring to her family, as she pulled on her stockings, drawers, and boots.

Mr. Edwards was crouching down, putting paint tubes back into the box, ignoring what she'd said. He didn't even look up.

Annabelle walked to him. "Did you not hear me? I said I don't care what they think. I'd run away with you if you wanted."

He went still.

"You don't know what you're saying. You don't even know me."

"Yes, I do."

"No, Annabelle. You *don't.*"

He returned to his task, quickly dropping the brushes into the box and closing it. He slid the box into her bag, then walked to the boat and set it inside.

Annabelle stood watching him, feeling hurt and confused. "I don't understand. Did you just come here every Sunday because you wanted a painting of yourself, and now that you have it, you're done with me? Or did you grow bored with me?"

She felt her heart breaking as she spoke the words. He wanted to end it. She could feel it coming.

He folded the easel and carried it and the painting to the boat, then came back for the lunch sack. "You know that's not true. I've enjoyed this as much as you have, but maybe we should be sensible and take some time to think about everything."

He returned to the boat and stood by it, waiting for Annabelle to get in, but she couldn't move. She was in shock over this change in him. It was as if the beautiful bubble of their love had just burst in front of her eyes.

"I don't need to think about it," she said, "but obviously you do." She strode toward him. "Just tell me why."

He did not respond. He simply gestured toward the boat. "Get in please."

"No. Not until you tell me why you're acting this way. Do you not care about me? Have I become dull?"

"You're not dull," he replied, sounding frustrated as he struggled for words. "It has just become too complicated, and I don't like things complicated. Now get in the boat please."

She was fuming now. She couldn't believe this was happening. How could a person change so quickly? What was wrong with him? And why had he let things go so far today if he wanted to end it? Why had he touched her like that and made her love him even more?

"Have you met someone else?" she asked, barely able to keep her voice from breaking.

"No." His tone was firm.

Not knowing what to say, because she was too angry to speak, Annabelle got into the rowboat. She braced her hands on the seat, while he pushed the boat over the gravel and into the water. Climbing inside, he picked up the oars, never meeting her gaze as he turned the boat around.

Annabelle glanced down at the painting. She had

worked so hard on it.

Soon they were coasting swiftly through the water, the boat propelled forward with every strong, forceful stroke. Mr. Edwards glanced at her occasionally while he rowed, but neither of them spoke. They both sat in angry silence, crossing the lake.

When they approached the dock, Annabelle grabbed hold of the post while Mr. Edwards climbed out and tied the rope. As soon as the boat was secure, she handed the painting and all the gear to him. He offered a hand to help her out, but she ignored it, awkwardly gathering her skirts in a fist while she climbed onto the dock without assistance.

"Annabelle...." he said, watching her pick up her things.

She did not speak to him. She couldn't. She was too angry.

She drew the lunch sack over her shoulder, along with her art case, then clumsily managed to get the easel under her arm.

"I'm leaving," she said as she started up the length of the dock. "You had better get going. You don't want to miss your train."

She heard him take a few steps to follow. "Annabelle, wait."

Her foot landed on the grassy bank before she stopped and turned. He was standing on the dock with the lake and their private island behind him. It looked so very far away.

Annabelle waited for him to say what he wished to say, but all he did was spread his hands wide in a shrugging gesture. Then he dropped them to his sides.

The noncommittal message infuriated her even more, and she could feel her cheeks coloring, her muscles clenching with fury.

"That's it?" she asked, shifting her load, barely managing to cope with the heavy easel under her arm.

He did not respond.

She looked away for a moment and shook her head. She had thought their time together had been special, but clearly, she had been wrong. All she'd been to him was a casual summertime affair, and now he wanted out.

"You've got your painting," she said icily. "The summer's over, and I think it's obvious that our friendship is over, too, because I for one *do* like things complicated."

When he still said nothing and did not even argue the point of their friendship coming to an end, Annabelle's anger mixed with heartache and disillusionment, and she had to fight not to let those feelings overtake her. As hard as it was to walk away from him—when a part of her wanted to drop everything, run back and beg and plead with him not to end it— she had to be strong. She was heartbroken, but she would not be pathetic.

She raised her chin and strove to keep her voice steady as she spoke over the painful lump in her throat. "Good-bye, Mr. Edwards. I will ask you not to contact me again."

With that, she headed for the path toward home, still thinking he might follow and tell her that he was sorry, and that he didn't mean it, and beg her to meet him again next Sunday. She wanted him to. The whole way along the path she listened for his footsteps, hoping, praying, that he would change his mind and come running after her.

But he did not come running. The woods were quiet as she tramped along the footpath, forcing herself to accept the truth—that she had been very wrong when she thought he loved her. He had been using her for his own pleasure and amusement.

Annabelle walked as fast as she could, fighting the tears that filled her eyes, but as soon as she reached the privacy of the forest, she couldn't go any farther.

She stopped on the path, dropped to her knees and wept into her hands.

Chapter 7

URING THE WEEK THAT FOLLOWED the painful end of her summer affair, Annabelle kept
mostly to herself. She slept late, feeling no desire to
get out of bed, and she excused herself from her aunt's
company in the afternoons, to nap in her bedchamber,
though she never really napped. She merely lay in her
bed, experiencing extreme—and sometimes conflict-
ing—degrees of emotion.

One minute she hated Mr. Edwards like she'd never
hated anything or anyone.

The next minute she missed him desperately and
longed to see him again—to touch him, to feel his
hands on her body, to taste his kiss. She wanted to
hear his voice and his laughter. She wanted to sit in
the boat with him and watch him row.

Most of all she wanted to feel the joy and freedom
she had felt when she was with him. She had never felt
more alive, or more herself.

Annabelle cried many tears that week, and on the
following Sunday she did what she'd promised herself

she would not do. She ran through the woods to the lake, whizzing past bushes and branches, hoping he had missed her, too, and would be there.

But when she emerged from the shady path the boat was empty, bobbing up and down upon the choppy water and knocking against the dock and she hated herself for being so weak. She hated herself even more for waiting there all afternoon, hoping he would appear and apologize for their argument.

That had been a sad, humiliating afternoon.

But it was nothing compared to the final time she saw him two weeks later, on a rainy Monday morning in London, when she experienced one of the most traumatic events of her life.

Hopping out of a hansom cab and into a puddle—after sneaking out of her brother's Mayfair mansion without her chaperone—Annabelle made her way across the cobbled street to the bank where Mr. Edwards had told her he worked. She dashed quickly through the rain to the front door.

Stopping under the overhang to catch her breath, she lowered the hood of her cloak and paused a moment, looking down at her muddy skirts.

She didn't know what she was doing here. She knew better than to try and see Mr. Edwards again, after he'd made it abundantly clear that he wanted to cut her loose. But she couldn't help it. She had spent the past three weeks wondering what had killed it for him, and she began to cling to the belief that he felt he was not good enough for her and thought he was doing the right thing by ending it.

If that was all it was, she would convince him it was *not* the right thing. She would convince him that he *was* good enough, no matter what her family thought.

She took a deep breath and swallowed hard, straining to hold on to her courage. All she wanted was an honest answer, even if the truth was not what she wanted to hear. If she had that, she believed she would have an easier time getting over him.

Just then, an older gentleman in a dark coat and top hat came running to reach the shelter of the overhang and paused a moment, brushing the raindrops off his shoulders before pulling the door open. He smiled at Annabelle and gestured for her to enter first.

"Thank you," she replied, forcing herself to cross the threshold.

Once inside, she glanced around the large bank and up at the high ceiling and brass chandelier. The floors were shiny black-and-white marble, and the desks and counters were all dark tiger oak.

There was a general echoing chaos of masculine voices, all speaking at the same time, and a bell rang from somewhere, signaling something. Toward the back, at least two dozen desks were arranged in rows, and each had its own lamp.

Feeling suddenly uncomfortable and out of place, she was about to turn and walk out when a young man in a bright blue tie approached.

"Good morning," he said. "Do you have an appointment?"

Annabelle squeezed her reticule in front of her and tried to appear relaxed. "No. I'm looking for someone. Mr. Edwards. John Edwards."

The young man's brow furrowed. "Is he a customer? Were you supposed to meet him here?"

She shook her head. "No. He works here, but he's not expecting me."

The man glanced uncertainly around at the array of desks at the back. "I am not acquainted with anyone by the name of John Edwards. Is he new?"

Her heart was beginning to pound. She shouldn't have come here alone, she thought, and certainly not to see her former secret lover. She felt as if this man knew she was sneaking around and doing something very wrong, and he was about to blow a whistle and turn her in.

"No, he's been working here for two years," she explained.

"Two years," the man replied with some confusion. "You are certain that's the man's name? Because there is no John Edwards here. What does he look like? Perhaps you have the wrong bank."

Annabelle began to feel a sickening knot tighten in her stomach. He had told her he worked there. Had he lied about that? But why would he lie? And if he did not work there, where did he work? How would she ever find him again?

Just then something drew her attention away from the young man before her, as if someone had called her name, though no one actually had.

Her gaze swung toward the back corner of the bank, where it remained fixed on the man walking toward her. All the sounds of the bank faded away, leaving only the whisper of her blood in her veins. The whole world seemed to disappear for a moment while she stood immobile, watching the man—Mr. Edwards—walk toward her.

He did not look pleased.

"Here he comes," she said in a fog, barely aware of the young man leaving her side and moving away.

Mr. Edwards came to a slow stop before her and spoke flatly without emotion. "What are you doing here?" He glanced uneasily at a coworker who was watching them. The coworker quickly went about his business.

Annabelle fought a feeling of intimidation as she looked up at her former love. There was no softness in his eyes, only displeasure. If she did not know him, she would believe him to be a cruel man. Perhaps he was. Perhaps that was why her heart was pounding and her hands were trembling. She actually felt afraid of him. This was not what she had expected.

"I just wanted to talk to you," she managed to say in a deceptively confident and assertive voice.

"About what?" he replied icily, as if she were a great bother to him and he had no time for her. It was shocking to her, the way this was unfolding.

All at once anger filled her. He had no cause to be so rude to her, to make her feel so troublesome. All she wanted was a few minutes of his time.

She squared her shoulders and copied his icy tone. "That man said there was no John Edwards here. Why would he tell me that?"

He stared down at her for an intense few seconds before moving past her toward the door and indicating for her to follow. "Come with me."

Still shocked by his inconceivable rudeness, Annabelle followed him outside, where they stood in front of the bank window. The rain poured hard on the street beyond the shelter of the overhang, hissing as it misted on the ground.

"I just want to understand what happened," Annabelle said, determined to get this over with as quickly as possible. "And why that man didn't know you as John Edwards."

"Let it go, Annabelle. This sort of thing happens all the time. Flirtations occur, and then they come to an end."

"Flirtations?" She could not control her voice. She had practically shouted the word. "Is that all it was to you? Because it was much more than that to me. I fell in *love* with you."

Something flashed through his eyes. Regret? Anguish?

No. It was shock. Love was a strong word.

"And that is why I had to end it," he said. "It went further than I ever intended it to go."

Her stomach whirled with dread and anxiety as she contemplated what he was saying. "So even in the beginning, you just wanted a casual affair?"

He paused, his brow furrowing as if he were in physical pain. "Yes."

"But when you came to see me that first time in my garden, you led me to believe it was much more than that. Were you toying with me? Is that something you do? Lead women on, only to discard them when their feelings become engaged?"

Annabelle realized she was clenching her fists.

"Lower your voice, please," he whispered, glancing

around. "It had to end. You know it as well as I do. I thought it kinder to end it sooner rather than later."

"Kinder! I don't want your pity."

"No, you wanted something else. You wanted too much, Annabelle, and I always knew it could never happen. You must have known that yourself."

"No! I told you I didn't care what my family thought."

He was quiet for a moment. "You need to let it go, Annabelle, and move on. Forget about me."

He turned to leave, but she grabbed hold of his arm. "Wait a minute. I don't believe you. You *did* love me. I couldn't have been so wrong about that."

Oh, how pathetic she sounded. How wretched and tragic. She wished she could take back every word she'd just spoken.

He glanced around with unease. "You're making a spectacle of yourself."

A spectacle? That did it. She could have throttled him.

"Tell me why you ended it," she demanded to know. "The real reason, and I want the truth."

The rain came down harder suddenly, roaring on the roof of the overhang and pouring onto the ground like a thick curtain beside them. But neither of them noticed. Their eyes were locked on each other's, while this painful moment of heartbreak played out.

Magnus was having trouble breathing. He knew the time had come that he must tell Annabelle the truth, and he nearly fell to his knees in despair.

He didn't want to hurt her, nor did he want to lose

her forever, but he couldn't let her go on believing that they could be together. He couldn't do that to her. He couldn't rip her from her beautiful privileged life and put her in the middle of a war between himself and Whitby. For if she defied her brother, she would be exiled to hell, just like he had been.

Shame flared in his gut. He should never have started this. He should have changed seats on the train that first day, as soon as he'd learned who she was. He should not have let himself be pulled in.

His voice shook when he spoke. "Fine. You want the truth? Here it is. My name isn't John Edwards. It's Magnus Wallis. I am Lord Whitby's cousin."

Annabelle felt her eyes grow wide. It felt as if her thoughts were draining out of her and washing away in the muddy flow of water down the street. She was stunned.

Cousin Magnus? No, he couldn't be.... It wasn't possible.

"Have you heard of me?" he asked. "Do you know that Whitby's father and my father were twins?"

Yes, she did know. She knew the whole sordid story about Magnus's father being sent away as a young boy because he was violent and dangerous. He had threatened the very life of his brother—Whitby's father. But she couldn't speak. Her brain was muddled, her mouth didn't seem to be working.

"It's a vile story, isn't it?" he said, his voice low and controlled, but seething with resentment. "My father was cut off from your high-browed family as I have always been, and it is no secret your brother and I despise each other."

"Why didn't you tell me?" Annabelle asked in a numb, shaken stupor.

"Because I knew it would cut our summer short, and...."

Magnus hesitated. A knife plunging into his heart would have been less painful to him than what he was about to say to Annabelle.

But he had to say it, because if he didn't, she might cling to some tiny shred of hope. He had to make sure she would let go of that and never come back here. For her sake.

"And I was enjoying a very satisfying jab at Whitby," he ground out.

Annabelle's face went pale, and her voice trembled when she finally spoke. "You were *using* me?"

He paused again, his jaw clenching. "Every minute we were together."

"But I loved you."

"I'm sorry to hear that, because I didn't love you."

He nearly choked on the words.

Annabelle sucked in a breath. There it was. The cold, hard truth, and hearing it spoken out loud knocked the wind out of her.

Magnus was staring at her, his eyes dark and expressionless. "I didn't want to say it, Annabelle, but you forced me to. So, there it is. Now you should go home."

Annabelle thought about what she knew of Magnus. She'd heard that he had inherited his father's jealous, violent nature, and that he was responsible for the death of Whitby's older brother, John, who was the heir to the earldom before Whitby. He had been found dead in Hyde Park when he was sixteen. His head was cracked open on a rock, and everyone knew that he and Magnus had seen each other that day and fought, as they always did.

Magnus had a bloody nose when they caught up with him afterward, but of course he denied having anything to do with what happened. They'd had no proof, and it was concluded that John was simply thrown from his horse.

John. John Edwards. Whitby's first name was Edward....

Her mind spinning with horrifying revelations, Annabelle felt faint and unsteady on her feet. "I cannot believe I was sneaking around behind Whitby's back to be with *you.*"

Magnus stiffened visibly, then his expression turned to a cold mask of stone. "But you were, and I helped you do it."

Annabelle could barely breathe. She had believed herself in love with a bank clerk named John Edwards, but it had all been a lie. He was her brother's enemy and he had used her and manipulated her for the sole purpose of vengeance.

"My brother is right," she said, glaring at him with hatred and loathing. "You *are* a monster."

She turned to leave, the rain pelting her face as she stepped out from under the overhang.

"Are you going to tell him about us?" he shouted after her. "I hope you do. I only wish I could be there to see his face."

Because Magnus never hated Whitby more than he

did at that moment.

Hearing that, Annabelle stopped. She didn't care that she was standing ankle deep in a puddle, nor that she hadn't bothered to pull up her hood and her tiny hat was soaking up the rain. She turned on her heel, marched back to Magnus, and slapped him hard across the face.

He took the punishing strike without flinching, then bowed his head very low.

"I will tell him," she said, "because I won't give you the satisfaction of knowing there is a secret between my brother and me, or that you know something he doesn't. And heaven help you when he finds out."

That was the last time she had ever seen or spoken to Magnus, her brother's enemy.

From that day forward, Magnus was *her* enemy, too.

Chapter 8

June 1892

*A*NNABELLE OPENED HER EYES AND found herself still lying on her back, staring groggily up at the leaves of the oak tree. The wind had died down and the sun had almost disappeared beyond the horizon. How long had she been asleep?

She sat up and reached for the timepiece on her chatelaine. The gold hands indicated seven-fifteen.

Annabelle scrambled to her feet, packed up her easel and painting, and hurried down the hill with everything in tow. She didn't want to miss dinner. If she did, everyone would be worried about her, for she never stayed out this late, unless she was painting a sunset.

But she hadn't been painting a sunset today, had she? No, she had been remembering the past.

She entered the house at the back and climbed the main staircase to her rooms, then rang for her maid, Josephine. Annabelle had already removed her bodice and overskirts herself when Josephine knocked and entered.

"Thank goodness you're back, Miss Lawson. I was concerned."

"No need to be. I fell asleep on the hill under the oak tree while the paint was drying."

Josephine disappeared into the dressing room and quickly returned with Annabelle's dark green dinner gown. Annabelle stepped into it and turned so Josephine could fasten it in the back.

"Your hair," her maid said, looking flustered.

Annabelle started pulling the pins out herself, while Josephine fastened the last few hooks at the back of her dress.

A minute later Annabelle was sitting in front of her mirror, watching her maid pull her troublesome hair into a knot on top of her head.

"The emerald earrings?" Josephine asked.

"Yes."

Josephine was passing them to her when the loud dinner gong rang, signaling the family to gather in the drawing room. Annabelle and Josephine exchanged a relieved glance. They had been very fast and efficient.

Rising from the chair, Annabelle smoothed out her skirts, while Josephine picked up Annabelle's afternoon dress, which was draped over the foot of the bed.

"Wait!" Annabelle said, hurrying to reach into the pocket of the skirt before Josephine took it away. "I need something." She reached in for the folded letter, then managed to feign a smile. "You can have it now."

As soon as Josephine was gone, Annabelle took the tiny key out of the locket around her neck and walked to her desk. She sat down and pulled her miniature cedar chest out of the top drawer, set it in front of her on the desktop and inserted the key into the lock. When the box clicked open, she raised the lid and stared at the first letter from Magnus, received almost two weeks ago.

She touched a finger to her lips.

He had written to tell her that he had returned to London and purchased a gallery, and that he wished to meet with her. Naturally, she had not replied, for she had been in shock, for one thing. Secondly, she had not wished to meet with him then, just as she did not wish to meet with him now.

A knock sounded at her door and she jumped, then slammed the box shut, for she had not told anyone about the letters. Though she certainly should have. She should have informed Whitby. The fact that she had not done so had troubled her for two weeks. It was not like her to keep things from her brother. But so many things about Magnus were secreted away in her heart. So much of what had happened that summer she would never share with anyone.

"Who is it?" she asked.

"It's Lily."

Annabelle quickly shoved the box back into her desk drawer. "Come in!"

The door swung open and her brother's wife entered with a hand on her swollen belly, for she was due to deliver her fifth child in the next few weeks. "I saw you come in late and wondered if you needed any help preparing for dinner."

"No thank you, I'm fine," Annabelle replied, her hands fidgeting on the desk. "Josephine was very astute. She had my gown ready and waiting for me."

Lily approached and rested a hand on the corner post of Annabelle's bed. She appeared hesitant, and her eyes held a hint of concern as she tilted her head to the side.

"Forgive me, Annabelle, but I must ask—are you feeling all right? You've not seemed yourself these past few weeks."

She should have known she could not hide her feelings from Lily, for they were best friends, and had been for the past eight years, since the day Lily married Whitby. Indeed, she had confided in Lily then, about what had occurred with Magnus, but this new development with the letters, she had kept to herself.

Leaning back in her chair, Annabelle sat in silence for a moment, then opened her drawer and reached for the cedar box. Setting it on the desk, she removed the two letters and handed them over.

"What are these?" Lily asked.

"They're from Magnus."

Lily gasped in astonishment, then fumbled with the letters, hurrying to read what they said.

"He's in London," she blurted out. "He can't do that. The allowance from Whitby requires that he remain in America."

"I know," Annabelle cut in. "I don't understand it. I am not sure what he's trying to accomplish."

Lily considered it, then moved toward an uphol-stered chair. With one hand on her belly, the other reaching behind her, she lowered herself onto the cushioned seat. "Have you replied?"

"Of course not. I was in shock, and I certainly don't wish to see him, or have any contact with him whatsoever."

Lily's cheeks paled as she considered the broader ramifications of this.

"Honestly, I can't believe this is happening," Annabelle continued. "I'd thought he was gone forever. For the past eight years it was almost as if he didn't exist. I've been content living here with you and Whitby and the children, and I thought all that was behind me, but now he's come back and...." She didn't quite know how to say it. She didn't even fully understand it herself. "I'm afraid hearing from him is stirring up old feelings."

Lily's eyes clouded with worry. "What feelings?"

Annabelle thought about how she'd just spent an entire afternoon reliving the past, feeling the excitement, the joys...and the overwhelming pain and heartbreak.

"Mostly my anger toward him," she replied. "Today I was recalling that summer we spent together, and I...." She hesitated, fighting to keep her voice steady. "I was so in love with him, Lily."

Lily gave her a consoling look. "I know you were."

Annabelle felt tears threaten, but forcibly crushed them. She stood and walked to the window. "Of course that was before I knew the truth about him— that he was lying to me and using me to satisfy his vindictiveness. He was so cruel that day in the rain, at the bank. It's remarkable how quickly love can change to hate."

Lily was still holding onto the letters. She flipped through them again. "What do you think he really wants? He can't just be here to open a gallery. There must be a more personal motivation."

Annabelle raised an incredulous eyebrow. "He's a snake. He's probably here to enact some other ruthless scheme."

Lily ran a hand over her belly. "I met him once in the village, remember? Eight years ago, just before he left for America. It was five years after he'd jilted you, and I know you and Whitby thought I was naive, but I didn't think him duplicitous."

"That's his talent," Annabelle explained. "He knows how to charm when he needs to, but he can knock you onto your back the very next instant. And are you forgetting that your coach overturned immediately after you encountered him?"

"There was no proof that he was involved," Lily argued. "And he denied it to Whitby. It could have been a coincidence."

"Just like there was no proof about how Whitby's brother John ended up with his skull cracked open on a rock when he was sixteen?"

Lily lowered her gaze. "Oh, Annabelle. Must you."

Annabelle closed her eyes, feeling ashamed for saying such grisly things. She faced her sister-in-law. "I am so sorry, Lily. That was my anger spewing out of me."

"It's all right. I understand."

Annabelle went to sit next to Lily on the sofa and rubbed the back of her neck to ease the tension she was feeling.

Lily handed the letters back. "Have you considered," she said, "that no matter what Magnus's motives are, this is an opportunity for you to be included in an art exhibition? It's something you've always wanted, and at least this time you would know exactly who you're dealing with."

For some unknown reason, Annabelle laughed. "But of all the paintings I've done, he wants to show the one I never wanted to see again."

"Which one is that?"

Though Annabelle had confided in Lily about many things, she never told her—or anyone—that she had painted Magnus that summer. She supposed she had not wanted to talk about it because, unlike the painful memories, it was not something she could erase.

"It's a painting I did of him on the lake, while he was in the boat, fishing. But I hate that painting. It's not representative of my work. It's artificial because I was painting a lie, and what I really want is to get it back and destroy it. Perhaps I could buy it back from him, or even give him another in exchange."

Lily pursed her lips. "That's a possibility."

For a moment Annabelle thought about everything, then she spoke in a gentle tone. "Do you know why I've never married? Because I have never been able to trust a man who was trying to be charming."

Lily's lips curled up in a grin. "All men try to be charming when they wish to impress a lady."

"I know that, but I believe I will always be sus-picious and skeptical, regardless. When a man is attentive or looks at me with interest, I feel immediately contemptuous of him. It's my downfall. My weakness. It's why I'm thirty-four and gathering dust on a shelf."

"In that case," Lily said, "you should definitely go and meet him. You're older and wiser now, and skeptical, as you say. This time, you know who and what you are dealing with. You'll be able to tell whether Magnus is sincere or seeking further vengeance. You will see it in his eyes."

Annabelle leaned back on the sofa. "I don't know. I can't conceive of it—actually seeing him again, discussing an art exhibition, of all things."

"If it makes you feel any better," Lily said, "ask if he'll show another one of your paintings, but at least go and find out his true purpose."

It was difficult to imagine walking into a gallery and seeing Magnus face to face again after all these years. What would he look like? Annabelle wondered. Perhaps his hair would be speckled with gray. Perhaps he'd grown bald and fat. She could only hope.

Either way, Lily was right. She was older and wiser now. She would see through his charm this time, and most assuredly the love she once felt for him no longer existed. For thirteen years she had felt nothing for him but hatred.

"Very well then, I will go," she said. "Under one condition. You cannot tell Whitby."

Lily sucked in a breath. "I beg your pardon? I can't keep a secret from him. We share everything."

"Please, Lily. Just this once, because if he knows that Magnus is in London, he will try to talk me out of going, and he'll go straight to Magnus himself. And you know what happened the last time when I told him what Magnus had done."

"Yes."

Of course Lily knew. Years ago, Annabelle had told her sister-in-law how Whitby had taken his coach out in the dead of night and gone to Magnus's home. He'd pounded on the door, and when Magnus answered, Whitby grabbed him by the lapels and shoved him across the entryway, up against the opposite wall. Heated words were exchanged, threats delivered, and Whitby had punched Magnus.

From what Annabelle had been told, Magnus took the blow and did not fight back, and after a second persuasive punch in the stomach, he doubled over, fell to his hands and knees on the floor and said simply to Whitby, "There. Now get out."

Even now, when Annabelle imagined that row, she cringed. Perhaps it was the unsettling idea of her brother conducting himself with brutality, because there was no man in the world more kind and loving than he. She knew that without a doubt. His fury must have been exceedingly potent that day.

Aside from that, she could not deny she disliked the image of Magnus being beaten, despite his appalling treatment of her. It made her feel slightly ill.

"Please don't tell Whitby yet," she said to Lily again. "Just wait until I see Magnus. I will tell him myself immediately afterward. You have my word."

Lily shifted her posture, her expression strained with misgivings. "I will *try* not to say anything, but I can't promise it. Now let us go to dinner. I could eat a team of horses, harness and all."

Lily pushed herself out of the chair and made for the door, but Annabelle went to her desk. "I will join you in a few minutes. First, I want to send a note to Magnus and tell him that I will meet him, before I change my mind."

Lily left the room, and Annabelle put both his letters back into the box, dipped her pen in ink and began to write.

> *Mr. Wallis,*
>
> *I received your letters but have one request. I would like to offer another painting to you in exchange for The Fisherman, as I would like to have it back. I will bring to your gallery, for your perusal, a selection of my other works. I hope you will find one of them suitable for your exhibition.*
>
> *Sincerely,*
> *Annabelle Lawson*

Two days later, Annabelle's letter arrived at the Grand Hotel in London and was delivered up the stairs on a gold-trimmed silver salver—to the largest, most luxurious suite in the building.

Magnus Wallis answered the door and accepted the letter, then carried it toward the roaring fire in the marble hearth, where he stood for a moment, after recognizing the penmanship immediately.

He tore it open, his heart pounding violently with curiosity and anticipation as his eyes scanned over it.

She was coming. Tomorrow.

Exhilaration flooded his veins at the thought of seeing her again, after all these years. He tipped his head back, closed his eyes and exhaled heavily.

A moment later he set the letter on the red cushioned chair and crossed to the sideboard, where he poured himself a brandy. He swirled it around in his glass a few times before taking a sip, wondering what he would say to her when she first walked into his gallery. There were a thousand things he wanted to say, but he knew he would have to tread carefully.

He supposed, since she was coming to discuss the exhibition, he would have to address that particular issue first and convince her to let him show *The Fisherman,* because he knew it would garner a superb response. He'd been waiting a long time to show it to the public.

He was disappointed, however, that she wanted it back. What did she mean to do with it? Did she have a plan for it, or did she simply not wish *him* to have it?

Sweeping that notion away—for it would do him no good tonight—Magnus continued to stand by the sideboard, staring at the wall. He took another sip of his drink. A log dropped in the grate, but he barely noticed because he was thinking only of one thing—Annabelle's pain and anger outside the bank that horrific day thirteen years ago, and his own unbearable agony.

He had wronged her, and he knew that, but he had wronged himself as well, for he had not believed himself worthy of her.

Downing the rest of his drink, he reminded himself that everything was different now. He had made something of himself in America, and finally put the misery and indignity of his old life behind him.

Most importantly, he had crossed an ocean for Annabelle, and nothing was going to stand in his way.

She didn't know it yet, but this time, no matter what it took, no matter how long, he was going to fight for her. And he would be relentless in that fight—forever—until the glorious, blessed day she was truly his.

Chapter 9

WHEN TUESDAY FINALLY ARRIVED, ANNABELLE rode the train to London for her dreaded meeting with Magnus and spent the entire trip rehearsing what she would say and how she would say it.

She had already decided that she would speak about nothing but the exhibition, and she would be aloof, indifferent, somewhat cool—so that he would understand that she did not trust him—but not to the point of rudeness, for he was a gallery owner and possibly her *entree* to the exclusive London art world.

She hoped she could convey those things, and not let him see that she was nervous or tense. Or still affected by what happened in the past.

Glancing down at the fashionable heeled boots she'd borrowed from Lily, which were uncomfortably tight, she wondered with a frown who she was trying to delude. She was beyond nervous or tense or affected. She was terrified that she would take one look at Magnus and remember the inescapable attraction, and feel the heartbreaking, devastating loss of those wonders all over again.

Oh, she was dreading this. She took a deep, shaky breath and let it out slowly, and promised herself that she would only remember that which was foul.

The train slowly chugged into Victoria station, and Annabelle got up and lugged her large case down the aisle. She stepped onto the noisy platform, where dozens of people milled about, then she walked through the station and onto the street, where she climbed into one of the hansom cabs lined up outside.

"Two twelve Regent Street, please," she told the driver, who closed the door and returned to his seat. Soon they were on their way, clattering through the busy streets of London.

Annabelle glanced down at her black case and felt a pang of nervous butterflies. She wondered if she were being foolish, trying to get *The Fisherman* back. It was hardly the act of an indifferent woman.

A short time later the cab pulled up in front of the gallery, which on the outside looked like any other shop. It had a large-paned window and a sign over the door that read, umbrellas by maillet, but the paint was faded, and the space looked as if it had been empty for quite some time. Was this supposed to be the gallery?

Annabelle frowned. Perhaps she had been gullible to trust Magnus even this much. Perhaps the gallery itself was another ruse, another deception.

She got out and paid the driver, then walked to the front door and entered.

Inside, the walls were painted soft white and there was an aroma of fresh paint and sawdust. The floors were newly polished oak. Supplies were littered on the floor in the far corner—a carpenter's box full of tools, a few cans of paint, and brushes.

There was a large maple desk at the back, which looked like it had just been delivered, and when she looked up, she saw that the lights were yet to come, for there were a few holes in the ceiling with new wiring.

It was true, then. It *would* be a gallery.

Annabelle could not deny that it would be marvelous when everything was finished. And the location—in the most exclusive shopping district of London—was simply inspired. It was perfect for an unknown artist just starting out.

Wondering if Magnus was there, perhaps behind the closed door at the back, she cleared her throat and called out, "Hello!" No one responded, so she tried again. "It's Annabelle Lawson. Is anyone here?"

At last the door opened and a man stepped into view. He remained there, at a distance, just standing there, looking at her.

It was Magnus, and she froze. Her breath caught in her throat at the sight of him. He wore a black suit and tie, his hair was thick and wavy, and when he began striding slowly across the gallery toward her, she felt a little lightheaded. He looked older than the young man she remembered from many years ago, but otherwise the same—still strikingly handsome, still wielding a raw, charismatic power that no other man in the world could rival.

He came to stand before her with his hands at his sides, and she fought to remember how he had once used, hurt, and deceived her.

"Good afternoon," he said.

"Good afternoon," she replied.

They both stood motionless, staring, until Annabelle finally took a breath and recovered herself.

"I'm sorry, I don't understand," she said. "I was very surprised to receive your letters, Mr. Wallis. What, may I ask, are you doing in London?"

She had wanted to be aloof and behave with indifference and speak of nothing but business matters—most importantly his interest in her paintings—but clearly that was not going to be possible.

"You promised never to come back," she added, "and Whitby pays you to stay away."

Magnus was speechless for a moment, and she thought she saw a loss of composure in his eyes. No wonder. He probably hadn't expected her to bring up the past, at least not in the first ten seconds. She hadn't expected it herself.

"I am aware that I am in breach of that contract," he replied. "But I intend to terminate it while I am here, because if I wish to travel to England, I will not have anything stand in my way."

Annabelle raised her chin and took a moment to try and regain her own composure, which seemed to have drained into her boots. "Why *did* you come?" she asked. "I hope it was not to have another jab at Whitby."

Magnus shook his head, his voice low as he spoke with a deep, almost forceful sincerity. "No, Miss Lawson, that is not why I am here. I don't care about Whitby. I only wanted to see you."

His words caused a commotion in her, and she realized her heart was racing uncontrollably. "Maybe this was a mistake," she quickly said. "I think I should go." She turned to leave, but he followed.

"Please, Miss Lawson, wait. Just hear me out."

Annabelle stopped with her back to him, her hand on the door handle, wondering uneasily why she was not already outside on the street, hailing a cab. Because she hated Magnus—now more than ever—for showing her how much of a hold he still had on her. Just the sight of him had knocked all her best-laid plans from her mind and turned her into a pathetic woman, still suffering from a thirteen-year-old heartbreak.

He moved to the door and stood beside her, and it took considerable effort to turn her eyes to meet his. Slowly, he brought a hand up to place over hers on the doorknob, then gently lifted it off.

Annabelle snatched her hand back. She did not want him to touch her.

"What is it you need to say?" she asked, noticing for the first time some differences in his appearance. He had developed lines around his eyes, and he was dressed differently. Expensively.

His broad shoulders rose and fell as he exhaled. "I will explain, if you will only come away from the door."

She took a moment to consider it, then did not even try to hide her lack of enthusiasm as she turned around.

"Perhaps we could go into my office?" he suggested. "I have chairs, and I could make tea."

"I don't want to go into your office," she replied

while she labored to quiet the workings of her body, but it wasn't easy when she was so terribly shaken by the fact that this meeting—which was supposed to be about an art exhibition—had spiraled so swiftly out of control.

"Please," he said again, holding up a hand to direct her toward the back.

For a moment Annabelle stared at him, for she did not want to do anything he asked of her.... But in the end, she did move away from the door—albeit reluctantly—for no reason but one: She had come here to learn his intentions and his true reasons for returning to London, and if she did not learn those things, she would leave there feeling very much in the dark. And she did not wish to be in the dark. That had been her downfall with him the last time. All summer long.

Not waiting for him to ask again, Annabelle set down her art case, crossed to the back and entered the office. It was a small room, but impeccably furnished, with a new sofa and two matching chairs on a Persian rug, and an empty space at one end, presumably for the desk outside the door.

Magnus entered behind her and walked to the cabinet in the corner. He opened one of the doors and withdrew a kettle.

"How are you going to make tea?" Annabelle asked. "You have no stove."

"It's an electric kettle," he replied. "I picked it up in Chicago last year."

Annabelle watched him plug it into the newly wired outlet on the wall. An electric kettle. What a brilliant invention. In any other circumstances she would have asked questions about it, but at present she was in no mood to talk about kettles, even if they *were* electric.

While he bent forward to withdraw cups and saucers from the bottom shelf of the cabinet, Annabelle took note of his finely made black suit and how it complimented his strong, muscled form. He was, and always would be, an attractive man who moved with a masculine grace all his own, and she hated the fact that she could still think so. Hence, she decided it would be better not to look at all. She turned toward the window.

It was at that moment she saw it.

The painting.

It hung on the wall adjacent to the window.

Annabelle froze on the spot, her gaze moving slowly across the canvas as she took in the dramatic mix of color, the light and delicate shadows. She could almost hear the fishing line slicing through the air, the hook landing on the water. She smelled the lake, the worms in the bait box, and the smelly trout.

Barely aware of the teacups clinking on saucers behind her, she moved closer to the painting, her emotions welling up inside her.

Good heavens. It was unlike anything she'd ever done before or since, and that undeniable fact filled her with yearning and a feeling of despair as she stared at it. She couldn't believe *she* was the artist.

Suddenly Magnus was standing beside her, gazing down at her profile. She hadn't even heard him approach.

"There it is," he said, turning his eyes toward the painting as well. "I know you said you'd like to exchange it for another piece, but I'd really rather not."

Suddenly she remembered that she had wanted to destroy it, and she could have wept at the thought. What had she been thinking? She couldn't possibly, not after seeing it again.

"I had forgotten what it looked like," she said in a bit of a daze.

They both stood in silence, staring at the painting, while the clock ticked steadily on the opposite wall. Then Annabelle remembered where she was and with whom she was standing.

"I am surprised that you kept it," she said. "I thought you might have sold it by now."

His tone was calm and surprisingly tender. "I never wanted to part with it."

It was a flattering reply, but Annabelle didn't entirely trust it.

Saying nothing more, she went to sit on the sofa. Magnus took a seat in one of the chairs, facing her. They sat in awkward silence for a moment or two before Magnus spoke.

"You look well," he said.

They were going to engage in small talk, were they?

"Thank you," she replied coolly. "I have been keeping busy."

"Painting?"

As he sat back waiting for her answer, Annabelle wondered why they were doing this. They were surely beyond normal social graces, especially after she'd asked all those forthright questions just now.

Perhaps he was seeking to bring some normalcy to

this conversation, which might not be a bad thing. She did not wish to feel uncomfortable. She wanted to be as calm and indifferent as he appeared to be.

"Yes, I paint often," she replied at last, "and I spend a great deal of time with my nieces and nephews."

He was nodding, looking genuinely interested, but she did not trust that, either.

"And how is Lady Whitby?" he asked.

"Very well. She and my brother are expecting their fifth child in a few weeks."

"Ah. That's wonderful news."

Annabelle felt her brow furrow with dismay. Magnus had been her family's enemy for as long as she could remember, accused of causing the death of Whitby's older brother. Yet he was asking after them like an old friend, acting as if he cared.

Which he could not possibly. He was a villain. A hateful human being. And this was ridiculous.

Nevertheless, when another awkward silence descended upon them, Annabelle found herself slipping into the familiar safety of polite conversation again, because she could not bear the noise of her heart drumming in her ears while he simply looked at her.

"America agrees with you?" she asked without enthusiasm.

"Yes. I have a house in New York and another in South Carolina. I prefer the southern weather in the winter months."

She pondered this news. He had two homes, and he had purchased this space, furnished it with some very fine pieces, and his clothes.... Well, he looked immaculate, with shiny Italian leather shoes and a shirt that was clearly made of the finest linen money could buy.

What had he been doing since he left England?

He must have seen the question in her eyes, for he answered what she was thinking. "I am in business in America," he explained. "Shortly after I arrived there, I discovered I had a knack for buying and selling property."

He was leaning an elbow on the armrest, his forefinger resting on his temple. He appeared very relaxed now, with one long leg crossed over the other, gazing calmly at her.

Annabelle knew he was doing this just to ride out her shock from seeing him again, and despite her agitation, she found herself breathing a little slower.

"I started out by purchasing a building not much bigger than this one," he continued, "which had a good location but was run-down. I rebuilt it almost from scratch, doing most of the work myself, and sold it at a profit. Then I did the same thing again with a larger building each time, and now here I am."

"Congratulations," she said, only because it was the appropriate thing to say. She looked around the room. "Did you do all this work yourself?"

"Most of it, yes," he said, "which I greatly enjoyed, because I haven't done this sort of thing in a while. The projects became too complex, and there were too many at once. I have people now who do the work for me."

"I see." She was quiet for a moment, pondering what he had just told her, thinking about this building. "Why a gallery?"

He inclined his head. "I have an interest in art."

"You didn't when I knew you," she said. "You knew nothing about it when I met you on the train."

He did not seem surprised or shaken by the slight note of accusation in her tone. He remained cool and collected. "No, but since then, I have acquired an appreciation."

Another tense silence ensued. Annabelle could almost feel the weight of her painting hanging on the wall behind her. She turned around and looked at it again.

"Someday that will hang in the National Gallery," Magnus said. "Or perhaps in the Met in New York."

"I hardly think so," she replied, even though she knew the painting was exceptional. More than exceptional, and it felt strange to think such a thing, because she never marveled at any of her other paintings. She was always so critical of her own work. But this one....

She still could not believe she had painted it.

At the same time, she was a woman, and the art world wasn't exactly an open door for members of her sex.

"Is this your first gallery?" she asked, wanting suddenly to redirect the conversation back to him. She didn't want to talk about herself or her life or her work as an artist.

"No. I own two others in New York. They're labors of love."

Labors of love? This whole conversation was surreal. This was Magnus. Magnus!

Annabelle strove to get her head on straight and decided it was time to take control of this meeting and learn his true motivation for returning to England. And to learn why he had asked her to hear him out.

"Mr. Wallis," she said, properly and primly. "Let us get to the heart of the matter, shall we? What is it that you wanted to say to me when you would not permit me to leave just now?"

He leaned forward in his chair. "Yes. Indeed. Well. I apologize for that, but I wanted to tell you that I have some regrets about what happened between us all those years ago, and I wanted you to know that."

Annabelle squeezed her hands together on her lap. "Regrets?"

"Yes."

"I see." She lowered her gaze. "I do appreciate the sentiment, but I am sure you will understand it when I say that I am having a hard time believing you."

He nodded and sat back again. "I suspected that might be the case. But I hoped it would not be."

Her eyes lifted. "You hoped it would not be? You treated me appallingly, sir. You used me and discarded me, knowing from the very beginning that you were going to break my heart, but you did not care in the least. So you must forgive me for finding it difficult to believe that such a heartless man might be remorseful."

They were harsh words, and yet it felt enormously satisfying to say them.

He frowned. "I am not heartless, Miss Lawson, and I mean to prove that to you."

She drew back slightly and scoffed. "Prove it to me? How in the world do you intend to do that?"

"To begin with, I will tell you that I am sorry,

and that I never meant to hurt you. It was not my intention when I came to see you, that first time, at Century House. When we spoke in the rotunda."

Annabelle's mouth fell open. Perhaps she was being a tad vindictive herself, but good God! Did he think he could just waltz back to London and say he didn't mean it, and she would simply smile and say *"How kind of you"* and he would be absolved?

"It took you thirteen years to realize that you had been unfeeling and unscrupulous, and that I deserved an apology?" Her anger was rising like a tidal surge.

He spoke with fervor. "I was not unscrupulous, but merely stupid and naïve for thinking that we could be friends. And it did not take me until now to realize that I had wronged you. I always knew it, even that day at the bank."

"Yet you followed through regardless, and said terrible, hurtful things to me. So why apologize *now?*"

When he didn't respond right away, she stood up. This was absurd. She wanted to leave.

He stood, too. "Please, Miss Lawson. Sit down. Allow me to finish."

She hesitated, fought to subdue her temper, then reluctantly did as he asked.

"Thank you," he said, sounding genuinely contrite.

Annabelle took a moment to breathe and calm her nerves.

"I find it odd that you claim you were not unscrupulous," she said, "when you told me in no uncertain terms that you were using me all along. Explain that, if you will." She frowned at him as she remembered his brutal, merciless words: *I was enjoying a very satisfy-*

ing jab at Whitby...I didn't love you...

Just thinking of it made her breath come short. He had cut her so deeply. There had been no kindness in his manner. He had not even tried to be gentle about it.

"I thought it was my only choice, to say those things to you," he said, "because I wanted you to forget me. But I did care for you, and I was not using you for vengeance against Whitby. I ended it because I was your family's enemy, and I knew I could not provide a proper life for you. I said what I said because I knew you loved me, and I believed it was the only way to make you leave me. Because I felt you deserved a better man than me."

She stared at him in astonishment as the kettle began to hiss on the side table.

"Your water is boiling," she said, because she was at a loss for words otherwise.

Magnus rose to pour the water into the silver teapot. He carried the small round tray to the coffee table between them and set it down.

Annabelle sat forward to pour her own tea. "Are you not going to have any?" she asked, sitting back.

"No."

Exhausted and weary from this trying conversation, Annabelle brought the fine china cup to her lips, but the tea was too hot to drink, so she set it back down and contemplated what Magnus had just said to her.

All her life she had been told certain things about him and his father—that they were both dangerous and conniving. Magnus had proven that sentiment to be true. He had admitted it that day in front of the bank, so how could she trust anything he said to her now?

Suddenly in no mood to drink tea, Annabelle stood and walked to the back window, which looked out onto a narrow lane. She focused not on what was outside, but on the window itself—the way the little bubbles in the glass held the light.

Then she heard Magnus rising from his chair, too, and heard his quiet footfalls across the carpet. Just the sound of his approach caused a fire to burn through her body, and she found herself remembering the excitement of being with him at the lake, and in the woods on the island, and how she had melted from the bliss of his presence alone.

He still possessed that same power, that same magnetic pull, and she hated that she was affected by it all over again.

Fighting hard to bury the memories—because she could not let him use his charm to trick her again— she squared her shoulders.

He came to stand beside her, so immensely disturbing to her in every way, but she refused to look at him. She did not take her eyes off the glass.

"Miss Lawson," he said, his voice changing to a soft, tender whisper. "*Annabelle*...I know you don't want to hear this, but I must say it. I must." He leaned closer, so that she could feel the moist heat of his whisper in her ear. "I regret what happened between us. I regret how it ended, and I assure you, I have not able to forgive myself. Nor have I been able to forget you."

Her emotional response to those words was devastating to her, because they reminded her of all the nights she had cried herself to sleep after their breakup, when she wished it could be nothing but a bad dream and her wonderful Mr. Edwards would return to her and say those very words—that he was sorry and none of it was true and he could not forget her.

But as quickly as the memory bloomed in her mind, it disappeared again, because she had the good sense to remember that what happened between them had not been a bad dream. It was very real, and she had to protect herself as she had not so many years ago.

Annabelle raised her chin. She wanted to be confident and defiant, but when she spoke, her voice was not strong. It shook. "You're right about one thing. I don't want to hear it."

Perhaps he recognized her weakness. He leaned closer still. "But Annabelle, not a day has gone by that I haven't thought of you and wondered how you are. Sometimes I dream about you, and the dreams are so real that I wake up in a sweat, thinking for days afterward that you might be missing me too. Every time I look at *The Fisherman*, I ache."

Annabelle closed her eyes, digging deep for the will to remember how cruel he had been that day at the bank, and to consider how cruel he might be again. She could not let herself fall so easily for him a second time.

"I have not been missing you," she told him.

Though she could not deny that she often looked for his face in a crowd.

With the back of a finger, Magnus stroked her arm lightly. His voice was gentle and soothing. "I will say it a hundred times if I must. I am sorry for hurting you. If I could go back, I would handle it very differently."

Suddenly Annabelle couldn't speak. Her chest was heaving with a desperate need for air. A lump had formed in her throat and she struggled to swallow over it and force it back down, for she could not allow herself to be fooled by his blatant attempt at seduction.

She turned and faced him, imposing an iron will on herself. "But you can't go back, Magnus. What's done is done."

"I know," he replied. "But perhaps someday you will find it in yourself to forgive me." His penetrating gaze did not waver. "I am not the man I was thirteen years ago. I promise you that."

She frowned, wondering what was really going on in his mind. Was he truly sorry? Was he being sincere? And even if he was, did it make a difference? "You expect me to believe you, simply because you say it?"

"No, I hope you are able to see it for yourself."

She looked him over from head to toe, still working hard to hold on to her caution, to be skeptical. "Because you have money? Is that it? A gallery? An expensive suit? Is that how I am supposed to see that you've changed?" She walked away from him. "I am afraid you're going to have to do better than that, Mr. Wallis, because I don't trust you. You could be the richest man in the world, and nothing you could say or do would ever change that."

He frowned as he digested her reply.

"I should go now," she said, before he could say

another bewitching word to her.

She walked out and he followed. They crossed the empty gallery, and Annabelle realized with a start that they hadn't even begun to talk about the art exhibition.

Perhaps it was just as well because she was not sure she could survive seeing him again. It was too painful. Too confusing.

She picked up her art case containing the three extra paintings she had brought.

He glanced down at it. "But wait...."

Annabelle closed her eyes. He was not going to let her get away so easily after all.

"I know this is probably too much to ask," he said, "but I am opening this gallery in a few weeks, and I would still like to include *The Fisherman*." He glanced down at the case again. "But perhaps, with your permission, I could look at what you brought?"

Annabelle was befuddled after all that had just occurred, but when she glanced around at the cream-colored walls and the shiny oak floor in this superb location, she could not let Magnus hold her back from this. She had wanted to be indifferent, didn't she?

Hence, she forced herself to hand the case over to him. He accepted it and carried it to the desk. Not entirely sure she had done the right thing, Annabelle stood back while he removed the first piece, which she called *Amber Grass*.

He held it at arm's length before him, silently studying it while Annabelle tried to forget that he was Magnus, the only man she had ever loved. Right now, he was a gallery owner making a judgment about her paintings.

He set *Amber Grass* on the floor against the wall before withdrawing the next piece: *Autumn Forest.* Again, he held it at arm's length, studying it for a long moment while Annabelle waited.

"Do you have arrangements with any other artists to show their work?" she asked, glancing around suspiciously.

He didn't reply right away. He continued to look at *Autumn Forest,* then set it on the floor against the wall, next to the other one.

"Yes, I brought a few works done by some American artists. Have you heard of George Wright?" He reached into the case for the third painting.

Surprised, Annabelle took a step forward. "George Wright? You're showing *his* work here?"

He was one of her favorite painters. He had a style of brushstroke like no one else, and he rebelled openly against convention.

"Yes," Magnus said, holding up the last painting. This one was a seascape that she called *Fierce Waters.*

Finally, Magnus turned to face her. "This one is the best."

"The seascape?"

"Yes. You have a gift with water."

Annabelle didn't know what to say. She was still staggered by the fact that Magnus had, in his possession, a painting by George Wright, and he was asking to include her work in the same exhibition.

"My home in South Carolina is on the coast," he said lightly, "and it has a spectacular view of the

ocean." He set the painting down beside the others.
"You would like it."

"Would I indeed?" she replied, not wanting him
to think he knew her personal tastes. But then she
remembered telling him once that she wished she
lived on the coast. Had he remembered that?

Magnus moved to the desk and sat on top of it, his
hands curling around the edge of it. "The paintings
are excellent, Annabelle. Can I show them? All of
them?"

She took a moment to think about it. If she allowed
him to show her paintings here, wouldn't that require
more meetings or correspondence with him? She did
not wish to have any connection with him again after
today because she did not trust him.

But then she thought of George Wright. She imagined her works hanging on the same wall, then
wondered if the promise of this was merely a ploy to
lure her in for some other evil plot against Whitby....

"How long do you plan to stay in London?" she
asked, wanting to understand what this would entail.

"I'm not certain," he replied. "I've purchased two
residences on Park Lane, so it depends how long the
improvements take and how quickly I can turn them
around."

She gave him a look. "You've returned to conquer
London, have you?"

"I suppose you could say that," he replied, his eyes
serious.

She imagined Magnus buying the houses on either
side of Whitby's London residence and turning them
into brothels. Then she chided herself for entertaining

such an outlandish thought. Surely, he would never be so blatantly ruthless with his vengeance. Would he?

"Regarding the gallery, however," he said, changing his tone, "I might only be involved with it for a few more weeks. I am looking for someone to manage it, and once it's established, I'll likely do what I do best."

"Sell it for a profit?" she asked.

He shrugged, somewhat apologetically. "It's what I do. And though I consider my galleries to be labors of love, I don't intend to remain in London forever, so it would be difficult to oversee."

She was quite relieved to hear that he didn't intend to remain in London.

"Well, it's obvious that you've put a lot of work into this place," she said, glancing around.

"What can I say? I am a man who enjoys rolling up his sleeves."

She suspected he was trying to tell her that he no longer coveted Whitby's position in society, that he had no respect for it and preferred his own position as a man of business. But she wasn't entirely sure she believed that.

"It's probably futile to ask," he said, "but I don't suppose *you* would be interested in managing the gallery for me?"

Yes, it was most certainly futile.

"I have no experience," she replied.

"But you know art."

But she could not work for Magnus. "I'm sorry, I don't think so."

He grinned at her, and it was the first time she had seen even the smallest hint of a smile. It was familiar and stirred those memories again, so she turned her face away.

"I had to ask," he said.

"I'm flattered you thought I might be qualified," she replied, striving to sound businesslike.

"I have no doubt that you would be."

The temperature of the room seemed to escalate suddenly as Annabelle stood before Magnus, who was still sitting on the desk, now paying her compliments.

He had paid her compliments once before, though, hadn't he? To seduce her and get what he wanted.

"But you haven't answered me about the paintings yet," he said. "May I show them?"

Annabelle thought about it. Despite her hostility toward Magnus and her desire never to see him again, she knew this was an opportunity she could not refuse—to be shown in the same gallery as George Wright, when it was next to impossible to break into the London art world, especially for a woman.

She could not let her personal feelings keep her from a dream such as that, could she? If she did, she would surely live to regret it.

Besides, Magnus had said he planned to hand the gallery over to someone else, so she would likely be dealing with that person after he returned to America.

After another moment's consideration, she finally gave him an answer. "Yes, you may show them."

Magnus slapped both his hands on the desk before he hopped off it, looking exceedingly pleased, while

Annabelle wasn't so sure. "This is wonderful," he said. "I know your work will attract a great deal of attention."

"No, George Wright will attract the attention."

"Not for long."

She wished she could take the compliment at face value, but alas she could not. Not coming from him.

"I will escort you out," he said, walking past her.

When they reached the door, Annabelle stopped, feeling a sudden onslaught of anxiety over what she had just agreed to. She faced him. "Perhaps if there are any details to be discussed regarding the exhibition, we could correspond through letters, as I don't come to London very often."

It was a lie. She came all the time, and she suspected he knew it. She could see it in his eyes.

"Of course," he replied, nonetheless. "And I will let you know as soon as I find a manager. When I do, he will take over from there."

She stood in front of the door, waiting for Magnus to open it.

"Thank you, Miss Lawson," he said, bowing slightly, and she wondered what he was thanking her for, exactly. The paintings? No, it was more than that, but she did not wish to contemplate it further.

She simply nodded and walked out.

Chapter 10

*A*FTER ANNABELLE LEFT THE GALLERY, Magnus closed the door and stood for a moment with his hand still resting on the knob.

Well. That had not gone quite as swimmingly as he had hoped, but at least he had broken the ice.

Leaning back against the door, he closed his eyes, feeling grateful for one thing at least—he finally knew what she looked like, after wondering for years how she might have changed.

Not surprisingly, she was just as beautiful as she had always been. Perhaps even more beautiful, for the years had given her a certain indefinable vigor, for lack of a better word. She seemed self-assured and more sophisticated than before.

But her eyes were still the same—wild and luminous, her figure still voluptuously attractive. The only difference was that her manner of dress was more conservative. She had been wearing a sensible hat and gone were the clumsy boy's boots.

He wondered if she still wore them in the country,

when she was lugging her easel up and down steep hills, with her ferret, Helen. Did she still have a ferret? he wondered. Probably not. Nevertheless, he smiled affectionately at the thought of it, but then his smile faded as he reminded himself that he still had a steep mountain of his own to scale and conquer.

Pushing away from the door, he crossed the gallery to where Annabelle's paintings leaned against the wall. He crouched down to look at them again. By God, they were magnificent. He especially admired the creative mix of color—the blues and grays of the seascape, with hints of.... Was it mauve?

He also had to marvel at how the water seemed to surge and swell before his very eyes. How in God's name did she create such movement?

Then he found himself wondering why she had never shown her paintings to the public before now. What was she afraid of?

Rejection, most likely, which caused him some regret.

All that aside, she was without question miraculously gifted, and it only added to her allure. He was in awe of her, and he wanted her back in his arms.

But was that even possible? he wondered with a twinge of concern, striving to be realistic as he rose to his feet and returned to his office. He glanced at the sofa cushion where she had been sitting—she hadn't touched her tea—and recalled their conversation, how she had spoken to him with such cool detachment.

She had not forgiven him, but he was not surprised, given what he did to her and the number of years she'd harbored and nurtured her hurt. He had expected as much when he rose from bed that morning. He had expected there would be a quarrel of some sort.

He'd also expected her to think he was there to exact further vengeance upon Whitby.

Magnus had told her he didn't give a damn about her brother—which was God's own truth—but he doubted she believed that, because there was a time when he very much *had* given a damn. Those five years after their breakup had been the darkest of his life. He had hated Whitby more than ever, and his bitterness had been all consuming, eating away at him like a disease. There were times when he'd become a villain himself, taunting his cousin, just to inflict pain on him where he felt pain was due.

And once, when Whitby was gravely ill, Magnus had actually hoped he would not recover. That was how dark those days had been.

If Magnus hadn't left for America when he had, he didn't know what would have become of him. He would surely have continued to wallow in his anger, on a downward course straight into hell.

But those days were over. After eight years in America, his life was no longer dismal. He had made a success of himself, had learned to have hope, and because of that, he finally felt worthy of Annabelle.

Even though she had been unwavering in her antagonism today, he would press on. He would not give up. Rome wasn't built in a day, after all. He would simply have to be patient and lay one precious stone at a time.

Annabelle returned to Century House that evening, exhausted after the three-hour train ride from London. Carrying her empty art case with her, she greeted Clarke, the butler, and went straight to her rooms to dress for dinner.

A short while later she hurried into the drawing room to join Whitby, Lily, and the children.

"Annabelle, you're back," Lily said cheerfully, standing by the piano, holding John's hand—her youngest, at only three years of age. He ran to Annabelle, and she scooped him up into her arms.

"Auntie Annabelle!"

"Johnny," she said. "Did you miss me today?"

"No."

"No!" Annabelle replied, laughing out loud.

"Father took us fishing!" Johnny explained, squirming out of Annabelle's arms, forcing her to set him down before she dropped him.

Annabelle looked across at Whitby, who was sitting on the far side of the room, across from young Eddie at the chess table. "You went to the lake?" she asked.

"Yes," Whitby replied. "It was a perfect day, wasn't it, son?"

"Perfect indeed," Eddie replied distractedly, moving a chess piece.

"I didn't want to go," Dorothy said in a haughty voice, for Dorothy—Lily and Whitby's only daughter as of yet—was a very grown-up four-year-old, who would never be caught dead touching a fish. She preferred her dolls and hair ribbons.

"So, if you didn't go with the boys," Annabelle said, "what did you do today? Did you stay indoors?"

"No. I took Helen the Second for a walk in the garden," Dorothy replied.

"Well, thank you very much. I'm sure Helen enjoyed the exercise."

Dorothy nodded proudly, then Annabelle moved to the sofa and sat down next to Johnny and Lily. Her thoughts drifted back to the fishing excursion years earlier.

"That old boat still floats?" she asked, realizing she hadn't been in it since that long-ago summer.

"Like a boat should," Whitby said. "We didn't have to bail, did we, boys?"

"What's a bail, Father?" Johnny asked.

"It's when the water leaks into the boat and you have to scoop it out with a bucket so you don't sink."

"I wouldn't like to sink," Johnny said.

Lily messed his hair. "I should think not!"

Lily and Annabelle shared an amused glance as Johnny slid off the sofa and went to join young James, who was sitting on the floor playing with his army of tin soldiers.

"How did everything go?" Lily asked in a quiet voice, though her eyes were brimming with curiosity.

Annabelle hesitated, glancing across at Whitby. "It went fine. He liked my other paintings, and he's going to include them in the exhibition."

"That's wonderful."

Annabelle then told Lily about the American artist, George Wright, and how it was an honor to be shown in the same gallery.

"But how was everything else?" Lily asked in an even quieter voice.

Annabelle wasn't sure where to begin. "It was rather

nerve racking. We talked about what happened years ago."

"You don't say."

"Yes, and he apologized to me, Lily. Can you believe that?"

Lily sat back. "I thought perhaps he might."

"Did you really?"

"Yes. Why would he come all this way and contact you unless he had something important to say?"

Annabelle gazed pensively toward the boys playing with their little army on the other side of the room. "I am still not entirely certain he came here for the singular purpose of apologizing. He seemed very determined, as if he were on a straight path toward something."

She thought about what he'd said to her, that he had not forgotten her. Was it possible *she* was the something he wanted, and he was in London to claim her? Could he be that presumptuous?

Yes, he probably could.

"He's purchased two buildings," Annabelle told Lily, attempting to distract herself from the idea of Magnus actually "claiming" her.

Lily's eyebrows lifted. "He must have money beyond the allowance from Whitby. Did he say anything about that?"

"Yes, he said he doesn't want it anymore, and he intends to inform Whitby as such."

Lily gazed lovingly at her husband. "You are going to have to tell him everything, Annabelle. I cannot keep it secret any longer. He knows me too well."

Annabelle watched her brother playing chess with

his son. Eddie made a move, and Whitby shouted with laughter. "Brilliant play, Eddie! I did not see that coming!"

But there was something else he did not see coming, and she was not looking forward to explaining it.

Later that night, after the children had gone to bed, Annabelle returned to the drawing room with Lily and Whitby—as was their habit most evenings after dinner, when they would read or chat or play cards.

While Lily played the piano, Annabelle sat on the sofa with Whitby, but she barely heard the music, for her mind was occupied with thoughts of what had occurred that day and how she was going to explain it to her brother.

"There is something I must tell you," she finally said, "and I hope you will not be angry."

Whitby's brow furrowed with concern.

"Over the past few weeks," she began, "I have received two letters from...a gallery owner. He wanted to include one of my paintings in an exhibition."

Her brother touched her arm. "That's wonderful news, Annabelle. Congratulations. But why would you think I would be angry?"

She bit her lip, then decided to cease her stalling and meet the problem head on. "Because the letters came from your cousin Magnus, and you're not going to like this, Whitby, but Magnus has returned to London."

For a moment her brother stared at her as if he wasn't quite sure he'd heard her correctly, then his eyes darkened with worry and he looked across the room at Lily, who was tapping away on the piano.

Annabelle understood her brother's anxiety. He had lost many loved ones in his lifetime—which was why he'd always been so protective of his wife—and he considered Magnus a serious danger to her.

"He wrote you letters while posing as a gallery owner?" Whitby asked.

Annabelle looked down at her hands upon her lap. "Well, he wasn't exactly posing. He really does own a gallery, and I went to see him there today."

Whitby stared at her in disbelief. "Did you know it was him when you agreed to meet?"

"Yes, of course," she assured him. "I'm sorry I didn't tell you, but—"

Whitby regarded her with outrage. "Why didn't you? Who knows what could have happened? You shouldn't have gone there alone."

He stood up, looking as if he wanted to dash out of the house that very instant, find Magnus wherever he was, and confront him again, just like he did the last time.

The music stopped suddenly. Lily turned to them. "Is everything all right?"

"Magnus is in London," Whitby told her directly.

"Oh dear," Lily replied.

For a long intense moment, he stared at his wife fixedly. "You knew."

Lily's lips parted. "Well...."

Annabelle felt guilty for asking Lily to keep something so important from her husband, but that was apparently not Whitby's first concern. He strode to the window, contemplating what all this meant.

"He should not have come back. He is in breach of our agreement."

"Please, Whitby, sit down," Annabelle said. "Let me tell you what happened."

Thankfully, he returned to the sofa, and Lily sat across from them to listen in.

Annabelle decided to start at the beginning. "That summer that we spent together thirteen years ago, I painted Magnus in the boat fishing, and that's the painting he brought with him—the one he wants to hang in the gallery."

"Wait a moment," Whitby said, holding up a hand. "You painted him? You never told me that."

"I didn't really want to talk about it."

He gazed off in the other direction, as if lost in a memory. "I saw that painting over his mantel once— on the day I offered him a settlement to leave England. *You* painted that?"

"Yes."

"It was one of the most beautiful paintings I'd ever seen, Annabelle," Whitby said. "I didn't recognize it as one of yours. Not that I don't think your work is exquisite, but it was different."

"I almost didn't recognize it myself," she said, "when I saw it again for the first time today."

Both Lily and Whitby waited in silence for her to continue. She took a moment to decide where to begin and what, in particular, she should tell them. It all seemed rather smudged together presently.

"When I met him today, he explained that he regretted the way he had treated me all those years ago, and that he hoped I could forgive him."

Whitby's jaw clenched visibly. "You didn't believe him, I hope." It was not a question, but rather a very strong suggestion.

"No, not really."

Where had that come from? It should have been a firm "Absolutely not."

"Not *really*? You're not sure, Annabelle?" Whitby's tone was laden with disbelief.

Annabelle felt suddenly frazzled. "No.... I mean of course I am sure. And I told him so—that I could never trust him, not in a hundred years."

There was no mistaking the fact that Whitby relaxed somewhat upon hearing that. His fist opened on his lap.

"I'm relieved to hear that," he said. "Did you get your painting back? He doesn't deserve to have it. We can hang it here. In a prominent place."

Nervous butterflies invaded her belly as she prepared to answer. "No, he still has it, and I left three more with him as well."

Whitby's hand slid up and down his thigh, as if he were trying to wipe something from his palm. "Why?"

"Because he is opening that gallery soon, and I want my work included in the exhibition."

Whitby chuckled bitterly, as if he had expected things to unfold exactly as they had. "But don't you see? That was his plan. He bought the gallery for the singular purpose of seducing you with it. That manipulative scoundrel."

Annabelle frowned as she fought to understand the reasons why her brother was so afraid for her, when he already knew she hated Magnus for breaking her heart.

"Tell me something," she said. "Why do you still hate him so much after all these years? I know you blame him for your brother's death, but everyone knows there was no concrete proof that—"

"Are you falling in love with him again, Annabelle? Is that what's happening?"

She sat up a little straighter. "No, of course not," she assured him. "I just want to know what I am dealing with. You believe he has returned for further vengeance upon us as a family—but vengeance for what? Surely he does not still harbor hatred because of how his father was cut off from the family. That was two lifetimes ago, and he seems to have moved on."

Whitby paused a moment before he spoke. "But you already know why Magnus has always been rejected here."

Annabelle sat with her back poker straight and squeezed her hands together tightly on her lap. "You told me that his father was dangerous, that he tried to harm your father when they were children. But how exactly?"

"Among other things, Magnus's father tried to set my father on fire."

Annabelle covered her mouth with a hand. "Good heavens."

"The bed went up in flames, and my father suffered burns on his arms and legs, but thankfully managed to get out of the room alive."

Annabelle flinched at the cold, disquieting tone of her brother's voice. "But what did Magnus do?" she asked, needing more specific information. "Why was he also cut off from the family?"

Whitby raked a hand through his hair, his eyes clouding over with disdain. "From what I understand, no one even knew of Magnus's existence until he was nine. His birth was kept secret from us."

"How did you find out about him?"

Whitby sat forward, elbows on knees. "When Magnus's father died, his mother took it upon herself to demand financial support from us, and promised my fourteen-year-old brother John—who had just become earl that year—that if he didn't give her what she wanted, she and Magnus would make all our lives a living hell. Then they did. Magnus threatened and even attacked John dozens of times over the next few years, and it didn't stop until John was dead."

Annabelle's blood chilled in her veins. "But Magnus would have only been a child."

"His father was a child when he lit my father's bed on fire. He was mad, Annabelle. He was jealous and hateful, and Magnus was the same. You know it yourself. You know what he did to you, how he used you. You know his heart is as cold as ice."

She began to feel ill.

Whitby blinked slowly at her. "You were only an infant when Magnus came into our lives," he said.

"I was three when John died," she added. "I barely remember him. All my life you have been my only family. And now Lily and the children, of course."

Yes, Whitby had been her guardian for as long as she could remember. Her protector. He had taken care of things when he learned how Magnus had used and discarded her, and he had held her while she wept.

Annabelle squeezed Whitby's hand. He was a good man, and now he was a husband and father. He loved his children with every inch of his being and would gladly lay down his life for any one of them. There was no one in the world more devoted and loyal to those he loved, and Annabelle was thankful to be one of those fortunate people.

If she had to decide whom to trust—Whitby or Magnus—of course it would be Whitby. There was no question.

"Do not worry about me," she said. "The only thing I care about is that my paintings will hang beside George Wright's paintings, and he is an artist I greatly admire. And I will not be seduced. I am not the foolish, trusting girl I once was. I assure you that it will be impossible for Magnus to ever win back my esteem. Especially after what I've heard today."

Whitby closed his eyes and pinched the bridge of his nose, while Annabelle glanced uneasily at Lily, who shrugged helplessly.

They all sat in silence for a minute or two, until Whitby spoke. "There is still the issue of my contract with him. He is in breach."

"He knows it," Annabelle said. "But he told me he didn't want your money anymore. He is prepared to terminate the agreement."

Whitby looked up in surprise, as if he couldn't believe any of this and almost found it humorous on some strange, outlandish level.

"Well, it's not up to him, is it? Whether he likes it or not, the payments stop now."

Annabelle merely nodded.

"Where is this gallery he purchased?" Whitby asked.

"Two twelve Regent Street," Annabelle replied, knowing full well why Whitby wanted the address, and she was not going to stand in his way. If he had something to say to Magnus, he could say it. It was none of her affair. She didn't care. They were both grown men.

Though in truth, they had always been more like two bulls locking horns, ramming into each other at every opportunity.

Whitby stood. "I will be traveling to London in the morning."

"I suspected as much," Annabelle replied.

He turned to leave, but Annabelle stopped him. "Wait, Whitby."

Her brother faced her, and she briefly mulled over what she wanted to say to him.

"You might find him different now," she said. "He has money."

Her brother stared at her briefly before his eyes narrowed. Lily nervously cleared her throat.

"Rich or poor," Whitby replied, "I will not find him any different." Then he turned and left the room.

Chapter 11

$\mathcal{M}$AGNUS WAS LEANING OVER A table he had
purchased at an auction that morning, pushing hard upon the sander—back and forth, back and
forth—taking pleasure in knowing that when he was
finished, this piece would be exquisite. He would set
the gallery cards upon it.

Feeling the strain in his back and arms, he straightened and wiped an arm across his brow. It was hard
work, sanding paint off mahogany, but well worth it.
And he'd always enjoyed working with his hands.

Just when he was about to lean back into it, the gallery door opened, and who should walk in but Lord
Whitby.

Bloody hell. Magnus set the sander down and let
out a deep sigh of frustration, for he did not want to
stop what he was doing, especially not to confer with
his cousin, but he knew it was inevitable and necessary. Best to get it over with.

He pulled off his gloves and tossed them onto the
table, then crossed the gallery to address Whitby.

They stopped in the middle of the room, facing each other, but after a short time, Magnus grew tired of the bravado. He had no interest in this sort of thing, which was rather astounding. At one time he had lived for it—especially during the five years after his summer with Annabelle. His bitterness over that loss had simmered and raged inside him for a long time afterward, and his resentment toward Whitby had reached its peak.

Thank God he had left for America when he had.

"I was expecting you today," he finally said to his cousin.

"Were you indeed?" Whitby replied.

"Yes. I suspected you'd want to discuss our contract. And I knew you would wish to have a word with me about Miss Lawson."

Whitby glared at him briefly before turning and wandering around the gallery, looking with a critical eye at the new wiring in the ceiling, the fresh paint on the walls. "I will always be looking out for Annabelle," Whitby said, "as she is my sister."

"Not by blood," Magnus replied curtly, realizing it was a point he'd often revisited with a sense of relief—the fact that Annabelle was not born of the same ilk as Whitby and John and their insufferable father. Their grandfather, too. He could certainly not forget to include him.

Whitby merely glanced at Magnus and ignored the comment. He walked to the front window and watched a few people walk by on the street, then spoke with a note of superiority. "A gallery. How out of the ordinary. You certainly chose a promising location."

"I always do."

Magnus watched his cousin saunter leisurely around the gallery again and recognized his intent to demonstrate how relaxed and confident he was—as if Whitby considered Magnus to be a mere nuisance, nothing more.

Yet he had come all the way to London without wasting a moment, hadn't he? Perhaps Whitby was not as impervious as he pretended to be.

Not that it mattered to Magnus at all. His cousin could throw himself off a tall building, for all he cared. All Magnus wanted was to get back to his work.

He glanced impatiently down at the sander, which sat idle on the table.

"Look," he said, taking a step forward, "I've got things to do, so let us get through this, shall we? Yes, I have returned to England, and by doing so I have broken our contract, so why don't we render it void as of three weeks ago, the day I stepped off the ship? Feel free to have your solicitor draw up papers for me to sign."

Whitby faced him. "Just like that, you are going to give up ten thousand a year? I hope the visit was worth it."

"It was," Magnus replied with absolute honesty.

Whitby frowned. "Why? What could possibly be worth that much money?"

"Why I returned to England is none of your affair," Magnus replied.

"It is my affair when you break a contract with me."

Magnus struggled to keep his impatience under

control, for this conversation was going around in circles when he only wanted to be done with it. "I told you I don't want your money anymore. I don't need anything from you."

"Except for Annabelle," Whitby said flatly.

All at once the tension in the gallery shot up to the ceiling. Magnus felt the muscles in his forearms tighten beneath his sleeves, and when he spoke, his tone was distinctly firm. "But she doesn't belong to you, does she?"

Whitby's expression clouded over with a grave, stony warning. "She is my sister and therefore under my protection."

"But can she not have thoughts or conversations of her own? She is a woman now, Whitby. She can do as she pleases."

Whitby offered no reply, but Magnus could see the displeasure in his eyes.

Oh, Magnus was getting tired of this. He didn't come to England to fight with Whitby. He came for Annabelle, and that was all that mattered.

"Is there anything else you wish to say to me?" Magnus asked. "Because I have work to do."

Whitby pondered the question. "Yes, as a matter of fact, there is. I will have you know that my sister is off limits to you, and if you lay one finger on her or hurt her in any way, I will hunt you down like a dog. Do you understand?"

Magnus stiffened and swallowed hard over the bile rising up in his throat. He had thought things were going so well since his arrival in England, but this was most assuredly a setback. And quite out of line for

Whitby to make such threats.

Evidently his cousin had not changed over the years. Not in the slightest.

"Do not attempt," Magnus said clearly and succinctly, "to tell me what I can and cannot do. You do not control me, nor are you above me."

"Maybe not according to American ways, but in England I am very much above you."

Magnus clenched his hands into fists. He could barely comprehend how quickly his hatred toward Whitby awakened and shot to the surface.

But he would not be dragged back down into the fight. That was behind him now. He was here for Annabelle.

"If you will excuse me...." he firmly said, turning away.

Whitby walked to the door. "Don't say you weren't warned."

Bloody hell, that was it. Magnus had tried to be civil, but there were limits to his forbearance, and he couldn't take this insufferable arrogance. Not anymore. Not on his own property.

He strode forward. "You always have to have the last word, don't you?"

Whitby raised a triumphant eyebrow at him and walked out, but as Magnus watched him go, he realized with a most disturbing sense of unease that where Whitby was concerned, he preferred to have the last word as well.

"What happened?" Annabelle asked, hurrying to meet her brother at the door the moment he walked into the house.

"Nothing of consequence," Whitby replied. "Magnus and I reached an agreement regarding our contract and his financial expectations."

Whitby handed his coat and hat over to the butler.

"That's all?" Annabelle asked, knowing there had to be more. She had been waiting all day for the details, praying he was not going to return and tell her they ended up in the street, wrestling on the ground. It wasn't as if it hadn't happened before, or so she'd been told.

"You really want to hear it?" Whitby asked.

Was he daft? Of course she did.

Taking her by the arm, he escorted her through the entrance hall to the stairs. "As it happened, your name did come up, and I informed Magnus that if he ever laid a finger on you, or hurt you again in any way, he would have to answer to me."

Annabelle stopped on the stairs. "You didn't."

Whitby stopped also, seeming surprised. "You didn't think I would fail to mention it, did you?"

Annabelle lowered her gaze. She understood why her brother felt compelled to speak to Magnus; they had their own issues. But she did not need Whitby to fight her battles anymore, and now she was worried that Magnus was going to change his mind about showing her paintings.

"I am a woman now," she said. "I told you I can take care of myself, and any connection I have with Magnus involves my paintings and his gallery and nothing more. You did not have to tell him that."

Her brother looked taken aback. "And here I

thought I was being your hero."

"I don't need a hero," she said irritably, then regretted her sudden moodiness. But ever since yesterday she had been feeling anxious and edgy, as if the floor were about to collapse under her feet.

Whitby faced her on the stairs, one hand on the railing. "Well, I suppose I have nothing to worry about then."

"No, you don't," she said, despite her uncertain mood. "Except for your youngest son, who seems to have discovered what's inside the sugar bowl."

"Sugar," Whitby said matter-of-factly.

"Yes. All over his face and down between the sofa cushions."

Whitby gave her an affectionate look that suggested they exonerate each other. Then he chuckled and hurried up the stairs.

Annabelle went in the opposite direction, however, because she couldn't very well be around other people when her nerves were so distressingly frayed.

For a full week Annabelle heard nothing from Magnus regarding the exhibition—not a single word—but neither did her paintings come hurling back at her, so she could only assume that no news was good news and everything was going ahead as planned.

She spent most of her time in her studio, working on a new painting—a waterfall surrounded by moss-covered rocks. She had sketched it a few months ago and was only now beginning the actual painting, though she was having some trouble with the water. Annabelle nevertheless continued blocking in the colors.

At the start of the second week, a footman brought her a letter on a silver salver. The letter had come from the Regent Street Gallery, and the mere sight of the address gave her heart palpitations, for this was all so much more complicated than just the gallery exhibition.

She waited for the footman to leave before she broke the seal and began to read:

> *Dear Miss Lawson,*
>
> *It has been one week since our meeting, and I felt compelled to write and thank you for the opportunity to show your paintings in the gallery, and to inform you of my progress.*
>
> *I have met with three other London artists who have agreed to be a part of the exhibition, and as of this morning, I now have in my careful possession, all of the various works.*
>
> *Tomorrow I will speak to a gentleman from the Times, who will write something about the opening, so I am hard at work on the final details.*
>
> *I have enclosed an invitation for the opening on the evening of the twenty-seventh, and I hope you will choose to attend. All of the other English artists will be there.*
>
> *Sincerely,*
> *M. Wallis*

A shiver of apprehension rippled through Annabelle's veins as she examined the invitation—an ivory card with a paintbrush done in watercolor in the top right-hand corner, and all the information printed in fine gold script just below.

She flipped it over, and on the back saw a list of all the artists. George Wright was named at the top, of course, and below in alphabetical order were the rest. Her name was in the middle.

She was ashamed to admit that despite all her fears and reservations about working with Magnus, she couldn't deny the fact that it was a thrill to see her name listed with so many fine artists.

But should she attend? she wondered uncertainly. If she did, she would have to socialize with Magnus in a friendly, affable way.

Annabelle sat down at her desk and reminded herself that this was a dream come true. How many years had she imagined her work being included in an actual London art show? And hadn't she already decided that she would not let her personal feelings hold her back?

The answer seemed clear. She should go. There would likely be a crowd anyway, and Magnus would be busy as the host. That would make it easy to avoid him.

But what would she wear? Good heavens. What did one wear to a gallery opening? A ball gown? Would it be that formal? No, surely not.

She checked the date again. At least she had time to acquire something. It was three weeks away. Plenty of time.

Annabelle stood and crossed to the window, not really seeing anything beyond the glass. She was very distracted. Then it occurred to her that she should reply and let Magnus know that she would be attending. Yes, that was the proper thing to do.

She sat down at her desk again and withdrew her personalized stationery from the top drawer, dipped her pen in ink, and began to write:

Dear Mr. Wallis,
I was pleased to hear of your progress with the gallery. Thank you for the invitation to the opening. I would be delighted to attend.

Sincerely,
Annabelle Lawson

She set down her pen and blew upon the ink, rereading what she had written.

...delighted to attend.

She sat back in her chair. *Delighted? Pleased to hear of your progress?*

She closed her eyes and blinked, as if that would bring reality back to her brain. This was Magnus she was writing to. In all her excitement, she had forgotten that rather sticky fact. She felt her brow furrow with confusion.

Annabelle looked down at her reply again and remembered their meeting one week ago at the gallery. She had been somewhat hostile toward him, aloof at best. Perhaps she should rewrite the note and try to convey that tone instead.

In the end, she shook her head at herself. Why was she giving this letter so much importance? It was a reply to an invitation, nothing more. If she were truly indifferent, she would not be analyzing it so carefully.

With that, it was decided. No more doubts and

uncertainties. She sent the trifling letter as it was.

Three days later Magnus sat down at his desk in the gallery office and read Annabelle's reply. She was coming. No. Even better, she would be *delighted* to come.

He leaned back in his chair until the front legs came clear off the floor and stretched his arms over his head. Ever since his meeting with Whitby, he was sure he had been hung out to dry. He'd imagined himself the topic of many heated conversations in the Whitby household—most of which would involve his misdeeds and flaws and general overall offensiveness. He'd even expected Annabelle to change her mind about letting him show her paintings. Every day, whenever a knock had sounded upon the gallery door, he'd expected it to be a footman, come to ask for them back.

But no footman had come, only this letter. This very satisfying letter.

Magnus sat forward, the chair legs landing hard upon the oak floor. There were still so many things left to be done—one of which was the printing of the exhibition labels, and since the paintings were being offered for sale, he did need to understand Annabelle's expectations regarding price.

He supposed he could have asked her that in the last letter, but now he was glad he had not, for it gave him another excuse to write to her.

Dear Miss Lawson,
I will be placing exhibition labels on the walls next to each

painting, and we must determine an asking price. It is my recommendation that you ask £200 for each of the three paintings you brought when you came to the gallery and £500 for The Fisherman. *Would that be acceptable to you? My commission is ten percent.*

M. Wallis

As soon as Annabelle read the letter, she dropped it on her desk. Five hundred pounds? Surely he was not serious. She was no one special. She had never sold a single painting in her entire life. She couldn't possibly ask that much.

She picked up her pen....

Dear Mr. Wallis,
While I am flattered by your confidence in my work, I wonder if a more modest price would be more appropriate. Perhaps £25 each? And £50 for The Fisherman?

A. Lawson

Magnus read her note and smiled. Dear, sweet Annabelle. She was modest, and completely oblivious to her talent as an artist. How could she not know?

Not that he was complaining. He was more than pleased that he would be the one to help her see it. *Yes, one stone at a time, carefully laid....*

Dear Miss Lawson,
I received your reply regarding the asking prices of your paintings, but I must plead your indulgence to trust me in this regard. I have seen many paintings come and go through my New York galleries, and I can assure you, these amounts

are not unrealistic for works as exquisite as yours. If any-thing, I would like to ask more.

I am honored to be the one to show them for the first time, as I believe you have a rare talent. The gentleman from the Times *was most impressed with your work, and singled you out among the others, and I was not at all surprised.*

So please, I ask you, let me print those prices? Anything less would be an injustice.

M. Wallis

Annabelle sat on the edge of her bed to read the letter, and as soon as she finished it, she flopped backward, sinking into the soft feather mattress. Staring up at the ceiling, she wondered if she should pinch herself.

Were the paintings really that good? She had no idea. She felt totally incapable of judging her own work. All she felt when she looked at them was a frustration over the things she wanted to change.

She was never completely satisfied with any of her paintings and felt them nothing special at all, even after she was long finished with them.

Except perhaps for *The Fisherman*. She had not wanted to change a thing on that one—which had been a novel experience for her.

But still... £500? Could she possibly allow Magnus to ask that much?

She supposed he had an interest. He wouldn't want to ask something insignificant because he had a commission to earn. But nor would he want to ask anything outrageous, because if the paintings did not sell, he wouldn't earn a farthing.

But surely, if he was as wealthy as he appeared, his commissions were of no consequence. He had called his galleries labors of love, hadn't he? Yes, he had, and he now had a great deal of experience in the art world.

Then it occurred to her—he couldn't be toying with her, could he? Flattering her as a means to an end? In a devious scheme to seduce her for some hidden purpose? To injure Whitby again?

Old fears and uncertainties came bubbling to the surface, because she *had* been flattered by all of this, and she caught herself chewing a fingernail.

Then again, if he *was* asking a high price just to flatter her, she would find out at the opening, wouldn't she? She would know very quickly if people thought the prices were unreasonable.

Annabelle sat up again and finally decided to take a risk and let Magnus ask whatever he wished. As difficult as it was, she would trust him—at least in this regard. And she would use the gallery opening as a way to test him, to see if he had been deceiving her.

She walked to her desk and penned him a quick note to approve his suggested prices, then dressed to go and visit Madame Dubois in the village, who required Annabelle's presence for one last fitting of the dress she had designed for her. Annabelle could hardly wait to see it.

Chapter 12

O N THE NIGHT OF THE gallery opening, Magnus
made his way through the crowd, greeting some
of the guests as they arrived.

So far, only a half hour into the evening, it appeared
to be a resounding success. There was a noisy hum of
conversation and laughter, some of the most respected
names in the art world were present, along with some
very prominent members of society, including the
Duke of Harlow, who was a well-known art enthu-
siast, and Baron St. Clair, one of the wealthiest men
in London since striking it rich in the American rail-
road, of all things. He was one of the few English
aristocrats with whom Magnus felt he had anything
in common.

But despite the impressive showing of prestigious
guests, Magnus felt no true satisfaction—for the one
guest who truly mattered had not yet arrived. He
hoped she had not changed her mind.

Then the door swung open and there she was—*his
Annabelle*—stepping into the gallery alone.

Magnus was jolted with a sense of urgency when he saw her, and was pleasantly surprised that she had come alone, for he had expected her to bring someone, perhaps even Whitby, which would have made a blatant seduction considerably challenging. This development, however, provided an unquestionable advantage.

She appeared nervous and flustered, so he interrupted the gentleman who was complimenting him on his choice of champagne and shouldered his way through the crowd to greet her.

"Good evening, Miss Lawson," he said, making a conscious effort to speak in a businesslike manner, though beneath his surface politeness he was struggling to harness a most uncompromising lovestruck state of mind. How in the world could he help it, when she looked so delectable in an elegant, plum-colored evening gown that accentuated the fullness of her breasts and the tempting, lavish curve of her hips?

Quite frankly, it was an injustice that he'd never seen her dressed this way before—in jewels and French heels and long, sleek black gloves. Even her fragrance aroused him. It was the sweet, spring perfume of lilacs.

"Good evening," she replied, handing her cloak over to the doorman.

Magnus waited for her to smooth out her skirt and take a perfunctory look around the room. "May I offer you a glass of champagne?" he asked.

"Yes, thank you."

Magnus caught the eye of the waiter and signaled to him. An instant later Annabelle was lifting a champagne flute off the shiny brass tray.

"Please come in," he said, guiding her through the crowd. "There are some guests who have been waiting to meet you."

Annabelle allowed Magnus to lead her into the gallery, and hoped that no one could detect how nervous she was, for not only was she attempting to enter into the London art world—when in reality she was a thirty-four-year-old spinster aunt who lived in the country, painting as her hobby—but she was also interacting with the man who was, and would always be, her first love. Her only love, really, although those old feelings were now mixed with so many others—like anger, distrust, and trepidation.

As she followed him through the crowd, however, she realized with a touch of anxiety that those off-putting feelings did not overrule the disturbing way she was reacting to him now—because seeing him again felt just as it had in the old days, when she would come to him at the lake after an agonizing week away from him and find him lounging back in the boat, looking handsome and virile.

Unfortunately, the very minute she laid eyes upon him tonight, her body awakened the same way—with exhilaration and desire, and she did not understand how she could possibly be feeling that way. How could she forget the antipathy that had crippled her all these years?

Magnus directed her to a group of gentlemen toward the back of the room, and they all stopped talking as soon as they noticed Annabelle. They studied her curiously, hesitantly, for there were not many women present, and one of the men in particular—older, with gray hair and spectacles—looked down the long length of his aristocratic nose at her before Magnus made the introduction.

"Harlow," he said, with a confident smile, "allow me to present Annabelle Lawson, my latest discovery. Miss Lawson, the Duke of Harlow."

The duke's eyes warmed instantly, his voice friendly and open as he spoke. "So this is the elusive new artist."

Annabelle felt her face flush with surprise, then she gathered her composure. "Your Grace, it is an honor."

He bowed elegantly. "My dear, the honor is all mine. I am enchanted to meet such a remarkable talent." The duke patted Magnus on the back. "My good man, you failed to mention that she was not only gifted, but lovely as well. Miss Lawson, will you be so kind as to discuss your seascape with me? I just acquired it."

Annabelle tried not to gasp. "You did?"

"You sound surprised," he said.

She felt Magnus's eyes on her, waiting for her reply.

"No, it's just so early in the evening. You must be confident in your tastes, Your Grace."

The duke seemed pleased with her answer and offered his arm. "Shall we?"

Annabelle smiled and wondered if this would answer her question—whether Magnus had been merely flattering her with his extravagant asking prices.

She supposed he could have exerted some influence and worked something out with the duke as part of his scheme, but then she feared she was being overly suspicious to the point of paranoia.

But Magnus had always possessed a talent for knocking her off kilter, hadn't he?

The duke escorted Annabelle across the gallery to where her painting was hanging on the wall next to a few others, none of which she recognized. She and the duke discussed all of them in addition to hers, and Annabelle soon began to relax.

She eventually met the other three local artists who were present, and they were all friendly except for one, who was a member of the Royal Academy. He seemed rather vain about his own work and spoke to her in a belittling tone.

"You may feel differently about Wright's work when you've gained more experience, Miss Lawson," he said to her, when she expressed her high regard for the American.

She did not bother to argue with him, for she could sense he was envious of Wright's talent. Instead, she turned her attention to the other gentlemen, who shared her appreciation, and enjoyed the delicious spiced shrimp *hors d'oeuvres*.

As the evening wore on, she realized that all her worries about seeing Magnus again were for naught, for he remained respectfully in other areas of the gallery, keeping his distance, leaving her to mingle on her own, and never once did he reveal that they had known each other before. He treated her exactly as he treated the other artists—with a professional reverence and respect.

She should have been relieved. She told herself she shouldn't even notice that he was ignoring her, but alas, she felt something very different, which was upsetting to say the least—for what she felt was disappointed.

The sad truth was, she had been acutely aware of his location every single second during the night. Despite all the terrible things she knew about him, she'd had to fight to keep from glancing over at him constantly, for the mere pleasure of watching him talk, laugh, sip champagne, or run a hand through his hair.

Yes, she still thought him the handsomest man in the world, the most intriguing, the most irresistible, and she could not deny the foolish yearning for him to merely glance her way. She wanted the excitement, the thrill of his eyes meeting hers. And even though she had done everything in her power to convince herself she didn't care and was only there for the exhibition, she had to accept the fact that she would always be drawn to him, and she hated such weakness in herself—for wanting something that had once been so destructive.

Later, as the evening drew to a close and the guests began to disperse, Annabelle stood alone in front of *The Fisherman,* looking curiously at the little red mark on the exhibition label and feeling weary of the battle going on inside her head.

She glanced across the room to where Magnus was speaking to some of the guests, and as soon as their eyes met, she knew she was simply incapable of fighting the attraction anymore. She felt a powerful surge of longing course through her and didn't have the strength to resist it. She had been suppressing her emotions for too long—thirteen years to be exact—

and she was exhausted.

Whether he felt what she felt, she did not know. All she knew was that he was picking up two glasses of champagne and blazing a direct path toward her.

She took a deep, steadying breath, not sure what would happen if she ever completely let herself go free.

"You did well tonight," he said, handing over one of the glasses. "Let's make a celebratory toast." He raised his glass, and Annabelle joined him by doing the same. "To a successful opening and the launch of your career."

Annabelle drank to his toast, then endeavored to initiate some relaxed conversation, for she did not want him to know how happy she felt, now that he was near.

"You may find this difficult to believe," she said, "but I never considered my art as a career. It has always been a hobby, though I've always dreamed it could be more."

"I don't find that difficult to believe," he said. "Because I remember."

It was the first spoken reminder of the past, and it was unsettling, to say the least, so she tried to change the subject. She pointed at the red mark on the label. "You told me, when I was in your office a few weeks ago, that you had never been willing to part with it, but now you finally have."

He gave her a sly look. "No, Miss Lawson. I am not parting with it."

Then she understood. *"You* bought it," she said with a grin. "But why? You already owned it."

"Ah, but I didn't truly own it," he explained. "You had asked for it back, if you will recall. So now that I have purchased it, I will be its rightful owner, and no one will ever be able to take it from me. Besides," he added, "I get a commission on the sale."

She laughed. "But it's *your* money."

He casually shrugged. "Now it's yours."

Annabelle shook her head at him. "I should refuse."

"Please don't. I will sleep better this way."

Annabelle continued to look at the painting while she sipped her drink, realizing with some surprise that she was feeling more relaxed now that they had actually smiled and laughed together. It had to be the champagne.... Her third glass.

"But if you take this painting back to America," she said, "I will never see it again. It feels strange to think of that."

"It will remain here in the gallery until then," he said. "You can visit it."

She nodded. "I wonder if I could paint another one like it." She tilted her head to the side. "Now that I see how I handled the brushstrokes I think I might be able to do it."

"I'm sure you could."

A few gentlemen came to shake Magnus's hand and thank him for inviting them, and they complimented Annabelle on her work.

"See?" Magnus said after they were gone. "You will be talked about."

A few others came to say goodnight, and before long there were only a handful of guests left in the gallery and it was much quieter.

Annabelle and Magnus wandered around the room, admiring the paintings and discussing each of them at length. Then, surprisingly, their conversation shifted to another subject.

"I know that Whitby came to see you," Annabelle said frankly. "He told me what he said to you."

"Did he indeed?" Magnus replied, not seeming the least bit surprised. "Which part?"

"The part about me. That if you ever did anything to hurt me, you would have to answer to him."

Magnus downed the rest of his champagne in one gulp, then set the empty glass on a charming little mahogany table and casually leaned a shoulder against the wall. His expression was playful and lighthearted, which surprised her.

"That's close, but not exactly it."

"What do you mean?" Annabelle asked.

"I mean, that's not exactly what he said. Let me see.... If I remember correctly, he informed me that you were 'off limits' to me, and if I ever laid another hand on you, he would hunt me down like a dog."

Annabelle drew a breath. "Goodness. He said those exact words?"

"As I live and breathe."

Of course she knew Whitby would never really hunt someone down like a dog. It had been an idle threat to emphasize how serious he was.

Nevertheless, if he had used those words, she should be extremely vexed with him. He could have foiled her opportunity to be included in this show.

She and Magnus continued to look at the painting for the longest time, and Annabelle felt as if she were back on the picnic blanket with her head next to his, staring up at the sky and seeing the same shapes in the clouds. The only difference was that back then, her shoes were far more comfortable. Feeling as if her toes were being squeezed and crushed, she tapped her heel hard upon the floor, but heard a small *crack* as her shoe gave way beneath her.

"Oh dear," she said, touching Magnus's arm to steady herself. "I think my heel just broke."

Magnus looked down, but her feet were hidden beneath her gown. "Is it still attached to the shoe?"

"Yes, but it appears to be dangling. Well, this is quite a pickle, isn't it?"

Magnus wrapped a hand around her gloved elbow to help her stay balanced. "Not at all. I have glue in my office. I can repair it right now, with your permission of course."

Thankfully, they were standing adjacent to the office door, so they discreetly went inside. The room was dimly lit by one Tiffany lamp in the corner. Magnus left the door wide open behind them.

He escorted her to the sofa but remained standing in front of her while she stared up at his darkly handsome face—the chiseled jaw, the fine straight nose, the soft, full mouth....

"Perhaps you could hand the shoe to me," he quietly said, startling her out of what felt like a trance, for she was alone with him now.

"Of course."

She slipped it off with her other toe, while a secret part of her wondered what would happen if he got down on a knee and removed it for her. She envisioned his large hand wrapping around her ankle, cupping her heel, holding the arch of her foot.

"Here you are," she said with forced calm as she strained to hide her thoughts. She handed over the satin, lace-trimmed shoe.

Magnus went behind his large desk and opened the bottom drawer. "This is carpenters' glue." He withdrew a half-empty jar and set it on the desk. "It should do the trick until you can have the shoe repaired properly."

He remained standing, spreading the glue on the heel while Annabelle watched his hands. They had always been callused and rough-looking, and despite his wealth and prosperity and the fact that he was the owner of a very fine art gallery, they were surprisingly still the hands of a common worker.

She could not deny that it was that very quality about his hands that had always excited her.

Magnus pressed the heel back into place, then set the shoe on the desk. "There. We'll just give it a moment or two to dry. Can I get you anything? Another glass of champagne?"

"No, thank you. I believe I've had enough."

More than enough, for she must be in some sort of drunken stupor to be feeling so attracted to Magnus after so many years of feeling nothing but the pain of his betrayal. Most confusing of all, she still felt that pain, right alongside the attraction, which made no sense.

"Tea perhaps?" he suggested. "Or I could go and fetch the tray with the shrimp that you seemed to like so much."

He had noticed. "Honestly, I couldn't eat another bite," she replied.

Just then an older couple appeared in the doorway, and the gentleman informed Magnus they were leaving. "It was a most enjoyable evening, Mr. Wallis. We appreciate the invitation."

"My pleasure, Stanford. Let me show you out."

Magnus turned to Annabelle and bowed slightly. "Will you excuse me for a moment?"

"Of course."

She watched him leave, listening to his laughter and conversation outside as she looked around the tastefully decorated office. There was another painting on the wall where *The Fisherman* had been hanging before. She didn't recognize it. Right in front of her on the coffee table was a vase of fresh chrysanthemums.

Her gaze then drifted to the large desk and ornate brown leather chair. The desktop was clear except for her lacy shoe and the jar of glue, and a basket containing a stack of letters and papers.

She leaned forward and glanced out into the gallery where Magnus was still conversing with the Stanford couple, and wondered how long he would be, because it was getting late, and she was beginning to feel more than a little uncomfortable with her all too intimate rapport with Magnus. Whitby would definitely not approve.

Besides, the room was clearing out, and she did not want to be the last person there.

Rising from the sofa, she limped on one foot to check her shoe. The glue wasn't completely dry, but at least the heel was attached. She could probably walk on it, if she kept most of her weight on her toes.

Annabelle set the shoe on the floor, and while she slid her foot into it, her gaze fell upon the basket of letters. One brief note lay on top, and before she knew what she was about, she was overcome with curiosity and found herself reading it.

> *Mr. Wallis,*
> *There is a problem with the wiring at Brownlow and Northington. Perhaps you could drop by in the morning.*
>
> *George Smith*
>
> *P.S. The electrical in the other building was finalized today.*

Well, that didn't tell her much, except that Magnus was installing electricity in the two buildings he was renovating.

"I doubt it's dry," he said, startling her as he reentered the office.

She became instantly flustered, not because she'd been reading his correspondence—though she did feel guilty about that—but because he was handing her a red rose.

"What's this for?" she asked, presuming he had just picked it out of the bouquet outside the door. She lifted it to her nose and breathed in the fragrant scent.

"It's to thank you for being here tonight," he replied.

"It wouldn't have been the same without you. Though I am sorry about your shoe. Perhaps you should have worn your other boots—the ones you used to wear at the lake. Do you still have them?"

He seemed to remember everything. "I have a newer pair, but they're similar."

They stood in the half-light gazing at one another for a quiet moment, until Annabelle checked the time. Her driver would be waiting outside by now, thank goodness.

"I appreciate everything," she said, struggling to smother the tension she was feeling. "But I really should be going."

Magnus's voice dropped to a slow, tantalizing hush. "Are you sure you wouldn't like to stay a bit longer?"

Annabelle imagined herself remaining there until all the guests were gone. What would occur?

Oh, she knew very well what would occur. They would end up on the sofa, and she would be lucky to keep her garters in place.

Struck with a sudden alarm, she fortified her resolve. "I am very sure, thank you."

He politely nodded. "When will I see you again?"

Feeling the heady combination of his masculine appeal and the lingering effects of the champagne, Annabelle raised an eyebrow. "That's rather presumptuous, don't you think?"

Magnus strolled a little closer. "Perhaps. But I know you, Annabelle, and I am quite certain that you are not oblivious to the spark that still exists between us. This cannot be the end."

It was astounding, how potent sexual desire could

be when it took hold with full force. It eclipsed all reason and sanity.

Thankfully, however, Annabelle did still possess some degree of discipline, so she cleared her throat and endeavored to cool this madness—because that's exactly what it was. Madness.

"If there is a spark," she replied in low voice, "I do not wish to act upon it."

Just then, two other guests interrupted and thanked Magnus for the evening. While he shook their hands, Annabelle managed to regain her sanity, realizing with a fright how quickly the situation had just spun out of control. A moment ago, she had imagined herself lying with Magnus on his sofa.

The guests left, and before Magnus could say another word to her, she brushed past him and started toward the door. He followed to walk her out.

"Please don't leave yet," he discreetly whispered, so as not to cause a scene.

"I must. My driver is waiting." She met the doorman, who retrieved her cloak from the front closet and held it up for her. She did not meet Magnus's gaze as she buttoned it. "Thank you. Mr. Wallis, for including my paintings in your exhibition."

"You are most welcome. I will be in touch."

In touch?

"About the sales," he clarified, as if he knew the workings of her mind. She supposed he had always been able to read her like a book.

Annabelle simply nodded. "Good evening."

She turned to leave, limping to keep from breaking her shoe again, but Magnus did not give up. He escorted her out onto the street where the coach was waiting.

"When are you going back to the country?" he asked, opening the door for her.

Annabelle climbed in and slid across the seat. "The day after tomorrow."

"Why don't you stay in London a little longer? We have to settle the sales, if nothing else."

The insistent fire in his eyes upset her balance, for it looked as if "settling the sales" was the last thing on his mind.

To be honest, it was the last thing on her mind, too, because the shocking truth was—she was still burning to touch him. He was the only man in the world she had ever truly desired, and now he had come back into her life and he wanted her.

He'd said there was still a spark between them, and it was true. It was raging brighter than ever before. But heaven help her, she could not be so foolish as to risk her heart a second time. Not with him.

"You can send me a bank note," she said at last, struggling to grab hold of her cautious, sensible self. "I think that would be best. Driver?"

But Magnus was still standing there, holding the door open.

"I must go," she firmly persisted, and shut the door on him before he could argue.

The coach lurched forward, and Annabelle turned in her seat to look out the window at Magnus, who remained on the sidewalk, watching her drive away. As soon as he was out of sight, she faced forward again and held up a gloved hand to see how badly it was trembling.

Quite badly indeed.

Annabelle inhaled deeply and wondered if she could relax now that the gallery opening was behind her. Perhaps she had survived the worst of it.

But then she pictured Magnus's face and heard his husky voice in her mind when he'd asked her to stay in London a little longer, and was forced to acknowledge the very disturbing possibility that the worst might still be ahead of her.

Chapter 13

*T*HE ONLY THING THAT KEPT Annabelle sensible through the night and into the next morning was her constant focus on all the wretched things she knew about Magnus. She thought of her brother's aversion toward him, and his reputation as a villain in her family, and naturally, she thought of the way he had treated her years ago.

But by doing that, she had to struggle to overlook the fact that last night she had not found him villainous in the least, nor did anyone else. He had been charming and considerate, and made her laugh and feel comfortable. Nothing he said or did seemed to match the opinions everyone held of him. Which only served to confuse her while she ate her breakfast.

Later, while sipping a second cup of coffee, Annabelle read the paper, but found herself distracted again by memories of the night before—her conversations with the Duke of Harlow and the other artists, the flavor of the champagne and the tang of the spiced shrimp, not to forget the image of Magnus repairing her shoe in his private, dimly lit office.

She thought of the letter she had read, about the wiring in the buildings he'd purchased, then recalled that during their previous meeting, Magnus had told her that his properties were located at Park Lane.

Annabelle sat back in her chair and stared at the wall. The letter last night had mentioned the corner of Brownlow and Northington. That was nowhere near Park Lane. Had Magnus lied to her? But why would he lie about something like that unless he had some darker purpose with his business ventures? If that were true, she would be terribly disappointed, because that morning, for the first time in thirteen years, she had actually let herself hope that she, and everyone else, might have been wrong about Magnus all this time.

It was a wish she had never let herself acknowledge before now, because she was certain it was a foolish one, but after last night, she wasn't so sure.

Annabelle sighed and reminded herself that she could not fall into that trap. She could not be too quick to presume that Magnus's amiable behavior was completely sincere. She had to keep her head and continue to be cautious.

And although she did not want to be unreasonably suspicious, either, given his past transgressions, she couldn't help but question this. Whitby certainly would.

Consequently, two hours later she was stepping out of a conveniently anonymous hansom cab at the corner of Brownlow and Northington, looking up at the building Magnus had supposedly purchased, for she was determined to find answers.

The property was a large home with paned windows and a wrought-iron fence all around. In the front yard, a bricklayer was making improvements to the walk.

Annabelle's cab drove away, so she crossed the street to take a closer look. When she reached the gate, she read the plaque set into the ironwork: Northington Street Orphans' Home for Boys.

An orphans' home? She looked up at the second story windows and wondered what Magnus planned to do with the property. He'd explained he bought and sold buildings for a profit. Would he sell an orphanage out from under the boys who had found a home there? It was exactly the kind of conclusion Whitby would come to. "*His heart is as cold as ice,*" her brother had said.

Finding it all very unsettling, but not quite ready to make any drastic assumptions herself, Annabelle opened the gate and approached the man who was on his knees, laying bricks. "Excuse me, do you work for Magnus Wallis?"

The man stood up and wiped his hands on his coveralls. "Yes, miss."

"I see that you're making some improvements," she said. "Do you know if Mr. Wallis is intending to sell?"

The man wiped a finger under his nose and sniffled. "No, miss, he doesn't own the place. He's just improving it. Having the whole place wired for electricity, and he's adding indoor plumbing as well. It's a changing world, wouldn't you say?"

Annabelle tried to clarify what the man was telling her. "But why would he make improvements to a building he doesn't own?"

"I reckon he's generous," the man replied. "Not like some people."

It was not what Annabelle had been expecting to hear, and she couldn't help feeling guilty for presuming the worst, when in fact Magnus appeared to be doing something quite charitable. He was renovating an orphans' home.

"Thank you," she said to the man, smiling politely before she turned to leave.

"He's inside if you want to have a word with him," the man called after her. "He's checking the electric."

Annabelle stopped. Magnus was there? Now?

She felt an odd mixture of excitement and apprehension, and turned to look up at the windows, wondering if he had already seen her out there on the walk, covertly interrogating his workers.

"Perhaps I will have a word with him," she replied, even though she knew she shouldn't. After last night, she should know better. But this charitable bequest—which seemed so out of character for a man whose heart was allegedly twisted—was petitioning her hopes.

Annabelle approached the front door and knocked. She was greeted by a plump older woman wiping her hands on her apron.

"I am here to see Mr. Wallis," Annabelle said.

"Come in. He's in the back garden. I'd take you, but I've got bread in the oven. Just go down that hall and there's a door at the end."

"Thank you," Annabelle replied.

There was a tingling in the pit of her stomach as she made her way toward the back of the house, but she tried to ignore it, for she was there only to ask him why he hadn't told her about what he was doing for this orphanage. Why had he kept it secret?

She reached the back door and stepped out into a covered entrance, where her gaze fell instantly upon Magnus. He stood on the grass with his back to her, playing cricket with a group of boys. He had removed his jacket and wore a white shirt with the sleeves rolled up, along with a dark patterned waistcoat. He was laughing at something, waiting for one of the boys to throw the ball.

Annabelle watched for a few more minutes, until one of the boys pointed at her and said, "Who's the lady?"

Magnus turned. Annabelle felt a jolt when their eyes met, and her pulse began to pound even harder when he walked toward her.

"That's it for me, boys," he said, his gaze intent upon Annabelle. "You'll have to finish the match on your own."

They all groaned, but quickly returned to their game.

"Well, this is a pleasant surprise," Magnus said, reaching the bottom step. He was slightly out of breath, and the hair around his face was damp with perspiration.

Annabelle inclined her head at him. "I hope you don't mind."

"Mind? I'm thrilled to see you." He climbed the steps energetically. "How did you know I was here?"

She hesitated before she answered. "I saw the note on your desk last night when I was putting on my shoe—the one asking you to check the wiring this morning. It gave the address, so I took a chance."

She refrained from telling him she had been wondering if it was all part of some dastardly master plan to harm her family.

"Well, I'm glad you did," he said. "Why don't we go inside?" He opened the door for her.

Annabelle entered and let him show her to the front parlor, where she smelled fresh paint on the walls. A few boys came bounding down the stairs, taking no notice of Annabelle and Magnus as they dashed toward the back door.

"Why didn't you tell me about this?" she asked when the house quieted down again.

"It didn't come up."

"But you told me you were making improvements to two buildings on Park Lane," she said.

He shrugged casually. "I am, and this is where the profits are going. Here, and to a girls' home across the river."

Annabelle's brow furrowed. This was not at all what she had expected. "I didn't realize you were such a generous philanthropist."

"I'm not really," he replied. "I just remember what it was like growing up in London, feeling like an orphan myself sometimes, having nothing."

Annabelle took a few steps closer to him, feeling as if there were many, many things she did not know about this man. All she knew was what Whitby had always known.

"You never told me any of that before," she said, "when I knew you as Mr. Edwards."

Where had that come from? She shouldn't have said it.

His eyes were wistful, yet surprisingly tender. "There were a lot of things I didn't tell you, Miss Lawson."

She continued to gaze at him, waiting for more.

"I was only nine when my father died," he finally explained. "And my mother.... Well, she wasn't much of one."

Just then two boys burst in through the front door, one shoving the other. "Bugger off!" the younger one said.

Magnus turned and watched them for a moment, and when the older one shoved the younger one again, he strode toward them. "Perhaps you could behave yourselves, gentlemen. There is a lady present." He put an authoritative hand on the older boy's shoulder. "Why don't you both go and join the cricket game out back. They're in need of a few extra players."

As soon as they were gone, Magnus returned to the parlor where Annabelle stood watching. "Boys like those two just need something to do."

She smiled and nodded in agreement.

"How did you get here?" he asked.

"I took a cab."

"Can I offer you a ride home?" he asked.

"That would be very kind. Thank you."

A short while later they were sitting across from each other in Magnus's luxurious private coach, heading down the street. Annabelle sat with her knees squeezed tightly together, her gloved hands clenched tightly upon her lap while she looked out the window.

She could not believe that she was sitting in a coach with Magnus, when for years of her quiet, uneventful life, she thought she'd never see him again.

Not to mention the fact that they had been lovers once. They had been intimate, then she was cut loose in the most brutal, excruciating way.

Strangely now, those unpleasant memories seemed rather distant, as if they had never really happened, and the real Magnus was the wonderful man she had come to know as Mr. Edwards—the wonderful man before her, who had been such a charming host the night before, and who was donating his business profits to orphanages.

Annabelle felt his gaze on her face. She turned her eyes from the window to look at him, slouched lazily on the red cushions across from her, his knees apart, one arm resting along the back of the seat.

All her womanly senses began to hum, for he was so impossibly handsome. And his eyes.... He stared at her as if he could see straight through to her soul, as if he *adored* her soul and knew her as well as only a lifelong friend could know someone.

Annabelle sucked in a little breath and tried to deny the part of her that felt happy—happy to be with him, the man who had, for a brief time been her most precious friend.

"Would you like to see my buildings on Park Lane?" he asked, and somehow, she knew that he recognized and understood her anxieties, and wanted only to put her mind at ease by distracting her.

She smiled and said yes, and the knots of tension in her shoulders began to unwind as she stopped fighting so hard against the part of herself that was happy.

A few minutes later, the coach pulled slowly to a halt on the elegant residential street, and Magnus stepped out to assist Annabelle. She climbed out and looked up at a large home. A number of workers on tall ladders were applying stucco to the exterior.

"This one must be yours," she said, linking her arm through his when he offered it.

Magnus stood on the sidewalk beside her, looking up. "Yes, but when I bought it, it was two narrow, unkempt houses side by side."

Annabelle examined the full width of the structure. "You turned two houses into one larger home? I would never have guessed."

He pointed from one side to the other. "I redesigned the exterior for a unified appearance. On the inside I knocked out a few walls and installed all the modern conveniences."

"What extraordinary vision you must have," Annabelle remarked, "to see such potential."

Magnus placed his hand over hers on his arm and leaned close. "There is an old adage about architecture that says visionary buildings come into being only when the designer reaches far beyond what is there."

The idea stirred Annabelle's blood, and she smiled. "You must allow yourself to see it as a blank canvas."

"Exactly." He gestured toward the house. "It's almost finished. Would you like to see the inside?"

"I'd love to."

They climbed the stone steps to the front door and entered the wide entry hall, awash with abundant sunlight beaming in through an enormous front window. Annabelle looked up at the high ceiling, the chestnut millwork, and the magnificent dangling light fixture.

"It's so bright," she said. "And so modern with all these daring colors."

He'd used saffron and burgundy and persimmon, which was a refreshing departure from the sea of aesthetic conservatism that defined English art and design. It aroused Annabelle's creative sensibilities.

Magnus closed the door behind them and let her wander into the parlor on her own. "It's definitely a bold palette," he said.

"Bold, to be sure." She pointed at the far wall, where the fireplace was encased in a marble mantel and flanked by chestnut columns. "I love how you've chosen different shades of the same color for different walls."

He followed her in. "Not many people notice that, Annabelle. It's very subtle."

"You know me. I am a painter. I am obsessed with color."

He smiled and nodded, then let her lead the way to another room. She walked through the parlor to the library and couldn't help but admire how the room was clearly masculine without any of the typical dark brown leather furniture and hunter green walls.

"Magnus, it's extraordinary. I've never seen anything like it."

He came to stand beside her. "I did my best to work

with the architecture already on hand. Most of the molding and paneling is original, though I've added some as well."

"You can't tell the new from the old. It's seamless."

"I'm glad you think so. Would you like to go upstairs?"

Annabelle's first reaction was to think of the bedrooms and worry that it would be completely inappropriate to say yes, but since there was no furniture in the house, she decided it would be only *slightly* inappropriate. Besides, she wanted to see what he'd done with the rest of the house.

They climbed the curved staircase and reached the second floor, and Magnus took Annabelle by the arm. "Now close your eyes," he said, leaning close again. "I have a feeling you're going to like what I'm about to show you."

She did as he asked and allowed him to lead her down the corridor. A door creaked open, and Magnus guided her into another room.

"Open your eyes."

Annabelle opened them and found herself gazing upon a veritable temple of hygiene—the most luxurious bathroom she had ever seen, complete with a hooded bath and spray shower encased in mahogany, a private water closet with a mahogany seat and matching cistern with hand-carved panels. The floors were polished marble. Gleaming tiles adorned the walls, and the water cabinet contained a basin of painted porcelain.

Awestruck, she walked all the way in. "This is spectacular!"

"I'm pleased you like it," he replied, casually leaning a shoulder against the doorjamb.

Annabelle went to touch the shiny brass fittings on the water basin. "I cannot begin to imagine how you could design all this and then put the house up for sale and let someone else live here. Aren't you ever tempted to move into the buildings yourself?"

He chuckled. "I like where I live."

"Do you have a bathroom like this in your home?"

"I do, actually. In both homes."

To some people it might have seemed as if Magnus was boasting to impress, but Annabelle didn't get that feeling. He was simply being honest with her. He enjoyed his work and he wanted to share it with her, for he knew she would appreciate it.

Which she did. Very much. How lucky he was, to be involved in such a creative profession.

All at once she was acutely aware of his manly presence in the doorway while he watched her wander around.

Laboring to redirect her interest back to the renovations instead of the man in the doorway, she continued to admire the fixtures.

"You have done very well for yourself," she said pensively. "You have everything."

His voice was calm, unemotional. "Not *quite* everything."

Annabelle knew instantly what he was referring to—that *she* was the one thing he didn't have—and when the initial shock of his declaration wore off, her body responded with a wave of attraction.

Not knowing what to say, and wishing she could

not be so easily beguiled, she turned her eyes in the other direction. But Magnus wouldn't let her look away. He pushed off the doorjamb and sauntered toward her, stopping in front of her, so close that she could smell his cologne in the air.

"Would you like to see the bedroom?" he asked in a soft, silky voice.

Annabelle's pulse quickened at the suggestion, and a flash memory of the day he had touched her intimately on the beach flew through her mind.

He was too close, too persuasive and enticing, and the mere mention of the word "bedroom" was highly inappropriate and made her go weak in the knees.

"That would be very nice," she said, regardless, with a surprising degree of aplomb.

He stared at her for a moment, as if studying her thoughts, then he turned to lead the way down the corridor. "It's this way."

Annabelle followed him into the large room at the end of the hall, and after seeing all the bold colors throughout the house, the restrained bedchamber came as a surprise, and perhaps a bit of a relief, for it was a soothing, dignified cream with polished, honey oak floors.

He faced her and inclined his head, and his voice was soothing as well. "I'm not sure where the bed should go. Any ideas?"

Annabelle smiled. "Here, I believe." She moved to stand against one of the walls and gestured with her hands. "A floor-to-ceiling headboard would be nice. The owner could sit up and look out the window at Hyde Park."

Magnus crossed to stand beside her, facing the window. They both imagined themselves sitting up on the imaginary pillows. "I think you're quite right. Here would be perfect."

Annabelle watched the leafy trees blowing in the wind outside and felt surprisingly calm and at ease. Then she turned her eyes to Magnus, who had been watching her profile.

He was so familiar, like a well-worn shoe. But much better looking.

Soon, the world diminished to a quiet heartbeat as his eyes held hers, and Annabelle wished desperately that things were different—that last night she had met him for the first time, that she had never suffered a broken heart because of him, and that her brother did not despise and distrust him.

Because heaven help her, she found him so immensely exciting in every way, and he awakened her senses like no other person in the world. She didn't want to go home. She wanted to spend the rest of the day with him and go on talking about his buildings and what he would do next. She wanted to know everything about his life now that things were different for him. She wanted to hear about his activities in America. What was the weather like? Did his galleries bring in many patrons? Was he happy?

But something stopped her from asking all those questions. Perhaps she feared that if she let herself drift into the intimate details of his existence, she would never be able to escape.

"I should go," she said abruptly, before she had a chance to change her mind.

The disappointment in his eyes was almost tangible, but she did not allow herself to be swayed by it. It was vital that she continue to be prudent.

"Of course," he replied, offering his arm. "I have kept you too long."

Soon they were climbing back into his coach and settling in for the ride.

It had been a perfect morning, Magnus thought as he sat across from Annabelle in the coach and admired the dazzling green of her eyes—not unlike the first day he'd met her on the train thirteen years ago, when he had become swept away by her lively, vivacious nature. Today he was pleased to discover that she had not lost that zest for life. She had been excited by his renovations, and her enthusiasm was contagious.

But she had always inspired him. If it weren't for her, he might never have gone to America to better himself. He wouldn't have bothered, and he had her to thank for the new direction his life had taken.

Soon they entered Annabelle's residential district, and he knew the coach ride would soon come to an end. Sliding smoothly across the small distance between them, he positioned himself next to her and stretched an arm across the back of the seat.

Annabelle gazed at him questioningly, but with a hint of a smile that pleased him, for it was an honest smile. It was the smile that belonged to the young woman he had met on the train, the woman who had stood on a beach and painted him in a boat.

"I am glad you came to see me this morning," he

said.

"I am glad, too," she replied. "I *think*."

Magnus chuckled, then ran a finger up her arm, from her wrist to the inside of her elbow, his heart thundering in his chest as he strove to control his desires—for what he really wanted to do was ease her onto her back right there in the shady confines of the coach and feel her soft, lush body beneath his own.

Her breathing changed, and he was pleased when he sensed a slight surrender. Since it was not in his nature to ignore an opportunity, he spoke frankly.

"Annabelle, I know that you are having a hard time trusting me again, but I wish you would give me a chance to prove myself worthy of your friendship. Why don't we have dinner together tomorrow evening?"

She looked him in the eye, studying him, searching for answers. "I am not sure that would be wise."

"Please consider it. We could start fresh and get to know each other all over again."

She looked down at her tightly clasped hands in her lap and was quiet for a moment. When at last she spoke, her voice was soft and gentle. "Magnus, I have spent the past thirteen years trying to get over what you did to me, and though I am grateful for the opportunity to be included in your gallery opening, and I enjoyed myself with you this morning, I am not sure that I would ever be able to let you back into my life. Or into my heart."

"But Annabelle—"

She shook her head. "It's not that I want to hold a grudge against you, or that I am unable to accept your apology. The problem is that I am afraid of getting hurt again. Love and the notion of handing my heart over to *anyone* makes me uneasy. I just can't do it. Not yet."

Magnus couldn't seem to move. A pain even more excruciating than he had felt that day outside the bank throbbed inside his chest as he listened to Annabelle speak. It forced him to contemplate from a very deep level what he had done to her. Remorse had become a part of his life, but it was never as potent as now, as he looked into her eyes and realized what he had cost her. He wanted so badly to fix it. If only he could go back.

"I'm so sorry, Annabelle," he said. Then he couldn't think anymore. He needed her to know how much he regretted the years they'd spent apart, and how desperately and passionately he still loved her.

He leaned close to try and tell her with a kiss.

A surge of relief coursed through him when her soft lips parted in response and she took his face in her hands. He had dreamed of this for so many lonely years, but he had never dared to imagine that it could really happen.

Astonished at the overwhelming intensity of his feelings—for he wanted her more than life itself—he curled his fingers around her gloved hands, inching closer to her on the seat, deepening the kiss. He wanted to take this further, to claim her for his own once and for all and never let her go again, but he knew he could not. She was a wounded creature, and he had to be patient, or he would scare her away forever.

Drawing back from the kiss, he touched his forehead to hers. "You don't need to protect yourself from me. You have my word. I will never hurt you again."

She shook her head, old fears and uncertainties resurfacing in her voice.

"But how can I trust your word? I trusted you once before and you betrayed me. Besides that, you are still my brother's enemy. That has not changed."

"But that shouldn't matter because he's wrong about me," Magnus replied, more than a little frustrated by his cousin's persistent influence upon her. "He has *always* been wrong."

Annabelle's cheeks became flushed with red. Her eyes revealed an inner turmoil. "But how can I take your word over his, when I have known him all my life, and I know he is a decent, honorable man? I don't know the same of you."

She looked down at the floor, seeming angry all of a sudden. Whether that anger was directed at herself or at him, he did not know.

"This shouldn't be happening," she said.

No.... She was retreating....

Magnus kissed her again, deeper this time, and surprisingly, she surrendered to him once more, parting her lips and moaning softly as he took her into a full embrace.

It was all the assurance he needed. She *did* have feelings for him, even though she was doing her best to resist them.

He felt the coach slowing and knew they had reached her brother's residence, so he gradually withdrew from the kiss.

"Tomorrow night?" he asked, feeling revived and rejuvenated. There was hope. He knew there was.

A shadow of fear filled her eyes. "No. I am expected back in the country tomorrow."

"Don't go. Stay another day."

"Magnus, please. I can't do this."

The coach rolled to a stop, and before he had a chance to get up and assist her out, she climbed over him and got out on her own, then stood at the open door.

"You *can* do it, Annabelle. Just give me one night."

She stared at him uncertainly. "Thank you for the ride." Then she shut the door in his face and ran off.

He considered going after her, but what if Whitby was at home? No. Magnus knew if he engaged in a confrontation with her brother, it would not help matters. It would spoil everything, for that situation was particularly volatile.

The coach lurched forward, and Magnus let his head tip back upon the seat, wondering how he was going to survive another day not knowing if Annabelle would ever find the courage to trust him again. And for the first time in many years, he felt the roar of his old resentment toward Whitby awakening inside him—like a sleeping lion he wished would keep still.

Annabelle slept late the following morning, for she had barely slept a wink during the night. She was too shaken by what had happened the day before and the way she had felt when Magnus kissed her—weak and utterly swept away. She had done what she'd promised herself she would not do. She had lowered her guard.

Resigning herself to the fact that nothing could be done to change it now, Annabelle sat up when her maid Josephine entered the room and drew the curtains apart to let in the light.

"A letter came for you this morning,"

Annabelle inched back against the pillows, trying not to sound too anxious or surprised, although she certainly was, for she suspected the letter might be from Magnus. Was it a bank note? Or something else?

"Where is it?" she asked.

"I have it here." Josephine reached into her pocket, withdrew the letter and handed it over.

When Annabelle read the return address, she waited for Josephine to leave the room before she tore at the seal and unfolded the letter.

Surprisingly enough, it *was* a bank note—for the full sum Magnus owed her—but there was more....

> *Dear Miss Lawson,*
>
> *I know you plan to leave for the country today, but I could not bear to leave things as they were when we parted in front of your brother's house yesterday.*
>
> *I know you have not forgiven me for what happened between us years ago, and I concede that it is your right. But please believe me when I say that I have suffered every day of my life for how I wronged you.*
>
> *I know it is far too much to ask, but please...a second chance?*
>
> *If only you would stay in London one more day. Please, Annabelle? We enjoyed each other's*

*company yesterday, did we not? We could enjoy
ourselves like that again.*

*I will remain at my hotel all day if you should
choose to see me. I sincerely hope you will.*

> *With Love,*
> *Magnus*

By the time Annabelle finished reading the letter, her heart was pounding so fast she could barely
breathe. She had never read anything like it in her
entire life. He was pleading with her. Pleading! And
she, in turn, was desperate for him—desperate for his
touch, his kiss, and so much more.

She had truly been swept away.

Slipping out of bed, she reached for her dressing
gown and pulled it on as she strode to the window,
which looked out onto the tiny, fenced-in garden out
back.

She wondered, after all that had happened, if she
could ever truly trust Magnus again. There had been
so much water under the bridge, and she would always
worry that her desire for him had prevailed over her
good sense.

She supposed the real problem was that she was torn
between her unstoppable passion for one man and her
deep devotion to another—the adoptive brother who
had raised her. A man she had always trusted.

And wasn't trust at the heart of all this? Whitby was
warning her to stay away from Magnus. He believed
him unscrupulous.

Annabelle didn't know what to believe, and that
frightened her. She feared she was losing her mind.

Wanting suddenly to return to her home where she felt safe and secure and could think about all this, free from Magnus's dangerous temptations, Annabelle picked up her pen and withdrew a sheet of paper from her desk drawer.

> *Dear Mr. Wallis,*
> *I'm sorry, but I must go home to my family today. Please do not wait for me. I cannot see you. I need time to think.*
>
> *Annabelle*

She sealed the letter and rang for her maid again. A moment later Josephine knocked and entered.

"Josephine, please send a footman to deliver this letter personally to the Grand Hotel," Annabelle instructed. "And when you're finished with that, go and pack your things. I want to go home, and I don't want to miss the midday train."

"Yes, Miss Lawson."

Josephine left the room, while Annabelle quickly went to retrieve her traveling case.

Passengers were already boarding the train by the time Annabelle and Josephine arrived at the station and purchased their tickets.

"I'll be so glad to get home," Annabelle said, leading the way along the platform, walking the length of the train to reach their proper carriage.

"But you enjoyed yourself at the gallery opening, didn't you, Miss Lawson?" Josephine said, hurrying to keep up. "Everyone liked your paintings."

Annabelle smiled over her shoulder at her maid. "Yes, I suppose I did. It was a very successful evening."

They finally reached the carriage where they were to be seated, but before they stepped on, Annabelle stopped to check her reticule for the tickets. Then something caught her eye—or rather, someone. A man came darting out of the station and stopped abruptly on the platform.

The world seemed to disappear for a moment as Annabelle focused on him. It was Magnus—there to say good-bye, or to stop her from leaving, or to plead with her one more time for another chance.

The fact that her maid was now looking at him, too, did nothing to wrench Annabelle out of her stupor, because heaven help her, she could not take her eyes off him.

He was so darkly handsome in his open black coat, the collar of his white shirt contrasting sharply with his thick, wavy black hair. Despite everything, he was the most captivating man she had ever known. In all her life, no one had come close.

His eyes met Annabelle's across the distance of the platform, and he merely stood there, seeming almost arrested himself.

Annabelle fought to understand the workings of her mind and body. She wanted to escape his power over her. She wanted to go home where she was safe with the family who loved her, but she couldn't move. She could barely breathe, for that matter.

Josephine continued to look at him as well. "Miss Lawson? Are we still going home?"

The words took a moment to register in Annabelle's mind. Somehow the young maid understood what was happening, though Annabelle had never confessed anything to her. She supposed it was rather obvious.

As the train blew steam not far from where they stood, Magnus continued to hold Annabelle in his gaze. And that was the moment she knew—there was no way on earth she could turn from him and step on the train.

She would have liked to say she had thought it out and come to the conscious conclusion that she *could* trust Magnus, or that she had chosen her own happiness over her loyalty to her brother, or simply that she deserved some passion and pleasure in her life. But none of those things entered her mind. She was aware only of her blood pounding through her veins and the noisy rush of lust that dashed like fire through her body, urging her to go to him, damn the consequences.

"No, we're not going home," she said. "Not today."

Somehow, practical thoughts found their way to the fore, and she gave her maid clear instructions. "Take the bags and return our tickets. Then use those funds to obtain transportation for yourself back to the house in Mayfair. Make excuses for me."

Without another word to Josephine, Annabelle started off across the platform toward Magnus.

Chapter 14

ANNABELLE WALKED THE LENGTH OF the train, and Magnus began walking, too. They met face to face not far from a uniformed guard.

"Is your coach waiting?" Annabelle asked.

Magnus did not reply. He simply held out his hand, and she took it. Before she knew what she was doing, she was hurrying to keep up with him as he led her through the crowded station.

A moment later they crossed the street and he ushered her into the privacy of his coach. Magnus tapped the outside to signal the driver as he climbed in beside her, slammed the door, and drew the curtains.

It was instantly dim. He sat for a second or two, staring at the floor as if searching for his bearings, then he turned to Annabelle and enfolded her in his arms in one smooth, sweeping motion. He buried his lips in the crook of her neck and held her for a long, shuddering moment, while her gloved fingers dug into the thick wool of his coat.

At last his lips found hers in a devouring kiss, and it

was familiar, so much a part of her dreams that Annabelle could have wept with joy.

The coach lurched forward, and they were knocked off balance. They each took the opportunity to pause and gaze at each other, and it seemed impossible to believe what was happening.

Then his lips were on hers again as the coach rattled down the street. The feel of his body beneath her roving hands forced Annabelle's wild and careless desires beyond the lines of reason.

"I'm so glad you stayed," he whispered, kissing her neck as he eased her onto her back on the seat.

He was her lover, her only lover. How had she lived without this kind of intimacy for so long? How had she survived?

Then he was on top of her, holding her close, and they moved awkwardly, struggling to find a comfortable position on the seat. She took his face in her hands and relished the heat of his mouth, while he tugged her skirts up and slid his hand up her leg. Annabelle gasped at the thrill of his touch.

"Are you still a virgin?" he asked.

"Yes," she replied.

He closed his eyes and rested his forehead upon hers. "Good. Because I can't bear to think of you ever loving someone else."

Annabelle sighed as he held her and made love to her with his hands and mouth, kissing her everywhere. Soon her body was trembling with excitement and she grabbed hold of his coat and squeezed the fabric in her fists as pleasure washed over her like an ocean wave. All she wanted was more, despite the fact that her brain was screaming at her to stop and think. To be careful.

It wasn't long before she was able to ignore those incessant warnings and relax into the delights that Magnus offered. She pulled off her gloves, yearning to touch him as she had never done before. He closed his eyes and rolled slightly to the side to allow her better access, but movement was awkward on the narrow seat. Nevertheless, her hand found its way into the warmth of his breeches, to the center of his passions, where she soon learned how he liked to be touched.

A moment later, drowsy with desire, Magnus opened his eyes and wrapped his hand around her slender wrist.

"You'd better stop, or I might lose my head."

"I want you to," she replied breathlessly, kissing his neck, inhaling the musky fragrance of his skin, thinking this was the most wicked thing she'd ever done, but she wanted so much more. She felt no need to hold anything back, which gave her a moment's pause.

This was Magnus, and she had vowed not to give in to him. She was so afraid of another heartbreak like the last time....

But whenever he kissed her, all of that went away. She simply had to have him, at any price. She wanted to give her body to him completely, to know what it felt like to make love. And why shouldn't she know? She was thirty-four. Quite decidedly on the shelf. What could she possibly be saving herself for?

The carriage bounced over an unexpected bump, and Magnus dragged his lips from hers. He grimaced as if straining to regain control, then sat up and leaned toward the window. Pulling the curtain aside with one finger, he looked out, then sat back. "We're close to my hotel. Will you come in?"

Annabelle hesitated. Should she?

He kissed her again and continued to kiss her until the coach slowed and rolled to a stop, at which time they both quickly sat up. Annabelle pushed her skirts down to cover her exposed legs, while Magnus buttoned his coat. He combed his fingers through his hair.

"Are you all right with this?" he asked, taking her hand in his and kissing it.

She couldn't speak. All she could do was nod.

"Will you come in, Annabelle?" he asked a second time.

"Yes."

Was she really going to do this? With Magnus?

He picked her gloves up off the floor and handed them to her. "Put these on." She did as he asked. "When I open the door, step out and go inside, straight up to room twenty-one. Here is the key. I will follow a moment later."

She nodded and accepted the key from him. He opened the coach door and she got out, then he closed the door behind her and remained inside.

Annabelle walked through the lobby of the hotel and straight up the stairs, as if she were a guest and knew exactly where she was going and what she was doing, though she hadn't a clue. She knew what room, of course, but the rest of it?

She found room number twenty-one and glanced

up and down the corridor before she inserted the key into the lock and turned it. Pushing the door open, still worrying that she was making a foolish mistake, she entered the large, luxurious suite. A brass bed was dressed in a crimson and gold cover and enough pillows to get lost in. The drapes were open, and a vase of fresh flowers had been placed on a table in front of the window. Annabelle breathed in their clean, summery scent.

She walked all the way in and touched Magnus's shaving supplies on the washstand, then glanced toward the dressing room and imagined his clothes hanging inside. She wanted to touch and smell them—she could barely believe she was in his room—but before she had the chance, she heard a noise and turned.

There he was, standing in the open doorway, seeming out of breath, as if he had just run up the stairs. He was so handsome, so achingly beautiful, he almost brought her to tears.

He gazed at her for a moment. "I was afraid you might change your mind and leave before I got here."

"No."

His shoulders seemed to relax, and he came in and closed the door behind him, locked it, then walked to the window and pulled the drapes shut.

Sauntering toward her in the smoky light cutting through the narrow space between the curtains, he unbuttoned his overcoat and shrugged out of it. He tossed it onto an armchair by the bed, then reached Annabelle and took her face in his hands.

"You can trust me," he said. "We won't do anything you don't want to do."

She knew what he was telling her. He was saying that she should not be afraid, because he would not take her virginity if she did not wish it.

Nevertheless, she was very afraid.

Struggling to overcome it—for she did not want to act a fool with him—she guided his hands away from her face and down over the top of her bodice to her breasts.

He gazed at her uncertainly for a moment. She was uncertain herself. She didn't know what she was doing, only that she wanted him to touch her. The rest, she would deal with as it came.

He took her face in his hands again and pulled her close for another kiss. She let out a little moan, while he backed her up against the side of the bed, stopping briefly to remove his jacket, waistcoat, and shirt.

While he unbuttoned her bodice, she gazed in awe at his chest, smooth and muscular, then slid her open hand across his shoulder and down to the coarse hair below his navel. She followed the line of hair into his breeches again.

Oh, she was beyond hope. She'd never imagined she would experience this with Magnus, the man she had loved and lost. She felt faint and dizzy with longing. She wanted all of him—urgently—so she allowed him to undress her without the slightest resistance.

At long last, she stood before him, naked while he looked at her, which he did, for a prolonged moment. Annabelle couldn't wait any longer. She stepped forward and wrapped her arms around his neck. The next thing she knew, he was sweeping her off her feet and laying her down upon the soft bed.

Her body burned as he came down heavy upon her. "I don't want you to have any regrets," he said.

"I won't."

In truth, she was not certain she would be completely comfortable with this afterward, because she was still unsure of so many things, but she didn't want to worry about that now. All she wanted was to be with him at last, after all this time....

He rolled to the side and removed the rest of his clothing. The next thing she knew, he was easing himself between her thighs, nudging her legs apart.

Annabelle's heart was pounding. She had no idea what to expect.

"You're nervous," he whispered.

"A little."

"We could wait," he replied, giving her one last chance to change her mind.

"No, I've waited long enough."

His chest heaved against hers as he contemplated what was happening. "If we do this, I promise to do right by you."

She knew what he was saying. He was telling her that he would marry her. But Annabelle didn't know what she wanted outside of that moment.

"Just make love to me," she pleaded, shaking those thoughts away, because she was ravenous for his body and would not be deterred.

He nodded and positioned himself while kissing her, holding her, loving her and distracting her from what was to come. Magnus paused and kissed the tip of her nose, then down the side of her neck. Annabelle lay still, trying to calm her racing heart until she felt the pain of penetration and squeezed her eyes shut.

Annabelle clutched his shoulders, and eventually the pain began to subside, and she gave herself over to the miracle of what he was doing to her. She began to move with him in the dim afternoon light, her body surging with passion and desire.

Everything seemed to come naturally, and she held him as close as she could until they were both drenched in sweat. The pleasure reached a peak and crying out, she slammed her hands down upon the blankets and squeezed the covers in her fists. She realized with both fear and joy that her life was never going to be the same after this. Everything would change. How, after today, would she ever be able to live without this beautiful sensuous bliss?

Lying with Annabelle, feeling his heart pounding against hers, Magnus withdrew and rolled to the side. He was in shock. He had just made love to Annabelle, and it had not been a dream.

He laid his open hand on his chest over his heart, and for the first time in his life he felt vulnerable and exposed, yet strangely content. It was an unfamiliar feeling, for the difficult circumstances of his life, especially during his childhood, had required him to be tough and impervious. He never let down his guard. He lived in a suit of armor.

Not wanting to turn his head on the pillow and look at Annabelle—for he was afraid she might already be regretting what they'd done—he reached for her hand instead. When her fingers curled around his, he closed his eyes, relieved by that small offering, then finally turned toward her.

She was lying on her back with her eyes closed, her hand pressed over her forehead as if she were deeply troubled.

His gut wrenched and he braced himself. "Annabelle," he whispered.

He wanted to tell her that he loved her. He wanted to say it right then and there, but knew he had to tread carefully.

She took her hand off her head and opened her eyes. "I can't believe we just did that."

"I beg of you," he said. "Do not be sorry for it."

She shook her head. "I don't know what I feel, Magnus. I should be regretting it, because I am a respectable woman who just made love to a man who is not my husband, a man who is my brother's enemy, in a hotel room in the middle of the afternoon. But all I'm thinking about is the fact that it was the most wonderful thing I've ever done."

He gathered her hand in his, brought her fingers to his lips and kissed the soft pad of each one. He did not want this moment to end.

"I can't believe what it felt like," she continued. "I had no idea."

He kissed her with immense tenderness. Her eyes were still closed when he came away, and she was smiling.

"You surprise me," he said.

"Why? Because I was morally deficient just now, and I don't care?"

She was attempting to make a joke, but he did not laugh because he could see the anxiety in her expression, the uncertainty about her future. Instead, he ran his hand over her hair and wondered if it was possible that one day, she could fall in love with him again like she had the first time. If one day she would be free of all her doubts and reservations.

"It certainly was wonderful," he said. "I've never wanted anyone the way I wanted you today."

For a moment she looked into his eyes, then she glanced away. "I'm getting cold. Can we get beneath the covers?"

He sat back and pulled the covers down, and they both slid between the sheets, lying on their sides facing each other.

"This is very strange," she said.

"Which part?"

"All of it. Because I am in bed with you. Because I trusted you enough to get into a private coach with you. I trusted you to be gentle with me just now, and you were, and I am completely at ease with what we did. Sometimes I wonder if there are two of you. The man before me now, and the person who jilted me years ago."

She gazed at him pensively while their conversation was interrupted by the sound of laughter and footsteps in the corridor, followed by the closing of a door, then silence.

Annabelle reached up to touch Magnus's lips. He simply lay there, letting her explore his face with her gentle, caressing finger.

"Can a person really change so much?" she asked,

wanting it to be true.

"I believe so," he replied. "Especially if that person has something to live for. A hope. A desire."

"I must not have been enough of a desire for you the first time."

He took hold of her hand and kissed her palm. "Yes, you were, Annabelle, but I did not feel worthy of you. Everything changed when I went to America."

She rolled onto her back and draped a slender arm across her forehead. "It must be a remarkable place."

"It wasn't just the country," he said. "I could have gone anywhere, and the effect would have been the same. I just had to break away from the life I knew—when I was always keeping my head down—and become the man I wanted to be."

Annabelle's eyes darkened with emotion. "There is so much I don't know about you, Magnus. Why were you always keeping your head down?"

He paused a moment before he spoke, for he had never talked to anyone about his childhood. "Because I was treated with cruelty and brutality by people who had heard the stories about my father."

"But Whitby has always insisted that you were a villain and bullied his brother, and that you caused his death."

Magnus shook his head. "That is not true. John was the one who started the fights, and Whitby would always come along to help finish them—at least until I learned how to defend myself. And the afternoon John died, I was long gone. We had fought that day, yes, but he rode off afterward."

Annabelle sat up. "But what about your mother

demanding money from Whitby?"

He shrugged. "I know she asked John to take me in after my father died, but he refused."

"Whitby says your mother threatened John."

Magnus inhaled deeply. He didn't like talking about this, didn't like to think about his mother's odious conduct, or the fact that in this regard, Whitby was probably telling the truth.

"I wasn't aware of her threatening him," he said with a sigh, "though knowing her, she probably did. That would explain why John picked fights with me, wouldn't it?"

Magnus found it strange that he could feel so numb upon speaking of this. He supposed he had shoveled a great deal of dirt over his age-old bitterness.

"Sometimes I just don't know what to believe," Annabelle said. "I trust my brother. He wouldn't lie about things. But my feelings for you are so...."

She didn't finish. She merely closed her eyes and shook her head, as if she didn't know which way was up.

Magnus, however, *did* know. He leaned on one elbow and resolved to say what needed to be said.

"All of that is in the past, Annabelle. I have left it behind, and I need you to do that as well. Come to America with me. As my wife."

She blinked repeatedly, her face going pale before she replied. "Please don't ask me that now, Magnus. This is all happening so fast. I need time to let the dust settle."

"But what were you thinking when you saw me at the station and decided to come away with me? Surely something changed."

He had hoped she'd realized that she still loved him and was willing to move forward. In a way, he had wanted her to choose him over her brother.

"To be honest, I wasn't thinking beyond the moment," she said.

It was not what he wanted to hear.

When he raked a hand through his hair in frustration, Annabelle sat up, hugging the covers to her chest. "Please don't make demands on me, Magnus. Not now. This is all very new and very confusing, and I can't be impulsive about a decision that will affect the rest of my life. This morning I wouldn't even have believed I would be in your bed today. I still can't believe it."

He slowly rolled away from her and sat up. He thought about how angry she had been with him when she first came to his gallery. She had hated him then, and that was barely a month ago.

He picked his trousers up off the floor and pulled them on.

"Are you angry?" Annabelle asked.

He shook his head, strode to the window and pulled the drapes aside to look out. "No, but I suppose I am waiting for the axe to fall, one way or another."

He remembered something of the sort once before, when he was a boy. He recalled the stories his father used to tell him to distract him from the hunger pains in his belly when there had been no food in the house. He used to talk of a fairy-tale life that might someday be his.

But then his ailing father died, and his mother had

dropped the axe. She told him the truth about that fairy-tale family—that they had tossed out one of their own sons—Magnus's father—and banished him to hell because he had been a disappointment.

He had not been good enough for them. He had been weak. Sick. Not normal. And his mother had told him that they didn't want him, either.

Magnus heard the bedclothes rustling, Annabelle's tiny feet touching the floor and padding toward him. When he turned, she was standing before him, wrapped in the sheet.

"I just want us to enjoy ourselves," she said, the fresh afternoon sun bathing her in soft light, gilding the highlights of her wild, unruly hair. "I'm not ready to think about tomorrow, much less the rest of my life."

He touched her then, because he couldn't resist the rosy pink of her cheeks, still aglow from their love-making. Gently, he traced a line down her slender neck and delicate shoulders, then across her collar-bone, while marveling at the silky warmth of her flesh beneath his fingertips.

Watching her eyelids close, he recalled that he had once told himself he would do anything to have her—so if that meant making love to her tirelessly until she finally surrendered to him heart, body, and soul, he would indeed make love to her tirelessly, with or without promises.

"Look at me," she whispered, her eyes still closed, her breasts rising and falling with breathless yearn-ings. "I am trembling. How do you do this to me?"

He shuddered with anticipation and need and answered her with a kiss that quickened his blood like nothing he'd ever known. Then, driven by lust and the consuming need to possess her, he swept her off her feet, into his arms, and carried her back to the bed.

Chapter 15

ORTY-EIGHT HOURS LATER, ANNABELLE WOKE up in Magnus's bed and wondered if it was possible for a person to die from too much pleasure.

She sat up groggily and tried to make sense of the sheets, which were tangled chaotically at the foot of the bed. The pretty crimson and gold cover had been tossed aside early that morning and was piled on the floor near the window, while their clothes were strewn everywhere.

And her hair.... Well, it looked like some strange little creature had built a nest at the back of her head.

She yawned and nudged Magnus, who lay on his stomach, stretched out in a careless sprawl. Her gaze drifted over his sleeping form, the corded muscles of his back, the wavy black hair spilling heedlessly across his face, his well-built, broad-shouldered frame taking up more than half the bed. He was a gorgeous specimen of manhood, she reflected with a sluggish, blissful sigh, and even now, after two days of lovemaking, she was certain she could still manage a little more.

If it weren't for the niggling sense of responsibility to make contact with her family and assure them that she was still among the living, she most definitely would.

She nudged him again. "Magnus, wake up. They're going to think we died in here."

"Who?" he asked, still half asleep, his lips puckered against the pillow.

"The hotel staff, that's who." She swung her legs to the floor. "And my maid has probably contacted the police by now and reported me missing."

"Surely not. She saw you go off with me."

"Precisely," Annabelle replied, smacking her tongue against the dry roof of her mouth.

In all honesty, Josephine was probably doing everything she could to cover Annabelle's tracks, for she was extremely loyal.

"Come back to bed," Magnus said without opening his eyes or moving.

"No, I can't come back. You've done me in."

Hearing that, he rolled over at last. "You've done me in as well, woman. Do you think I'm made of steel?"

"There are times you appear to be," she replied with a smile.

"Well, not now. I'm spent."

"You need food."

"Food. I'd forgotten about food."

She returned to bed and lay down on her back, her body crossing diagonally over his. "Maybe we should get dressed and go out."

He lifted his head off the pillow. "You'd have to comb your hair."

"Where is a lady's maid when she is most needed?"

Magnus dropped his head back down. "What's her name? Josephine? Maybe you should let her go. She's been hopelessly ineffective. Look at this place. Your corset is hanging off the curtain rod, for pity's sake." He pointed. "Look at that."

"You're absolutely right. I will fire her tomorrow."

Two minutes later Annabelle had forgotten about her responsibility to her family, and both she and Magnus were making good use of the bed again.

"I can't just be your lover," Magnus told Annabelle that night, his voice heavy with desire as he made love to her again, gently, with great attention to detail. "I must be more than that. I want to be your husband. For life."

She inhaled sharply at the sound of those words. *Husband for life.* To be given that guarantee—that Magnus would be hers and she would be his and they would share pleasures like this forever—was beyond her imagination.

She cried out, a muffled sound of indulgence as her fingers dug into his back and her legs squeezed around his hips. "Don't stop," she pleaded, voracious for him, needing more of the rapture he offered.

"Marry me," he said.

She wanted to say yes. She wanted to scream it out loud, but she couldn't think. All she could comprehend was ecstasy and sensation.

"I love you," he whispered in her ear, his breath hot

as flame, his intense physical rhythm incomprehensible.

"I love you, too," she replied. "I don't care about anything else."

His movements stilled and he drew back, just far enough to look her in the eye. "Then marry me."

"I don't know, Magnus."

"Trust me. You know that you can."

There it was. That which was holding her back....

"I know that I *want* to."

"You want to trust me?" he asked. "Or you want to marry me?"

She considered the question but couldn't think because she was losing herself in a mounting flood of physical delight. "Both. I want both. *Yes.*"

The world outside of Annabelle's mind and body disappeared, and she surrendered to her yearnings once and for all, welcoming the force of Magnus's desires as he finally groaned and gave all his love to her.

He collapsed upon her, heavy and exhausted, and lay for a moment until their breathing returned to normal and their bodies regained their natural rhythms. Then he took her into his arms and held her close with a different kind of tenderness—the kind that felt like forever—until the sun rose in the morning and light spread across their bed.

Annabelle woke from a deep sleep as if an alarm bell had gone off inside her head. Groggy and disoriented, she sat bolt upright and looked around.

The suite was quiet except for the ticking of the

clock and a cart with a squeaky wheel rolling by outside the door. Light poured in through the space between the drapes, and the room was still a mess. She had no idea what day it was.

Gazing down at Magnus asleep beside her, lying on his back, naked under a single white sheet, one arm draped over his face, Annabelle suddenly remembered the words he had spoken the night before. He had told her he loved her. And somewhere in the wild, spinning magic of her passions, she had agreed to become his wife.

The old familiar doubts and fears came rushing back to her, and she wasn't sure she could move. What had she done? She should have taken more time to think about the full implications of her decision, but she supposed she hadn't exactly been thinking with her brain.

"Good morning," Magnus said, his hand coming to rest on her back.

Annabelle looked down at him. "Good morning."

For a moment he studied her face. He tossed an arm up under his head, and she knew that somehow, he understood what she was feeling. How could he not? He must have been expecting this.

His fingers began to brush lightly across her back. "Don't worry," he said.

Annabelle swallowed with difficulty. "Easier said than done. We've been out of our minds with lust the past few days, and last night I agreed to marry you. What will Whitby say when he finds out?"

Magnus's eyes clouded over with displeasure. "It won't matter what he says. We're together now, and I won't let anything—or anyone—tear us apart."

Still feeling unsure, she rested a chin on her knee and gazed pensively toward the window.

"Come here." He urged her back down to lie beside him.

Annabelle rested her head on his shoulder, and the heat of his body warmed hers. As she lay there in his arms, she contemplated all the misgivings that still hammered away inside her head, and a far worse fear came over her. She imagined taking Whitby's side and telling Magnus that she could not marry him. She imagined saying good-bye to Magnus and pushing him out of her life forever. Quite frankly, the thought of that was worse than death.

Nothing seemed to matter now but the joy he gave her. When he was holding her close like this, she didn't care about the past or what other people thought. She didn't want to be suspicious and worry that he was using her to hurt Whitby. She wanted to believe in him. She wanted to believe that he told her the truth—that he had come back to London for *her*—and revenge upon Whitby had nothing to do with it.

When it came right down to it, all she cared about was this crazy, mad love, and every instinct in her body was pushing her to trust him. Maybe that was all that mattered.

She leaned up on an elbow and looked down at him. "I don't want anything to come between us, either."

Magnus took her face in his hands. "I will make you happy, Annabelle. I promise. You will never want for anything."

"I don't need anything except you."

His eyes flashed with desire, and he pulled her down for a kiss, but Annabelle laid a hand on his chest to stop things before the kiss progressed to something more.

"We can't start this again," she said with a smile, "because we have to get up and get dressed. I'll need to go home today."

He settled back, disappointed. "Why?"

"Because I have to tell them."

His chest rose and fell with a deep sigh. "Why do you have to go back there? Why don't we just leave? You could write to them from New York."

"No, I could never do that," she replied. "They're my family and I care for them—Whitby, Lily, and the children. I can't leave without saying good-bye."

He sat up against the pillows, his dark eyes sweeping over her face with a measure of discontent.

"You don't have to come," she said.

"Oh, yes. I most definitely do. I will not have you going alone, as if you are ashamed of me."

"It wouldn't be like that," she assured him.

Magnus looked away toward the window. *"He* might think so. Or he might think I am afraid to face him. He'll certainly try to change your mind."

Annabelle felt a chill come over the room with this change in Magnus's mood. She wished he would look at her. "It won't matter what Whitby thinks," she said. "Nothing will change my mind."

Magnus continued to look off into the distance as if he hadn't heard her, then finally, he met her gaze. His eyes warmed, and she was relieved.

"You're right," he said. "It doesn't matter. I am only thinking of you. I hate that you must do something so difficult. If you like, I could do it. I could face him alone."

Annabelle tried to imagine that, but she could not. Whitby probably wouldn't even believe that she had consented to marry Magnus. Whitby would think it a lie, or that Magnus had kidnapped her or some other such foolishness.

She squeezed Magnus's hand. "No, you were right the first time. We must stand together. And I will do my best to convince my brother that he has been wrong about you. All along."

"He won't believe it."

"I told you, it doesn't matter. I will say whatever it takes. And if he doesn't like it, so be it."

Annabelle's stomach began to churn with a slow mounting dread. She rested a hand on her belly, thinking she would be very glad when this day was over.

Century House in Bedfordshire was hailed by some as one of the most majestic houses in England, and though Annabelle had lived there all her life, she never failed to be moved by its magnificence whenever she returned after some time away.

The coach rolled past the ornamental fountain and came to a smooth stop at the front entrance. Annabelle glanced briefly at Magnus, who was looking out the window in the opposite direction of the house.

He does not want to be here.

"Shall we?" she said, nonetheless.

"Of course," he replied. "Allow me."

He climbed out of the coach and offered his hand to Annabelle to assist her as she stepped down. She started off toward the front entrance but stopped and turned when she realized he was not following. He stood beside the coach, his dark eyes moving slowly from left to right across the front of the house.

"I haven't seen this place in eight years," he said, "and I have certainly never made it past the front doors."

Annabelle was uncomfortably aware of a change in him. There was no warmth in his eyes, no flirtatious spark or seductive appeal. Nevertheless, she spoke with confidence. "You will walk through those doors with me today."

He nodded and followed.

They were met at the door by Clarke, the butler, who politely greeted Annabelle, but as soon as he recognized Magnus, his expression turned to shock.

Annabelle removed her gloves as she spoke. "Mr. Wallis is my guest today, Clarke. We wish to speak to Whitby. Inform him, if you will."

The butler stared perplexedly at her before he closed the door behind them and recovered his aplomb. "As you wish, Miss Lawson."

"Tell him we will be in the gilded drawing room," she added.

Clarke bowed at the waist before he turned to go. Annabelle could see the panic in his gait. It was not something she had ever seen before.

When she faced Magnus, he did not look pleased.

"It's this way," she said, wanting only to get through

this as quickly as possible.

They climbed the stairs, and Magnus looked up at the enormous ancestral portraits on the walls, some dating back as far as the fifteenth century. He was barely watching where his feet were going.

When they reached the top and entered the drawing room with its ornately carved, gilded ceiling, Annabelle watched him with a mild sense of trepidation. His eyes scanned everything—from the massive gilt-framed mirror over the fireplace, to the Chippendale furniture, the statues, the harp, the grand piano, the gold wall sconces, and the tall tree ferns.

"You could feed half the orphans in London for a month with whatever it cost to furnish this room," he said bluntly.

Annabelle wasn't quite sure what to say.

"It's a far cry from the place where I grew up," he added, approaching the eight-foot portrait of his grandfather on the wall and looking up at it. "There he is." The derision in his voice was unmistakable.

Annabelle approached Magnus and linked her arm through his, seeking to remind him that the man in the portrait was part of the past, and it was time to leave all that behind. Isn't that what he had tried to tell her when he asked her to return to America with him as his wife?

"I never knew him," she said, looking up at the portrait. "He died long before I was born."

"Which was probably fortunate for you, because I doubt that he would have taken you in."

Startled by the severity in Magnus's tone, Annabelle shot a surprised glance at him.

His expression gentled. "I apologize." He shook his head at himself. "That was thoughtless of me. I just never expected to see the inside of this house. It brings back old memories."

He took her into his arms and held her, calming her misgivings with the affection in his embrace.

Just then a throat cleared from the doorway, and both Annabelle and Magnus stepped apart. It was her brother, Whitby. He appeared horror-struck. "Annabelle. What in God's name...?"

She gestured toward Magnus. "I've brought someone."

Whitby remained in the doorway. "I see that."

There was a long, drawn-out silence while Annabelle's gut began to churn, and her heart hammered against her ribs. These two men—both whom she loved—despised each other. They had fought as children, each blaming the other for unfortunate circumstances in their lives, and Annabelle wasn't sure it would ever be possible to change that.

She glanced anxiously at Magnus, who stood motionless, facing Whitby.

"Why don't we all sit down?" she suggested.

After a moment's hesitation, her brother slowly entered the room, and Annabelle took a seat at one end of the sofa. As soon as she was settled, Magnus sat beside her, while Whitby chose the facing chair.

"Where have you been?" her brother asked, sounding more than a little displeased. "We expected you home days ago."

She squeezed her hands together on her lap. "I apologize. I was...detained."

Whitby's piercing gaze flicked to Magnus. "Detained."

Magnus said nothing. He merely crossed one leg over the other and let Annabelle do the talking. She was very glad of that.

"Yes," she said, resolving to be firm and forthright, for there was no point dancing around the issue. "You see...Magnus and I have spent the past few days together and we have come to realize that...that we are still in love."

Oh, how foolish she must sound to Whitby, who no doubt could not believe his ears. She even sounded foolish to herself.

Whitby's tolerance seemed to snap like a tangible thing in the room. Annabelle almost feared the ceiling was going to blow through the roof.

"Please, Whitby. Try to understand," she said.

"Understand?" To her utter surprise, he spoke not with anger, but with gentle pleading, as if Magnus were not even there. "How can I? I've watched you go through your entire adult life without hope or optimism because of what he did to you. All this time, you've hated him."

"Only because I was hurt," she explained, though she did not feel confident. She felt ridiculous, for she had changed her opinions—opinions she had held for thirteen years—virtually overnight, even after Whitby had warned her that Magnus would try to seduce her. Which he certainly had done, quite effectively.

Whitby wet his lips and shifted in his chair. He appeared shaken but determined to convince her that

she was making a grave mistake and was merely confused.

Meanwhile, Magnus was sitting back with quiet
fortitude, watching everything unfold.

"No, Annabelle, you forget," Whitby said. "Do you
not remember the lies that you could not forgive?"

"I do remember that," she said, "but it was a long
time ago, and I am a different person now and so is
he." Magnus gave her an encouraging nod, and she
was so very, very thankful that he was there, because
she wanted to be with him. She did. She could not let
anything change her mind.

Whitby, however, watched the exchange from
where he sat across from them, and all his gentle
pleading flew out the window. He stood up. "Annabelle, you are not a fool. Use your head."

She shot him an exasperated look. "I *am* using it."

"No, I do not believe you are."

She stared dumbfounded at her brother. "You need
to give him a chance, Whitby. He is not the villain
you think he is. There have been misunderstandings,
and he regrets what happened between us. He never
wanted to hurt me."

She looked at Magnus then, needing him to inter-
vene, to defend what she was saying.

He recognized her entreaty and turned to Whitby.
"Indeed, I am not the villain here. And I do regret
what happened between Annabelle and me. But you
have played a part in her unhappiness, too, Whitby.
Annabelle has felt trapped here, as if she owes something to you because your family took her in. She
needs to feel that she is free."

"Is this true, Annabelle?" Whitby asked.

She paused. "You have been very kind to me, which makes it difficult to do something that will disappoint you."

Whitby shook his head at Magnus. "I am not going to apologize for being *kind* to her."

"Well, I have apologized to her," Magnus said, "and she has forgiven me."

Whitby's face screwed into a disbelieving grimace. "You cannot be serious, Annabelle! You believe him? Tell me that you were not so gullible. You assured me you were not."

"I was not gullible, Whitby. It is the truth. He is not the man you think he is." She fidgeted and cleared her throat, striving to maintain a confident tone. "I believe it's time you stopped hating Magnus so much and put the past to rest."

"Put it to rest." Whitby shook his head and strode to the other side of the room.

Annabelle felt like she was suffocating. She glanced desperately at Magnus, but he was sitting forward, watching her brother.

Finally, Whitby faced them again. "What do you mean to tell me today, Annabelle? Why did you bring him here?"

She sensed he already knew the answer to that question, but he needed to hear it just the same.

"We are engaged," she confessed, feeling her heart break at what should have been the happiest moment of her life.

The ensuing silence carried enough weight to crush the house.

Annabelle sat motionless, immobile. She was aware of Magnus beside her, waiting for Whitby to oppose the engagement, and she wasn't sure what would happen after that.

Whitby strode closer. "Are you blind, Annabelle? He came back here to use you again, so he could finally feel that he has won."

"No, you are wrong," she insisted, hearing her voice break because her brother's words were not what she wanted to hear, not after she had suffered so much, fighting against her doubts and fears.

"It's just because you are lonely," Whitby spat. "You are not thinking clearly because you are desperate for a marriage of your own."

Her lips fell open. "I am not desperate."

Magnus, to her left, stood suddenly, tall and ominous in the room. "I think I've heard enough."

"I beg your pardon?" Whitby said bitterly.

"Shall I repeat it for you, cousin? *I have heard enough.*"

Whitby slowly blinked. "May I remind you of the fact, sir, that you are not welcome here."

Annabelle stood also. "Yes, he is. It's my home, too, and he is my guest."

They both ignored her.

"Your sister is coming with me," Magnus said. "She has agreed to become my wife, and I will be taking her to America with me."

Whitby spoke through clenched teeth. "You will do no such thing."

Annabelle stood there stunned as she watched them, not knowing what to do or say.

"I will do exactly as I please," Magnus shot back.

"She belongs to me now."

"I don't belong to either of you!" Annabelle shouted, but again, they both ignored her. They were glaring at each other like a couple of growling wolves.

"You insufferable bastard," Whitby said, his voice low, but brimming with a dangerous, repressed fury.

The grandfather clock chimed once, and before Annabelle had a chance to say another word, they simultaneously charged at each other.

Chapter 16

$\mathcal{M}$AGNUS AND WHITBY GRABBED HOLD of each other in the drawing room, knocked over a plant, then slammed hard up against a tapestry on the wall. The heavy fabric jostled as they shoved each other, then they hurled each other back to the middle of the room, shouting as they fell against a table, knocking over a lamp, which smashed on the floor. They fell beside the broken glass and rolled in the other direction, grunting and cursing until Annabelle shouted, "Stop it! Both of you!"

Whitby pinned Magnus down and punched him in the jaw, then Magnus sat up and bashed his forehead against Whitby's. Her brother fell backward.

"Stop!" Annabelle shouted again, and suddenly Lily was beside her, grabbing her husband under the arms and scrambling to pull him off Magnus.

"What is going on!" she shouted in disbelief.

The sound of his pregnant wife's voice seemed to arrest Whitby on the spot. He sat back on the floor, cupping his forehead.

Magnus staggered to his feet and wiped the back of his hand across his bleeding lip. He was out of breath and panting. He jabbed a finger at Whitby. "I am warning you, Whitby. Do not try to come between us. We will be leaving for America tomorrow, and do not expect to visit your sister, because you will not be welcome in my house."

Shocked and shaken, Annabelle turned to her brother and sister-in-law, who were waiting for her to say something.

All the weight of the world descended upon her at that moment, and she wasn't sure she could find the words to speak.

Then Magnus's arm curled around her waist and he closed his eyes and pressed his face against her cheek, and she found herself holding tight to him. She wrapped her arms around his neck.

She looked back down at Whitby and Lily and felt a wretchedness of heart she had never imagined possible. "I'm so sorry," she said. "I have to go with him."

With that, she and Magnus left the drawing room.

They made it only as far as the staircase, however, before Annabelle stopped and took hold of the railing, her anger finally spilling over the edge of her composure. "What in the name of God was that?"

The fire from the struggle was still burning in Magnus's eyes. "What do you mean? He insulted you."

"How?"

"He said you were lonely and desperate."

Annabelle shook her head at Magnus and descended the stairs, hearing him follow fast behind her.

"That wasn't about me," she said accusingly. "It was

about you seizing the opportunity to fight him. You were waiting for it. Eagerly."

They were practically sailing down the stairs now.

"Oh no you don't," he said. "Do not try to blame me. I sat there calmly through all of that. It was your brother who wanted to fight from the first minute he set eyes on me. He wanted to crush me, like always."

Annabelle walked quickly across the entrance hall, her strides snapping her skirts between her legs. "You think it's him and he thinks it's you. I'm sick of it."

Magnus followed her out the front door and down the steps to the coach. She climbed in and sat down, and he climbed in beside her, slamming the door shut, but the coach didn't move.

"How can you be angry with me?" he asked. "I was a bystander."

"Oh, yes, you were very unassuming when you smashed him up against the tapestry!"

"I did it for you, Annabelle. I was defending your choice to marry me. I was not going to let him stop us."

"But I saw the fury in your eyes! You were out of control, and all this time you have been promising me that Whitby no longer has any power over you—that you had left all that behind, and the only reason you came back to England was for me. I believed you. I trusted that you were telling me the truth."

"Don't do this, Annabelle," he said. "Don't let yourself. You're so unreasonably loyal to him! Just because he took you in and raised you does not mean you have to live your life only to make him proud. You must find your own way and your own happiness. Be true to yourself. You do not owe him your whole future."

"It's not as easy as that. I trust him to know what is best for me and what will make me happy, when I don't really trust myself."

"Or me," Magnus said.

She did not reply.

"Say it, Annabelle. I am the reason you don't trust yourself."

"Yes!" she shouted. "I made an error in judgement years ago. I was fooled. Duped. And after what just happened, how can I not still have doubts? How can I believe that there is not some truth to what Whitby just said—that you want me because you want to feel that you have won. You simply want to take something away from him."

His eyes darkened with frustration. "That is not true. You are letting him influence you. Trust your heart, Annabelle. You know I love you."

"But you were still fighting the same battle today that you always were! What has changed?"

Magnus sat forward and wiped his lip again, examining the blood on his hand.

"Whitby is not a bad man," she told Magnus. "He only wants me to be safe and happy, and I don't think either of you really knows why you hate the other."

That statement caused Magnus to lift his head and look at her with dismay. "I know very well why I hate him, Annabelle."

"Why?"

"Because he has always taken pleasure in making my life a living hell. He has deprived me of my birthright, beaten me to a pulp on numerous occasions, spread cruel gossip about my father and me, causing us to be treated as outcasts and lunatics. As a child, I was spit upon in the streets, kicked and beaten by those who enjoyed thrashing a fallen aristocrat. But it was my father I pitied the most, because he died a broken man. That is why I will always hate your brother—for continuing his grandfather's legacy of heartlessness."

Stunned by Magnus's outburst, Annabelle could feel her throat closing up. "But you told me you didn't care about Whitby anymore, that that was behind you. How can I trust completely that there is not a part of you that *is* using me? Do you even know it yourself? I saw the satisfaction in your eyes just now when you told him I belonged to you, not him. At that moment, I was nothing more than a weapon to use against him. And I can see the hatred in your eyes now. I just heard it in your voice."

She looked out the coach window toward the horizon over the treetops in the distance.

"You cannot blame me for hating Whitby," Magnus said. "But it has nothing to do with you."

"But that's just it! I do blame you for hating him. It is not his fault that you and your father were cut off from the family. Your father *was* dangerous. He tried to light his own brother on fire."

The shock of hearing that seemed to stir Magnus's anger all over again. "That is a blatant lie! My father was not dangerous. He was sickly and weak. That is the reason why my grandfather did not want him. He lacked the appropriate stature of an aristocrat."

Annabelle felt her brows pull together in a frown.

"That is not what Whitby believes."

Magnus shrugged and looked off in the other direction, as if what Whitby believed was of no consequence to him.

Hope sparked anew in Annabelle's veins. "I feel a great need to get to the bottom of this."

He shook his head at her, as if he were puzzled by that desire. "Why? It's in the past."

"It is not in the past, because you are still bitter about it."

"I am bitter that you won't trust me!" he shouted, raking a hand through his hair in frustration. "You continue to trust Whitby over me, when what I need is for you to take a leap of faith. Just believe in me *now*. Forget about the past."

Annabelle shifted uneasily on the cushioned seat. "Perhaps I could talk to Whitby and tell him that there has been a mistake," she said. "That circumstances are not as he believes them to be. He might listen to me."

Magnus took hold of her shoulders. "Annabelle, it was a long time ago. It doesn't matter. Just trust me now and come away with me."

"I can't."

"Why? What are you looking for? Concrete proof that you can trust me? Because you will never get that. The trust has to come from here." He placed his fist on her chest, over her heart.

Annabelle gazed at him in despair. "But there is so much to be sorted out here."

He lowered his gaze. "Please, I am asking you.... Don't confuse all this with your fear of letting yourself love me. Just look in your heart."

He regarded her intently with eyes dark and beseeching, and she did as he asked. She *did* look into her heart, where she felt passion and love and hope and desire. She wanted Magnus with every breath in her body. She wanted to spend the rest of her life with him.

But he was asking her to take a blind leap of faith and simply believe him, when she could not. She was afraid to, especially when there were still so many unanswered questions.

She wished it were not so, but she needed something more than Magnus's word—his word against Whitby's—to hang her trust upon.

She lowered her gaze, knowing it was going to kill her to say this, and it was going to kill him to hear it....

"I'm sorry, but I can't."

Magnus tipped his head back on the upholstery and stared up at the dark ceiling of the coach. "You are going to trust Whitby's word over mine?" They sat in silence for a moment. "Please don't do this, Annabelle. Come with me now."

"No, not like this," she replied. "Don't make me choose between you and them when I am not ready. If it's me you love, you will be patient." She crossed in front of him to climb out of the coach.

"Where are you going?" he asked.

"Back inside."

"Please tell me you're going to collect your things."

She opened the door and stepped out. "No. I can't go with you today, Magnus."

She backed away from him, toward the house.

He climbed out of the coach, too. "Please, do not go back in there."

"I have to. I need to fix this."

"You can't fix anything!" he shouted. "Even if you find out there was a misunderstanding and my father was wronged, it won't give you what you are looking for. Why can't you accept that?"

She stopped and took a breath, overcome suddenly by self-doubt, but then she kept going, because she simply could not take that leap of faith. She wished she could, but she could not.

He called to her one more time. "Annabelle!"

But she kept going.

Magnus pressed the heels of his hands to his fore-head, then strode back to the coach and pounded his fist against the outside of it over and over. He grunted with fury and frustration as he kicked a wheel, then got back inside, slammed the door shut, and shouted at the coachman to drive off.

Gathering her skirts in her fists, Annabelle strode purposefully up the stairs and returned to the drawing room, where Whitby and Lily were standing together in front of the window. Whitby was holding a cloth to his forehead.

She stopped in the doorway, and Lily immediately came hurrying across the room to hug her.

"Oh, Annabelle."

When they stepped apart, Annabelle gazed at her brother, who was still standing at the window. He must have seen what had occurred out front.

"Thank goodness," he said, lowering the cloth and tossing it onto the marble table beside him. "I'm relieved you had the good sense not to leave with him."

Annabelle loved her brother, and she knew he only wanted what was best for her, but she had never, ever been more furious with him.

"I have not come back," she said, "at least not the way you think."

He shook his head at her, as if he couldn't get over her foolishness, then turned and faced the window.

Annabelle strode toward him. "How *could* you, Whitby?"

He faced her again. "How could *I*? You were the one who brought an enemy into our home and told me you wanted to marry him. Marry him, Annabelle! Of all the men in England, you had to choose him?"

Annabelle tried to explain. "I fought it every step of the way—honestly, I did—but then I just couldn't do it anymore. I am in love with him."

Whitby's eyes fumed with shock and dismay. "You are determined? You are going to choose that villain over us?"

"I have not yet made that decision," she said. "I am still unsure."

Whitby seemed to relax upon hearing that. "You still have reservations?"

"How can I help but have reservations? I've had a broken heart since I was twenty-one. I'm not capable of trusting *any* man." She sank into a chair and buried her face in her hands. "I am such a misfit."

Whitby crossed toward her and touched her shoulder. "You are not a misfit, Annabelle. You're just cautious, and wisely so."

"But I love him, Whitby. Why can't I just trust him? Why must I live in constant fear that the rug is going to be pulled out from under me, with no warning whatsoever?"

"Because that is what happened the last time."

Her brother's eyes softened with compassion, which Annabelle greatly appreciated because she felt very alone and was worried that she had just made the biggest mistake of her life, walking away from the man she loved.

She sighed heavily. "Maybe it would help if I understood more about why his father was sent away by your grandfather," she said, still fearing that Magnus was right—that she was using the past as an excuse, giving it more importance than it deserved because she was simply afraid of letting herself love him.

Whether or not that was the case, she did not know. All she could do was press on. "Magnus truly believes they were wronged."

"That is not what I know about it, and I've already told you everything I know," Whitby said.

He appeared less angry now, and she wondered if it was possible that he might take pity on her and help her.

"It appears to be your word against his," she told him. "One of you must be wrong, and I am tired of all the questions. I need to feel as if I know what I am doing."

But even if she did know the truth, would she *ever*

feel completely sure?

Annabelle spent the rest of the day questioning various members of the household about Whitby's grandfather and his twin sons, and everyone who had worked in the house at that time said the same thing—that the boy was sent away because he was violent and dangerous. One servant even went so far as to claim that the boy had "the devil in him," which did nothing to improve Annabelle's optimism. But it was so long ago that none of them could quite remember what he looked like.

Annabelle had the distinct feeling that people believed what they had heard through gossip over the years, and that the story had taken on mythic proportions.

Later, when all her questions turned up no new information, she spent the evening in her studio, distracting herself from the stresses of her life by working on the painting of the waterfall.

She still could not seem to get the reflections in the water to look the way she wanted them to, so she finally gave up, chalking it up to the fact that she was too anxious to concentrate.

That night, Annabelle went to bed feeling certain that she was wasting her time on this futile search. What was the point, after all, when Magnus said he didn't care about the past? What difference would all this make once they arrived in America, if she went with him? Whatever happened to his father had nothing to do with their lives now. If she was going to give her whole heart to Magnus, she would have to do as he'd asked and somehow find the courage to take that blind leap of faith.

Just then a quiet knock sounded at her door, and she leaned up on both elbows. "Come in."

The door creaked open, and there stood her brother, holding a kerosene lamp. He was still wearing his dinner jacket, but his shirt was open at the collar, his tie loose around his neck.

"I am sorry if I woke you," he said.

"You didn't. I wasn't sleeping."

He hesitated a moment. "May I speak with you?"

"Of course."

He closed the door behind him, walked to the bed and set down the lamp, then pulled a chair up and took a seat.

"Today, after you told me that Magnus believed his father was wronged," Whitby said, "I began thinking about it, and I remember whispers and gossip when I was growing up. Gossip about my grandfather."

Annabelle's pulse began to beat. "Pertaining to what?"

Whitby rubbed at the back of his neck. "Evidently, there was a parlor maid who worked here in the house, and she and my grandfather were intimate lovers."

"That sounds scandalous," Annabelle remarked.

"The maid was let go eventually, but I seem to recall hearing that she was sent away at the same time Magnus's father was."

A disturbing notion suddenly occurred to Annabelle. "Was she the mother?"

Whitby held up a hand and shook his head. "No, no. Nothing like that. Magnus's father and my father were definitely twins. That is certain."

Annabelle was not sure where her brother was heading with this, until he reached into his waistcoat pocket and handed her a folded note. "But perhaps this woman knows something and can give you some insight into what happened. If she is still alive, that is. I have no idea."

Annabelle unfolded the note and read the woman's name, Rose Michaels, along with a London address.

"I don't know if her family still lives there," Whitby said, "but it was all I could find in the employment records."

Annabelle tossed the covers aside and slid to the edge of the bed. "How can I ever thank you?"

He stood. "Don't be so grateful. I still don't trust Magnus, and I am hoping this woman will prove me right. I just want you to be sure of your decision, whatever it turns out to be."

Annabelle wrapped her arms around him, and he held her briefly before he drew away. There was a note of warning in his voice as he spoke.

"All I ask is that you be careful, Annabelle. Do not let your emotions rule your head. But heaven forbid, if you do, and you decide to go with Magnus, please know that you can always come home to us. We will be here for you no matter what."

"Thank you, Whitby. It is good to know."

He turned to leave but stopped in the doorway. "You should also know that if that man ever hurts you again, I swear I will cross the ocean to make him pay. I promise you that, Annabelle."

And she knew that if circumstances warranted it,

her brother would make good on that promise.

His head in a fog, Magnus entered his hotel room and looked around.

The maids had been there. The bedclothes were in order, the drapes were open, and everything was tidy. It was almost as if Annabelle had never been there.

Closing the door behind him and dropping the hotel key on a table, he slowly walked to the bed and rested a hand on the brass frame. He rested the other hand on his stomach, because he felt ill, as if he had been shot back there...into those dark times when he wanted to blame Whitby for everything that was wrong in his life, and crush him. Magnus had thought he was over that, but today had been very grim.

He was ashamed of himself—for his shocking, appalling behavior in Annabelle's drawing room. He had tried to crush Whitby again. He had felt such intense bitterness toward him.

Why had he even bothered to come back here and subject himself to this? He felt wretched, like that rejected boy who had been kicked and beaten and called the spawn of a madman.

He should not have come. Not even for Annabelle. She was too entrenched in that world. Magnus just wanted to leave, immediately, and go home to America.

But God, oh, God...he could not. Because he still wanted her with every inch of his soul, even though the likelihood of his ever truly having her seemed slim, because she simply would not trust him.

Granted, she had said she wanted to fix things, but

he didn't want her to go poking around in the past, finding out things he might not even want to know. What if she discovered something that would confirm what Whitby had always said, and it would make Annabelle fear and loathe him more than she ever had before—just as everyone else had all his life?

In all honesty, he was afraid of what she might find, because how well had he really known his father, after all? For all he knew, maybe his father *had* been a madman.

Chapter 17

ANNABELLE KNOCKED FIRMLY UPON ROSE Michaels's door and was greeted by an attractive woman in gold spectacles. Her gray hair was swept into a loose knot, and she appeared to be in her sixties.

"Good afternoon," she said.

Annabelle smiled politely. "Good afternoon. I'm looking for someone who lived here quite a few years ago, and I'm wondering if you might know her. Her name is Rose Michaels."

Annabelle saw recognition flash through the woman's eyes before she gave a melancholy smile. "Rose was my mother. But she died seven years ago."

Annabelle sighed and bit her lower lip.

"Perhaps there is something I can help you with?" the woman asked.

Annabelle wondered again if it was possible for *anyone* to help her. She was standing at a stranger's door, looking for answers about Magnus—a man who had no connection to these people. Rose Michaels was a ghost. She had never even met him.

"No, but thank you," Annabelle replied as she turned to leave. "I'm sorry to have bothered you."

"Wait, dear...." The woman took an anxious step forward. "How did you know my mother?"

Annabelle stopped on the front walk and turned around. "I didn't. My brother—the Earl of Whitby—gave me her name, because she once worked as a maid at Century House in Bedfordshire, and I wanted to ask her some questions about that. But it was such a long time ago."

The woman's eyes narrowed curiously. "Your brother is the Earl of Whitby?"

"Yes. Well, actually, I was adopted, but he is like a true brother to me."

The woman nodded her understanding. "I can guess what you wanted to speak to my mother about, but I am curious as to why, after all these years."

Annabelle swallowed uneasily. This was very awkward. A scandalous affair was not something one spoke about to a stranger. At the same time, it was important that she learn the truth, and she sensed that this woman knew something.

"Would you like to come inside?" she asked.

Annabelle accepted the woman's kindness.

"I am Hannah Pascoe," she said. "And you are...?"

"Annabelle Lawson." They shook hands, then went into the parlor and sat down. "I am looking for information about the former earl's son, Robert Wallis," Annabelle explained. "He was the younger of twins, and he would have been just a boy when your mother worked at Century House. The older twin was the heir to—"

"I know who he is," Mrs. Pascoe interjected. "He was the boy they sent away. The one they kept secret."

Annabelle sucked in a breath. "You *do* know about that."

"Only what my mother told me, but she asked me never to speak of it." She stood up, strolled to the mantel and took down a framed photograph, which she handed to Annabelle. "This is what she looked like a few years before she died. That's when she spoke to me about what happened at Century House. I suppose she had begun to long for certain things in her past, or perhaps she just wanted someone to know."

"Long for certain things?"

Mrs. Pascoe shrugged noncommittally. "She told me your brother's grandfather was the great love of her life, and she never really recovered from the heartbreak of being sent away. She longed for him until the day she died."

Annabelle stood up, reached for the picture, and looked at Rose's face. She was an elderly woman, and it was difficult to imagine what she might have looked like so many years ago.

Annabelle handed the picture back. "I believe I understand how she must have felt, because the reason I am asking about this is that I have met the man who is Robert's son, and he has also been ostracized from the family."

Mrs. Pascoe stared in silence at her for a moment, then turned and set the photograph back upon the mantel. "And you are in love with him."

The woman was very astute. Annabelle managed a smile. "Yes, I am. But I don't know what to do, because no one trusts him, and I am not sure that I should, either." She paused and looked hopelessly at the picture of Rose, then cupped her forehead in a hand. "I don't even know why I am here and what I hope to accomplish. *I'm* the one who needs fixing, not him, and not this feud between him and my brother."

"If you really love this man," Mrs. Pascoe said, "your heart should know whether or not you can trust him. What happened to his father should have nothing to do with it."

Annabelle smiled wretchedly. "You're not the first person to tell me that, and I know you're right. The real problem is that I still fear that his love is not genuine, and that he is lying to me about everything, and I am going to end up with my heart broken again."

Mrs. Pascoe inclined her head.

Annabelle swallowed hard and felt a need to shift her focus back toward something she could sink her teeth into, something that could provide real answers, because the rest of it was still very muddy in her brain.

"The last person I asked," she said, "told me that Robert had the devil inside of him."

Mrs. Pascoe sat down again, and her voice was sullen, but sympathetic. "The devil? No, that's not true."

Annabelle faced her. "What do you know about it, Mrs. Pascoe?"

For a long, tense moment, the woman was quiet. "Perhaps you had better sit down. This might take awhile, and I don't think it will be easy for you to hear."

Despite all her attempts to convince herself that none of this really mattered because it was in the past, Annabelle was overcome with curiosity, so she returned to her chair and sat down to listen.

Chapter 18

Dear Magnus,

*   I have just returned from a most fascinating meeting with a woman who knew of your father, and I have much to tell you. Could you come to the house in Mayfair as soon as you receive this letter? I will be waiting for you.*

Annabelle

MAGNUS STOOD NEXT TO HIS coach on the street outside Whitby's London residence, gazing up at the large stone mansion. He had stood in that spot many times as a boy and later as a young man, always an outsider wondering what the house looked like on the inside. He had longed for acceptance then, and he had wanted what Whitby had been blessed with—a family who was proud of him.

He felt a dim flicker of the old familiar feeling of isolation and loneliness, but knew it was merely the memory of those days, for he no longer cared that he was an outsider. In fact, he preferred it that way. He had no interest in being accepted by the people of this world, and no longer cared what this house looked like on the inside. All he cared about was Annabelle.

Besides, he had two homes in America that were just as fine. Finer even, for he had attained them—perhaps earned was a better word—through his own ingenuity and hard work.

But Magnus was not here to revisit his difficult youth. He was here to see Annabelle, because she had asked him to come. He would listen to what she had to say about his father. If the information was damning, he would ask her not to judge him by his father's deeds.

Magnus hoped she would be able to do that, and come away with him regardless, though after what happened the other day, he doubted that would be possible for her. She was not likely to take a risk with him. She had become far too cautious and guarded.

But that was his fault, he supposed, and perhaps he deserved this. He was now reaping what he had sown.

Magnus closed his eyes and stood listening to the wind in the trees. Deciding that he had done enough speculating, he stepped away from his coach and started off across the street. He reached the door and knocked and was more than a little surprised when the butler greeted him warmly. "Good afternoon, Mr. Wallis. Please come in."

Magnus crossed the threshold, and while the butler took his coat, he glanced across the main entrance hall and found himself looking up at the large portrait of Whitby and his wife and children.

Unexpectedly, despite his reflections just now about

not wanting what Whitby had, Magnus experienced a stabbing sensation in his gut. Maybe he didn't need Whitby's possessions, but he did need Annabelle at his side. He wanted a portrait just like this one to hang in his own home back in America.

"Allow me to show you to the drawing room, Mr. Wallis," the butler said. "Miss Lawson is waiting for you."

Magnus followed the butler up the stairs to the second floor and was shown into the room. He stopped just inside, his gaze falling upon Annabelle as the doors closed behind him. She stood in front of the window, wearing a sky-blue gown with white lace at the collar, and she was smiling at him.

No. She was more than smiling. She was beaming. Her eyes were glimmering with happiness; she looked like she could barely contain the joy that was bursting from her heart.

Instantly, he felt joyous as well. How could he not? She looked more beautiful than ever, smiling at him in that way, and he felt certain that she was going to say yes. That she had missed him the past few days just as desperately as he had missed her, and that she was ecstatic just to see him.

He took an anxious step forward. He wanted to close the distance between them and take her into his arms and promise her the world if she would only let him give it to her....

But all at once something stopped him. A movement to his left. Another presence in the room.

Magnus turned and saw Whitby rising slowly from the chair in front of the fireplace.

The elation Magnus had just experienced seemed to fall flat on the floor at his feet, and his whole body stiffened defensively.

"Magnus," Whitby said, his tone cool.

Magnus glanced uncertainly at Annabelle, not sure what he was facing.

Perhaps she recognized his unease, for she came forward to welcome him. "Magnus, I am so glad you're here." She gestured toward the sofa. "Won't you please sit down?"

So much for taking her into his arms, he thought, with a hint of annoyance at having his desires so swiftly curtailed. This was to be a formal meeting, evidently.

Whitby crossed the room to sit in a chair opposite the sofa, while Annabelle sat beside Magnus. She smiled again, which caused him to look questioningly at Whitby, who was not smiling. Not in the slightest. He looked as somber as ever, which was why Magnus did not know what to expect.

When Annabelle finally spoke, her voice was quiet but steady. "As you know," she said, "I have been asking questions about your father and why he was sent away, as I felt a need to understand this feud between you and my brother."

Magnus glanced at Whitby. His cousin merely stared back at him, revealing nothing.

"This may be difficult for you to hear, Magnus," she continued, "and I apologize in advance."

Difficult to hear?

He felt as if the air in the room were getting thinner. He turned to Whitby. "Do you already know what she is about to tell me?"

"Yes," he replied flatly, and Magnus clenched his jaw. He hated this. He hated being at a disadvantage.

Annabelle sat forward and continued. "I found a woman who is the daughter of a maid who was employed by your grandfather at Century House seventy-five years ago, when your father was born. She was intimate with your grandfather for five years, before she was forced to leave for that reason."

Perhaps he was being overly skeptical, but Magnus couldn't help but doubt the credibility of the source. "You found one of my grandfather's jilted lovers, and you're going to believe what she says?"

Annabelle squeezed her hands together on her lap, and Magnus instantly regretted his tone. But how could he help it? He had been accused of everything nasty and disagreeable all his life, and it was almost impossible not to become defensive. Especially with Whitby listening to all this in noteworthy silence.

"She couldn't say anything," Annabelle said shakily, "because she died seven years ago. It was her daughter I spoke to, but she knew a great deal about what happened to your father. May I describe it to you?"

He gazed into Annabelle's eyes and recognized her discomfort. Her brow was furrowed, her cheeks flushed. She wished to tell him something that was obviously going to be unpleasant, and she dreaded it.

"Yes, Annabelle," he said, more gently this time. "You may certainly tell me."

The tension in her body diminished slightly. "This woman, Rose Michaels, was deeply in love with your grandfather, and she knew why he sent his son away."

Magnus braced himself for whatever was coming.

"Your father was not dangerous," Annabelle said. "You were right about that. What happened was tragic and troubling, and he was indeed greatly wronged, just as you have been. You have been right all along, and Whitby knows it."

Magnus's gaze darted to his cousin, who was still sitting at his ease in the chair. He simply nodded at Magnus, then gestured with a hand toward Annabelle.

Magnus returned his attention to her, feeling oddly disconnected from his body while he waited for the rest of the story.

"According to Rose Michaels," Annabelle said, "your father was in fact your grandfather's favorite son. He was the gentler of the two boys, and perhaps because he was the younger one and would not have the advantages of his older brother, the heir, your grandfather doted on him. He spent more time with him, and he loved him very much."

Annabelle's expression darkened, however, with sadness and regret. "But there was an accident when he was four. Your grandfather had taken him into the stables one afternoon, and he was kicked by a horse."

Magnus felt his brows draw together with horror over hearing such a thing. "Kicked?"

Annabelle glanced uncertainly at Whitby, who said, "Tell him the rest."

She slid closer to Magnus. "Your father's skull was cracked, and he was never the same after that. He had seizures, and this is where the tragedy occurred. Rose Michaels said that your grandfather was so disturbed by the sight of the seizures that he kept your father hidden most of the time, so no one would know. Perhaps he feared an asylum, or perhaps he was ashamed. It's difficult to know."

"That's why he sent him away?" Magnus asked, barely able to believe what he was hearing.

"Yes. And it is very likely he was having a seizure the night he knocked over the lamp that caused the fire."

Shock held Magnus immobile. "But why would he be cut off in every way? Why did my grandfather not at least take care of him financially?"

"He did provide for him somewhat. He paid for the cottage where he was raised, and the woman who cared for him."

"But he received nothing after that, when he moved to London."

Annabelle's eyes glistened with tears and an unspoken apology. "I'm sorry. I know it was not enough. It was unfair, and I wish I could change how your father was treated. I was heartbroken to hear it, and there is nothing I can say to make it right."

"But why would he do that to the son he doted on?" Magnus asked, still shaken by all of it. "How could he have been so callous?"

"I don't know. Perhaps it was guilt."

"It sounds to me like he was worried about appearances. He didn't want a lunatic in the family."

A flood of memories came at Magnus suddenly—all the times his father had locked himself in a room and hid himself away. No wonder he had been ashamed and afraid to let anyone see the truth. He had been banished from his family because of it.

Magnus sat forward and dropped his forehead to the heels of his hands. It was an unforgivable injustice. His father had been abandoned for no fault of his own and removed from his home, torn from his family and made out to be something he was not. He was never cruel or violent. The only cruelty had been in the heart of Magnus's grandfather, who had valued appearances over the love of his son.

Magnus lifted his head and looked at his cousin. "Did you know about this?"

"No. Not before today."

They continued to sit in silence for a moment, until Whitby finally spoke. "You and your father were indeed wronged, Magnus, and I offer my most sincere apologies. I have every intention of making it right."

"Making it right?" Magnus ground out. "How can anyone make it right? My father is dead, and he lived a miserable life. So pardon me for pointing out that there is no way in hell you—or anyone else—can fix that."

Whitby dropped his gaze, his face drawn and pale. "All I can offer is my deepest regrets for the way you have been treated. If I had known...."

Magnus stood up. "You should have known, Whitby. If Annabelle could find out the truth so easily, why couldn't you? Or your brother, John?"

"We had no reason to doubt what we had always been told, and from what I had seen of your behavior—"

"*My* behavior? Fighting with your brother? Did you ever stop to think that he picked the fights with *me?*"

Magnus felt Annabelle's hand curl around his. "Magnus, I know you are angry, and you have every right to be. This must be a shock to you, but please sit down. There is so much more to say."

He labored to control his breathing, then slowly did as she asked.

Annabelle was quiet for a moment, presumably to let the news settle in. Then she reached for his hand again. "Magnus, I called you here today to tell you the truth about your father, but also to inform you that Whitby is now open to the possibility that you may not have been at fault regarding John's death."

"And what, pray tell, changed his mind about that?" Magnus asked.

"Because I trust Annabelle," Whitby said. "I trust her instincts. She was right about you telling the truth about your father, wasn't she?"

Annabelle shared an affectionate smile with her brother.

"Magnus," she said, "let us now tell you how Whitby wishes to make amends for everything. I know that no one can change the past, but we can at least affect the future."

Annabelle looked toward her brother, as if they had rehearsed this speech and it was his turn now to speak.

"There is a property near Peterborough," Whitby said. "It has been in our family for five generations, and it is an impressive country house with a number of prosperous tenant farmers. I would like you to have it."

Magnus turned his gaze back to Annabelle, who appeared pleased and proud.

Whitby continued. "I would also be honored if you would allow me to introduce you into society. I can put in a word for you at my club, and I can arrange a full social calendar for you, and you will likely receive a number of the very best invitations before the week is out. It is my wish to see you fully restored to your rightful position, Magnus. It is the least I can do."

Magnus felt Annabelle squeeze his hand and looked into her eyes. He had never seen her look so happy. She wanted this for him. She wanted him to take the house and join Whitby in his club.

Feeling almost numb, he shook his head in dismay. *"Do you even know me at all?"*

Annabelle's smile vanished instantly. "What do you mean?"

"I don't wish to sound ungrateful, Annabelle, but do you think I would want what your brother is offering?"

She blinked a few times, and her voice revealed her surprise. "But you have always felt cheated out of your birthright...."

"Not any longer," he replied angrily. "I am not the man I once was. How many times do I have to explain that to you? Did you not see it over the past few weeks? But I suppose you did not. You did not see deeply enough to truly believe I was not a monster. You had to go running around to hear it from other people. From strangers."

Her lips parted as she stumbled over words, in the end saying nothing.

Magnus shook his head at her. "I came back here so you could see the man I have become, but you still see only the man I once was. The man who broke your heart." He raised a hand, gesturing around the room. "And I don't want all this." He turned to his cousin. "I beg your pardon, Whitby. I realize your intentions are honorable and I thank you for your concern, but you must understand that I do not wish to become a member of your club, nor do I want the house in the country. I want to go back to America where I can work and enjoy the challenge of it. I don't want this life."

"But you are entitled to this," Annabelle said, her voice revealing shock and bewilderment, and Magnus felt the distance between them rise up suddenly like an ocean tide. Annabelle was entrenched in this world. Unlike him, she had not been born into it, but she had been raised within it, and her perspective was, in truth, very limited.

He was surprised and disappointed as he regarded her, because that was what he had always loved about her—the fact that she was not really one of them. He had always admired her unconventionality and had connected with her because she seemed to be an outsider, like him. She had not cared that he was a mere bank clerk when they met on the train so very long ago. He'd always believed they were similar creatures, and that she had loved him for what he was on the inside.

But now, looking into her eyes and seeing her desire to pull him into this world with her, he never felt more disconnected.

He had been wrong. They were not the same, and she did not know the real man he was deep down.

Magnus stood. Both Annabelle and Whitby stared at him, speechless.

"Annabelle," he said, "I must thank you for finally discovering the truth about my father. I am glad to know it. And Whitby, I appreciate what you wanted to do here today, but I am afraid I must turn down what you are offering me."

He turned and started toward the door.

"But Magnus!" Annabelle said, rising to her feet as well.

He stopped and faced her, but she couldn't seem to find any words. She merely stared at him, her eyes wide as saucers, looking utterly dumbfounded.

"Good day," he said, feeling only a suffocating need to get out of that room. He bowed slightly before turning again and walking out.

He had already received his coat from the butler and was making his way across the street to his coach when he heard Annabelle call his name again.

"Magnus! Wait!"

He stopped in front of his coach and shut his eyes, wishing she would just let him go. He didn't want to talk to her right now. He didn't want to explain himself, because he wasn't sure he could. He didn't even know how he felt about everything he had just heard.

Nevertheless, he waited.

She paused while a carriage crossed the street in front of her, then she picked up her skirts and dashed across. "Where are you going? Why did you leave so quickly?"

"Because I don't belong in there, and I couldn't sit and listen to Whitby offer me charity on a platter, as if what he was going to give me was the only thing that would make me worthy of your trust."

"That's not how it was," she said.

"No? That's how it looked to me. I'd never seen you so happy, Annabelle. All the reservations you had were gone because suddenly your brother approved of me and I was going to have social precedence as the grandson of an earl. I was going to be a respectable, honorable gentleman, sipping tea in drawing rooms— as if those things would erase what I had done to you. But nothing can erase it, Annabelle. *It happened.* I *was* that loathsome man who broke your heart, and that past we share is never going to disappear. What I need is for you to move past it and forgive me."

"But you don't understand. When I learned the truth, I wanted you to have what you should never have been denied."

"I never wanted that when I came back for you, but you couldn't believe it. You had to try to fix the past, when all anyone can do is live with it and learn from it."

He turned toward his coach and stepped inside.

"Wait a minute!" Annabelle shouted. "You can't blame me for not trusting you. What did you expect?"

He sat down but couldn't leave because Annabelle was holding the door open, preventing him from closing it. "I don't know."

She finally let go of the door and stepped back. "Will you go back to America?"

"It's my home now," he replied.

"When?"

He paused, staring at her. "Tomorrow. I've already

handed my properties over to my solicitor."

Rage found its way into her voice as she swiped violently at her tears. "So that's it? You're just going to leave? Why am I not surprised? You got what you wanted. You won. Whitby finally conceded. I will therefore release you from your obligation to marry me. A match between us is no longer necessary. And I am glad."

He looked into her eyes, which glistened with tears, and realized with aching remorse that she was still so very angry with him over what had happened all those years ago, and she almost seemed to be taking some perverse pleasure in being right. *That he was doing exactly what she had predicted he would do.* That she had been right all along not to trust him, or any other man, for that matter.

But how many times had he told her he was sorry, and why couldn't it ever be enough? All his life he had felt unworthy, and now she was looking at him as if he were a disappointing wretch. It took him straight back to the loathing he had endured in his youth.

He had been right. Annabelle solving the mysteries of the past had not changed a thing.

He couldn't do it anymore. He couldn't go on waiting for her acceptance and forgiveness. And now she wanted to end their engagement. It was time he found his own pride, with or without Annabelle's belief in him.

"If that's what you want," he said, tightening his grip on the door handle. He just wanted to get out of there. "Good-bye, Annabelle."

He shut the door and sat back in the seat, resist-

ing the urge to look out the window at her, because
heaven help him, despite everything, he still loved her
with all his heart, and he was devastated.

Chapter 19

"*Y*OU DON'T REALLY THINK HE'LL leave, do you?"
Annabelle asked Lily late that night while they
sat on Annabelle's bed.

"I don't know," Lily replied. "I have no idea what's
in his mind. The only time I ever saw you together
was the other day in the country, when I was pulling
him and Whitby apart."

Annabelle slid off the bed and padded across the
floor to the fireplace to warm her hands. "You must
think me a fool, then. All you saw was the man everyone has always described—angry, vengeful Cousin
Magnus."

"No, I don't think you're a fool. You saw something
in him that no one else saw, and because of that, you
uncovered the truth about this family's past, and you
proved that mistakes in judgment had been made.
Even Whitby believes it now—that Magnus was not
all bad, that he had been wronged and he had a right
to be angry."

"But despite what happened to his father," Annabelle said, "Magnus is still Magnus. It doesn't erase what he did to me thirteen years ago, or the fact that he just walked out on me again. Knowing the truth about the very distant past doesn't change what exists today. He told me it wouldn't. I should have listened."

Lily merely shrugged at her. "I don't have the answers, Annabelle. Only you can decide what you believe."

"Therein lies the problem." Annabelle returned to the bed. "What scares me is the fact that nothing he ever said or did made me trust him completely, because I am simply not capable of it. I am deficient."

"No, you are not."

"Oh, what does it matter anyway? He left me standing there in the street today and told me he wanted to return to America, apparently forgetting that he had proposed marriage."

"But it was you who ended the engagement," Lily replied, running a hand over her swollen belly. "Perhaps in his mind you were just having an argument and he had no intentions of leaving England without you."

Annabelle flopped onto the bed. "If he leaves on that ship in the morning, abandoning me a second time, that should answer the question."

For a long moment Annabelle stared at the ceiling in silence, wondering what she should do. Should she wait and see if he would leave without her, or should she search for the courage to take that difficult leap of faith, and do whatever it took to try and stop him?

Through the night, Magnus wrote four letters to

Annabelle, and in each and every one he apologized for something—for closing the coach door on her and driving away, for not taking the house her brother had offered, for saying things that hurt her. But when he read over each letter, he chastised himself for doing it again. For crawling back to her and pleading with her to accept him.

It was what he had been doing all his life—longing for acceptance into a family that didn't want him, until he had finally grown to hate them.

Would he grow to hate Annabelle eventually, if he spent his future striving to earn her trust? Never feeling good enough?

In the end he did not send a letter.

So it was with a heavy heart that he left his hotel room the next morning, traveled to the docks and boarded the ship, checking over his shoulder as he crossed the gangplank, gazing into the sea of faces on the dock, searching for her, wondering if she would come to stop him from leaving, or to tell him to wait for her, that she was coming with him....

When he stepped on board the ship, a porter showed him to his stateroom and saw that his trunks were delivered. Then Magnus sat down on the bed and held his gloves in his hand, tapping them upon his knee.

He felt rather nauseous, and the ship hadn't even left the dock yet.

He checked his timepiece. They wouldn't depart for another fifteen minutes. Perhaps he would go up on deck and look over the rail.

A minute later he was heading down the corridor

and pushing through the doors to the sunny upper deck. He walked to the rail and wrapped both hands around it, leaning over to peer down at the crowd on the dock. People were waving to others beside him. They were smiling and blowing kisses in return.

He experienced a burning panic suddenly, as if he'd just swallowed a red-hot lump of coal. Maybe he should get off the ship. It had been just an argument, after all. Perhaps he was being too hasty and stubborn.

Feeling his breath come short, he scanned the crowd again, then checked his timepiece.

Five more minutes.

Should he get off? he wondered again. Was there time?

He swallowed hard and leaned farther over the rail to see if the gangplank had been raised yet. It had not. He could still change his mind.

Then he saw a movement in the crowd. Someone running. A woman. He sucked in a quick breath and watched her shoulder her way through the tight crowd toward the gangplank. He couldn't get a clear view of her, but her hair was just like Annabelle's.

Magnus was off like a shot, running for the upper deck doors and flying down the steps, taking two at a time, darting down the corridor that led to the outer door.

If it was Annabelle, he would tell her he was sorry. He would get down on his knees and thank God in heaven that she had come, and he would pull her into his arms and never let her go again. Pride be damned. He would do whatever it took just to have her with him. What had he been thinking, leaving her again after they had come so far?

He stopped suddenly, however, when he reached the main door and found himself staring not at Annabelle, but another woman. She was just stepping on board, flushed and apologetic for being late.

The gangplank was raised, the doors were closed behind the woman, and a whistle blew somewhere behind Magnus. He stood there breathing hard, feeling as if he were floating in a murky haze or a bad dream, staring at the ship door, tightly closed.

"Can I help you, sir?" a porter asked, blocking Magnus's view of the door.

"I beg your pardon?" he replied.

"Is there a problem? Are you waiting for someone?"

Yes, he was. But she wasn't coming.

He stared blankly at the young man and knew that this was one of those moments in life. It was a fork in the road. Should he get off the ship? Or should he return to his stateroom and settle in for the voyage?

He imagined what would happen if he got off. He would return to the Whitby mansion in Mayfair and plead with Annabelle yet again....

The porter was still staring at him, waiting for his answer.

Magnus steadied his voice. "No. I am not waiting for anyone."

With that, he turned away from the door and headed back to his stateroom alone, fearing that in about an hour, he was going to be cursing himself and regretting his godforsaken stubborn pride.

It was with a burning sense of panic that Annabelle

came running onto the dock with barely a minute to spare before the ship left.

She had awakened that morning determined to stop Magnus. She'd dressed at lightning speed, skipped breakfast, and dashed out the front door, terrified she was going to lose him forever because she had been too afraid to take the blind leap he had wanted her to take.

But when she arrived at his hotel, he had already checked out, and the desk clerk assured her quite emphatically that he was bound for America that very morning.

That should have been enough, Annabelle thought miserably, as she pushed her way through the crowd on the dock, after first going to the wrong pier and getting lost. It should have been the answer she needed—that Magnus was abandoning her yet again, and she had been a fool to believe there was hope.

But it had *not* been enough. She was desperate to see him, without the slightest care for her pride or her fears. She had not been able to let go of the tiny fragment of hope that still flickered within her—that yes, he loved her and she could trust him. That she had always been able to trust him.

It couldn't be over yet, she thought as she reached the gangplank. It couldn't.

But then a porter blew his whistle and waved his arms over his head, and the gangplank was raised.

She stopped on the dock, watching, looking up at the people waving from the railings, searching for Magnus, unable to accept that he was actually on board.

She tried to make her way along the dock, shading her eyes from the sun as she looked for him. She walked the length of the ship, then found herself searching through the crowd on the dock, wondering if he had changed his mind and never even stepped on board.

But she did not see him.

Not long afterward, the ship blew its horn and the ropes were drawn up and everyone was waving goodbye. Annabelle stood among the crowd, watching in dismay as the ship steamed away from the dock. A cold, piercing agony spread through her like ice.

What a fool she was. She should have known better. How could she have put herself in this situation, to be rejected a second time?

And how could he have done this to her? How could he have made love to her with such tenderness and passion, then leave like this? It was unimaginable, and she didn't know how she would ever recover from such a betrayal a second time.

Somehow, feeling completely dead inside, she managed to turn around, walk back to her carriage and make her way home, though she remembered none of the trip.

When she arrived at the house, she asked the butler, "Did anyone pay a call? Was there a letter delivered?"

"No, Miss Lawson," he replied soberly.

She wondered if he knew whose letter she was hoping to receive. Either way, it did not matter.

Annabelle slowly climbed the stairs and went to her studio rather than her bedchamber, for she did not intend to fling herself on her bed and cry like she had all those years ago. She would not do that again.

All she wanted to do now was distract herself from the persistent hope that Magnus had not even been on the ship to begin with and that perhaps he would be knocking on her door within the hour.

She looked at the painting she had brought with her from the country—the waterfall surrounded by moss-covered rocks. With her body moving in an oddly mechanical way, Annabelle donned her smock and squeezed some paint onto her palette, creating a few different shades of brown and adding black, green, and white. Then she picked up a brush.

But as she stared at the water flowing over the rocks, she knew in her heart that she was too frustrated to paint, and besides that—this piece wasn't right, and it would *never* be right. She wasn't happy with the brushstrokes around the rocks, and the mist at the bottom was all wrong, as were the shadows on the trees. It didn't look real.

She needed to change it. It wasn't even close to being finished. It was a mess.

Annabelle took a step forward, dipped her brush and lifted it, but froze with her hand an inch away from the canvas. How could she paint now, when she was so angry because she had not been able to trust the one man who understood all her eccentricities and aroused her passions?

He was the only real world she had ever known, she realized suddenly, with a raw new heartbreak. He was the only person who had ever made her feel alive.

And he had left her.

Overcome by a fierce swell of frustration, she turned

her palette over in her hand and smacked it paint side down upon her canvas, smearing it back and forth over the waterfall, wanting only to destroy the painting, to turn it into a misfit, too. Just like her. She hated the way it was. She couldn't get it right. And she was so bloody, bloody angry!

After a few seconds she realized what she had done and winced as she pulled her hand from the palette—which stuck to the canvas briefly before sliding down.

Annabelle quickly reached for it, to keep it from falling onto the floor, not really caring that she had destroyed the painting. She hadn't liked it anyway, and it had felt so good to feel the thick paint smearing under the palette.

Finally, she peeled it back to see the anarchy she'd created.

It most certainly was a picture of anarchism. It was wild, unrecognizable mayhem—nothing but emptiness—just like her life without Magnus.

She stared at it for a moment, but then turned her back on it because she couldn't bear the loneliness it made her feel.

She set her brush and palette down on the table. Closing her eyes, she wondered if this creative agony was worth it. Perhaps she should give up painting altogether and give up being strange. She should replace these ugly boots with a pretty pair of shoes, and get a lapdog like other spinsters her age.

No. What was she thinking? She could never replace these boots, nor could she stop painting. And she would always prefer her ferret to a lapdog.

So she turned around and faced the canvas again,

and strangely, sadly, when she looked at the waterfall, all she saw was Magnus.

Struck by the sight, she reflected upon the state of her life and the confusing collage of her emotions. She still couldn't believe he had left her. She had been so sure that everything was different this time.

She supposed it *had* been different. But the situation she was in now was all her fault—for not being able to give him her whole heart, for thinking only of protecting herself and keeping her world safe, like her dull, uninteresting paintings.

Except for *The Fisherman,* of course. It was the one piece she was proud of, and she had painted it during the one and only time in her life that she had felt truly free to be herself.

Something prompted her to pick up her brush and palette—with its outlandish, muddled mixture of color—and approach the canvas again. She could still see Magnus in the waterfall.

Tilting her head this way and that, she dabbed at the image, moving the thick paint around to better capture what she was seeing—for she was seeing something very different that morning, and she was holding the brush in a way she had never held it before.

Three hours later, after wielding her brush swiftly and furiously without a single break to rest her arm, Annabelle stepped back and looked at the colors on the canvas. For the first time in her life she felt satisfied with her creation and set down her brush.

Chapter 20

❧

The London Times
April 30, 1893

Unknown Artist Turns London Art World On its Ear

The latest exhibition at the Duke of Harlow's Regent Street Gallery has been causing a stir among art enthusiasts here in England and as far as Paris, with the modern expressions of local artist Annabelle Lawson. Miss Lawson has risked her budding reputation as a landscape realist to produce a body of work so nonrepresentational that one simply must stop to study the themes of reflection and reality, so evident in the artist's passionate brushwork. It cannot be denied that no other English painter has yet dared to challenge the aesthetic sensibilities of the public, and in so doing, Annabelle Lawson has freed all future English artists from the tedious constraints of competition with the camera....

The New World

May 1893

Chapter 21

WITH A GLASS OF RED wine in his hand, Magnus stepped out of his bedchamber onto the second-story veranda that lined the rear of his South Carolina mansion by the sea. The sun was just setting, and it was a warm evening for November. He smelled the saltwater in the air, heard the power of the surf on the beach.

A sailboat was visible in the distance, and he raised a hand to shade his eyes and watch it heel impossibly in the wind, until the sails almost touched the waves. At the last minute it righted itself and turned toward the horizon.

Magnus took a slow sip of his wine, then sat down on the cushioned wicker chair. He lifted his feet onto the small table and crossed his legs at the ankles.

He sat there often in the evenings after dinner, watching the sun go down. It was his favorite time of day, and his staff knew not to bother him, for he worked hard from sunup to sundown and needed this time to rest and reflect.

As a result, he was surprised when his butler stepped through the door onto the veranda. "I beg your pardon, sir. Sorry to disturb you, but you have a visitor."

Magnus lifted his legs off the table. "Who is it, Bradley?"

"She didn't wish to give her name, sir, but she has an English accent."

Magnus knew that his butler was aware of what had occurred with Annabelle in England, though he never spoke about it directly. As a result, the comment caused Magnus to rise to his feet so fast he almost knocked over his chair.

"I didn't hear anyone arrive," he said.

"The surf is rather thunderous tonight, sir."

Magnus looked down at the waves crashing onto the beach. "Yes. I suppose it is." He set down his glass and straightened his tie, then glanced at Bradley and saw an emotion in the man's eyes he had never seen before.

Was it pity?

Magnus checked himself. Bloody hell. What was he doing, getting his hopes up like this again? How many times had he received a female caller and run downstairs hoping it was Annabelle?

And had it ever been her before? No. It was always some other woman, looking for a charitable donation, or someone visiting the area and looking for directions, and each time it happened, his anger toward Annabelle and everything that had occurred between them resurfaced.

He really needed to stop doing this, he told himself. It was over.

Even if she did come back to him, he would not wish to rekindle anything. He would not wish to return to constantly having to prove himself to a woman who simply could not believe in him. He believed in himself, and that was enough. He had finally put the past to rest.

"Thank you, Bradley," he said, relaxing his shoulders and speaking in a calmer voice. "I'll see what she wants."

"She's in the library, sir."

Magnus entered the house through his bedchamber and made his way to the main staircase and down to the ground floor. He peered out the front window and saw a carriage outside, then went immediately to the library.

He hesitated outside the door, however, for despite all his self-imposed lectures on letting go of the memory of Annabelle, he wanted to savor this moment, because he knew that as soon as he walked through the door, the dream would be snuffed out again, as always.

He supposed certain elements of his past would never be resolved.

Finally taking a deep breath, he pushed the door open and entered. A woman wearing a colorful floral scarf over her head stood across the room with her back to him, looking out the window at the ocean, perhaps watching the sailboat that was now just a tiny speck on the horizon.

She must have heard him walk in, because she turned and faced him. When their eyes met, Magnus felt his blood rush to his brain.

It was her. This time, it was Annabelle.

Neither of them said anything for several seconds, but it wouldn't have mattered if she'd asked him a thousand questions at once, because he couldn't speak. He couldn't even think, he was so shocked by the vision of her, looking more beautiful than ever before, and so different.

Her clothes were not the same. The scarf over her head was wild and vibrant, and her dress was unfashionably loose with fringe at the cuffs. She wore no gloves, and her hair was spilling over her shoulders in wild, uncontrolled waves.

The sight of her made his breath catch in his throat, and he struggled to steel himself against the attraction he felt toward her—because he had to protect himself.

When he continued to stand there without speaking, Annabelle lowered the scarf and draped it over her shoulders. She took an uneasy step forward, as if she weren't sure she should have come. "You're surprised to see me."

He swallowed over the elephant in his throat. "Yes."

They continued to gaze at each other while the sound of the waves crashing outside filled the silence.

"How have you been?" he finally asked, because he could not be rude, but he maintained a cool tone.

"I have been well, thank you. I've been painting. A lot."

He saw her gaze move discreetly over the walls of the library.

"It's in the drawing room," he said, somehow knowing she was looking for *The Fisherman*. "Hanging over the fireplace."

She nodded. "I see. I wasn't sure if you would still have it."

"Why wouldn't I?" he replied, his voice still cool and detached.

Annabelle shifted her weight uncomfortably from one foot to the other. "Well, after what happened between us."

Beneath her surface politeness, he thought he detected a note of apology in her voice, but he couldn't be sure, because he remembered all too clearly how they had parted and what she had said to him. She had believed he'd only wanted to triumph over Whitby, that he never really loved her, and she had looked at him with disdain.

The bitter memory of how she had not been able to trust him—despite everything he had done to prove that she could—made him steel himself yet again.

"What do you want, Annabelle?" he asked directly, deciding that he didn't want to play games or engage in small talk with her. It was too late for that.

She looked down at the floor before finally lifting her gaze to meet his. Her voice was steady, her chin held high. "You're angry with me."

He raised his hands at his sides. "Nothing has changed since we parted."

"May I inform you," she said, "that I have been angry with you, too, Magnus. You deserted me. After everything that happened between us, after I'd given myself to you, you left." Suddenly, she began spewing out every thought that must have been on her mind over the past few months.

"What if there had been a child?" she asked. "There

wasn't, thank God, but what if there had been? Did you not wonder about that?"

"Yes, I wondered about it," he told her. "But I thought that if there had been, you would have contacted me. On the other hand, if you had chosen not to.... Well, that wouldn't have come as any great surprise."

Her delicate eyebrows drew together in a frown. "What do you mean by that?"

"It would have been consistent with every other aspect of our time together if you had not believed I would act honorably, or if you had not wished to marry me because you did not trust that I would be a decent husband and father."

Her face softened slightly. "Is that what you thought?"

"Naturally, yes."

She turned and faced the window again, while Magnus stood waiting, still wondering why she was there. She hadn't really answered that question, had she?

He walked toward her and leaned a shoulder against the wall so he could look at her profile—her tiny nose, her deep-set green eyes and full lips. The truth was, he still thought she was the most beautiful creature on the face of the earth and being this close to her made his blood course through his veins like a raging river. That aggravated him, because he didn't want to feel that way about her. He wanted only to remember how angry he had been over the past few months.

"Why did you leave England so quickly?" she asked, facing him. "Were you just using me like the last time?"

"What a question!" he said, throwing his hands up in the air. "Of course I was not using you, but I am not going to stand here and try to convince you of that until I'm blue in the face. If you cannot believe it, or if you don't already know enough about me—"

"I do believe you," she said flatly, and Magnus wondered if the earth had just shifted under his feet.

"I must be hearing things," he said with a bitter laugh.

She gave him a stern look. "I've thought about it a lot over the past couple of months, Magnus, and I've been able to at least recognize the fact that I *was* incapable of trusting you, but only because you had hurt me so deeply the first time. Maybe you can't understand that...."

Oh, but he did understand it, because he was feeling that way himself at this very moment. He was afraid to trust *her*.

"Then why didn't you write to me?" he asked.

She hesitated. "Because it took me a long time to figure out what I wanted to say, and to be honest, for a long time I was too angry with you for leaving. You didn't even *try* to resolve things between us."

"I didn't *try?*" he burst out. "I'd been trying to resolve things since the first day, but nothing I said or did made any difference to you."

"But you didn't have to leave the very next day. You could at least have waited."

Frustration heated his face. "For how long? You knew I had booked passage on the ship that morning, yet you didn't try to stop me. I even stood at the rail and watched for you, but all I could think of was the fact that you would never be able to trust me, that you would always think ill of me. And when you didn't show up at the dock, I had to force myself to let go of the hopeless need for your approval or forgiveness."

Annabelle's eyes filled with tears. "I *was* at the dock," she told him, her voice full of pain and regret. "But I went to the wrong place, and then I was too late."

He felt his body shudder as he drew in a sharp breath. "You were there?"

"Yes," she said. "Despite all my fears that I would be rejected again, I went there hoping I was wrong. I was going to plead with you to forgive me for not trusting you, and I was going to tell you that I loved you. I wanted to prove to you that I could take the leap you always wanted me to take."

He shook his head skeptically. "But I was looking for you. I would have seen you."

"I got there just as the ship pulled away. I was there, Magnus."

He turned away from her and crossed to the middle of the room. "But for months I have believed otherwise. Why did you not come here sooner? Or write to me?"

"Because after you left, something changed in me, and I needed to understand it."

Magnus walked to the other window to look out, on the opposite side of the room from where she stood.

Annabelle let out a frustrated sigh. "I know this may sound strange, but part of the reason I came here was to thank you."

"Why?"

"Because I didn't really know who I was until you left me," she explained. "Something in me exploded that day—all my anger, my frustrations, my passions. I'd always known I was living by rules that didn't suit me, but I was afraid to break out and do anything risky. I've always thought myself a misfit, as you well know. But when I watched your ship leave, all I felt was anger and chaos, and those rules were broken. I was so angry, I didn't care about anything anymore. I was no longer afraid, because nothing seemed to matter, and it made me open my eyes to certain things."

He shook his head at her, and she crossed the room to the bookcase, bent forward and picked up her large portfolio. He hadn't noticed it there.

"Perhaps you'll understand when you see what I brought you." She set the case on the table in the center of the room and withdrew a painting. Oil on canvas.

Magnus looked at it from where he stood at the window. "It's me."

Though how he knew that, he couldn't be sure. It was hardly a conventional portrait.

But rules of portraiture aside, it was astounding. He walked toward it and took it in his hands, holding it up to the light to study it.

It was as if he were looking at himself through rain-covered glass. Or perhaps water. Yes, water. Deep, choppy water. There was movement, too, as if he were forever changing with the swells.

"My God, Annabelle. When did you do this?"

"The day you left."

He studied the image of his face, then let his eyes wander to the outer edges. He looked at the colors, the shapes, the shadows and contrasts. One rock in particular caught his eye....

He pointed at it, in the top left corner. "Good Lord, you *were* angry, weren't you?"

She smiled faintly. "Yes, but it was the setting that enraged me. I think this is my aunt Millicent." She pointed at a rather bulbous boulder in the bottom corner, and Magnus chuckled despite himself.

"I believe I see the resemblance. That must be her nose."

Annabelle laughed, and despite all their arguing just then, it was the sweetest sound he could ever imagine.

They stood in the library for a long while, side by side, looking at the painting.

"It's extraordinary," Magnus finally said. "I've never seen anything like it. Has anyone else seen it?"

"Yes. Most of London. Paris, too."

He chuckled with disappointment. "That's a shame. I would have liked to be the first to exhibit it."

Annabelle smiled, but there was a deep sadness in her voice. "I'm so sorry I didn't give it to you first, but I wasn't ready to show it to you, and I needed to...." She didn't seem to know what to say, so she returned to the window again.

"You needed to do *what,* Annabelle?"

She sighed. "To be free for a little while. I told Whitby and Lily that I needed to do something for myself, and they were happy for me and wished me well. So I went on my own to Paris and I spent three months there, painting every day."

He set the portrait down and followed her. "You went to Paris? Did you show your work?"

"Yes, and I spent time with other artists who shared my desire to paint in new ways. I was even included in an exhibition with Mary Cassatt."

His lips parted in surprise. "Extraordinary. You did well, Annabelle."

She shrugged, as if making light of it. "I'm surprised you hadn't heard about it. I thought you might have been keeping up with what was going on in the art world."

He shook his head. "I wasn't keeping up with anything. I retreated from all that after I returned. I still own my galleries, but I haven't set foot in either of them in quite some time. I suppose I also needed a bit of a holiday."

She sighed and faced him. "Magnus...."

All at once he wanted to touch her face, her lips. Everything about her was magical and vibrant. She was like no other woman he had ever met, and she had been brave enough to go to Paris on her own and show her work with Mary Cassatt. *Brava, Annabelle. Brava!*

But he resisted that emotional outburst and the surging rush of his desires, for he could not let himself give in so easily. She had not given him what he had needed last time. He had even begun to believe that his love for her had been a fantasy all along, that she was not—and never had been—the daring girl he remembered from his younger days.

But then she began to speak, and all he could hear in his mind was the sound of her laughter in that fishing boat on the lake, when the perch came flying out of the water.

"Magnus," she said with her eyes downcast, "when you came back to London and I saw you for the first time at your gallery, I was not the person I am now."

"That sounds familiar," he said.

She smiled, but there were tears in her eyes. "I was so worn out and unhappy, but you brought me back to life."

"But I was the one who killed your spirit in the first place," he said with regret.

"No. You just made me see that I had never really been living, and what I really *needed* to do was embrace my freedom. I needed to be pushed over the edge and to become fearless—have nothing to lose. I needed to learn that I could trust my instincts and take chances, that I could steer away from what was safe, and I did that through my paintings. Because of you. You unlocked something."

The physical world around them seemed to almost fade away as his eyes held hers and his heart began to beat very fast. "What are you saying, Annabelle? Why did you come here?"

She strode closer. "I came here to finally take that brave leap of faith with you, and I'm praying with all my heart and soul that you will take my hand and leap, too. That you will forgive *me* this time and find it in yourself to believe that I do love you. That I've loved you every day of my life." She walked to him and laid her open hands on his chest, and a shiver of need rippled through him. "And I would give any- thing to know that in spite of everything, you still love me."

She rose up on her toes and touched her lips lightly to his, and he was overcome by a love so potent that no amount of discipline or self-control could stop him from taking her into his arms.

He covered her mouth with his own and pulled her as close as he possibly could. Her lips were soft and warm and succulent, and all at once nothing mattered but his need to be with her. He picked her up and carried her out of the room.

"Where are you taking me?" she asked in a breathless voice, kissing his cheeks and mouth and neck as he headed toward the stairs.

"To my bed."

Burning with desire after months spent dreaming of making love to Magnus again, Annabelle gave no argument. She held tight to his strong, broad shoulders as he climbed the stairs and carried her down a wide corridor and through to his bedchamber, lined with dark oak walls and furnished with a massive mahogany bed. The room glowed pink from the sunset outside the window.

He laid her gently on the soft bed, then came down upon her, his body heavy and warm and insistent. She welcomed him with her heart open, thrusting her body close, sliding her hands down his back. She wanted him with every breath in her body, with every spark of passion that lived in her soul, and she couldn't wait a single moment longer. She had to have him, on any terms.

"Make love to me," she said. "Don't keep me waiting. I've waited long enough."

Obliging her reckless impatience, he didn't even take time to get undressed. He merely reached a hand down to unfasten his trousers, tugged her skirts out of the way, and lowered his body onto hers.

Annabelle sighed with rapture. She loved this man, she desired him beyond all else in the world, and a sheer, mad need for everything he offered compelled her to lift her heart and deepen the awesome, satisfying joining of their bodies.

"Oh, Magnus," she whispered, her breath coming short. "I can't lose you again."

Leaning up on one elbow so he could look her in the eye, he drove into her with a blissful rhythm until her mind and body quivered with ecstasy, then at last he spoke, his voice a deep, husky seduction in itself.

"You won't," he said, pressing his lips to her neck, whispering behind her ear. "This is it for me, Annabelle. You are all I ever wanted. I'll do anything for you. Whatever you want." Then he drove deeper still, propping himself up on his hands. "Marry me this time."

"Yes," she sighed.

Then she felt his release, deep inside her heart and soul. Holding him tight in her arms, delightfully exhausted, Annabelle marveled at the tears seeping from her eyes.

"You forgive me?" she asked, her voice shaky with love.

He gently withdrew and rolled to the side, resting his hand upon her cheek. "There is nothing to forgive. All that matters is that we're together now. Finally."

"Yes, finally." She touched his face also, running a

finger over his strong cheekbone. "I've missed you."

"I have missed you, too—every day of my life. But all that's over now, because you're here."

"Yes," she said with a tender smile. "I'm here, and I have never felt so happy, or so at home."

"It will always be your home," he replied. "Here with me, wherever we are in the world."

"It's what I always dreamed of," she said.

Then he rolled onto her again and filled her once more with pleasure.

Epilogue

"**I**S IT ALMOST FINISHED?" MAGNUS asked, reaching the top of the hill where Annabelle stood before her easel, paintbrush in hand. The sun was shining brightly overhead without a single cloud in the sky, and the wind had picked up, cooling her cheeks.

"Yes." She stood back to look with a critical eye at what she had done. "Come and see it."

She set her palette and brush down on the little table and held out her hand. Her husband came to stand at her side. Together, they looked at the painting—a bold mix of textures and colors, all sweeping together with swirling movement.

Annabelle inclined her head. She felt satisfied with this piece, for she truly believed she had captured— really captured—the passion and splendor of their seaside home.

Magnus slid his arm around her waist and continued to study the painting, while a breeze blew a part in his hair.

"I am in awe," he said, resting a hand over his heart.

"It makes me feel euphoric. Triumphant. It's the best thing you've ever done. I mean it."

Her eyes filled with tears as she smiled at him. "You say that about all my paintings."

"It's always true."

Annabelle returned her gaze to the painting and stared at it for a long time, feeling the genuine romance in the color of the sea, and the joyful warmth of the sunshine on the water. In the background, sailboats with bright spinnakers dotted the horizon, yet none of it was absolutely perceptible. All the images intermingled to form a rich, colorful whole.

"You once said I would love this place," she said to her husband as she gazed toward the Atlantic and felt the wind on her face, "and you were right. I have never been so happy. I never knew it was possible. I feel so at peace here."

He turned to her. "There was a time when you felt trapped. And now have made a commitment to be my wife until death do us part. I hope you still feel that you have freedom...creatively."

She sighed and reached for his hand. "Yes. Because of you, I learned to be free. You pushed me to learn it. And now that I am, I have been able to love you without reservation. Today I am fully alive, when I didn't really know how to live before. But what about you? Are you happy?"

He closed his eyes and inhaled deeply. "Yes, thanks to you. I will always be grateful that you found out the truth about my father, but more importantly because you made me see that we can all change and grow. You are a forgiving person, and I love you for that.

I've learned to forgive, too."

He took her face in his hands and touched his lips gently to hers, then drew back and looked at the painting again.

"We shall never sell this one," he said, "even though it would bring in a small fortune, to be sure."

Annabelle rested her head on his shoulder. "Perhaps it could hang in the front room."

"I know a better place." His voice had become playful all of a sudden.

"Where?" she asked, though she suspected she already knew the answer.

"Our bedroom. Not over the headboard, but next to the bed, where we can look at it in the mornings."

She grinned mischievously. "But that might be a waste. We've never been interested in looking at paintings when we're in bed."

Magnus considered the issue carefully, then nodded and went to pack up her paints and brushes. "You're right, as always, but I suggest we at least try it out. Let's go hang this masterpiece, then slide under the covers and see what we end up doing."

Annabelle laughed, and feeling quite euphoric indeed, and overcome with a deep, loving desire for her husband, quickly folded up her easel.

Author's Note

Thank you for taking the time to read *To Annabelle, With Love*. This novel was originally published by Avon/Harper Collins in 2006 under the title *Portrait of a Lover,* and that book has long been out of print, so I am pleased to reissue it with a fresh edit and new title and cover art.

This story is a follow-up to the first book in the Can This Be Love trilogy which begins with *Love According to Lily*. In that book, we are first introduced to Magnus and his longtime feud with Whitby. If you have already read that book, you will know that Magnus was the villain in that story, and I wasn't entirely sure if I could redeem him and turn him into a worthy hero, but as in life, every story has two sides, and how you understand it depends on your point of view. Through Magnus's eyes, Whitby becomes somewhat of a villain in this story, but thankfully, we get to see him through Annabelle's eyes as well, and he remains heroic most of the time.

If you are interested in reading about Whitby's growth as a character, you might want to start at the beginning with *To Marry the Duke*, book one in my American Heiress trilogy. His relationship with Lily is introduced there, and it reaches a crescendo in *Love According to Lily.*

The next book in this trilogy is *Where Love Begins,* which is about Martin Langdon, Lily's brother. A description of that book, along with an excerpt follows, and then you will find a complete list of all my historical romances, as well as my contemporary women's fiction novels, each of which has a love story at its heart.

If you would like to stay informed about my future releases and take part in my monthly autographed book giveaways for newsletter subscribers, please visit my website at www.juliannemaclean.com. I would love to send news to you.

Lastly, if you would like to know when an e-book edition from my backlist goes on sale for 99 cents (or is occasionally offered for free), please go to my author profile on Bookbub and click the "follow" button. You'll be sent an email whenever there's a flash sale. You can also follow me on Amazon to be informed of discounted e-books for your Kindle.

I am also on Facebook and Twitter where I chat with readers most days.

– *Julianne*

Where Love Begins

Can This Be Love Trilogy – Book Three

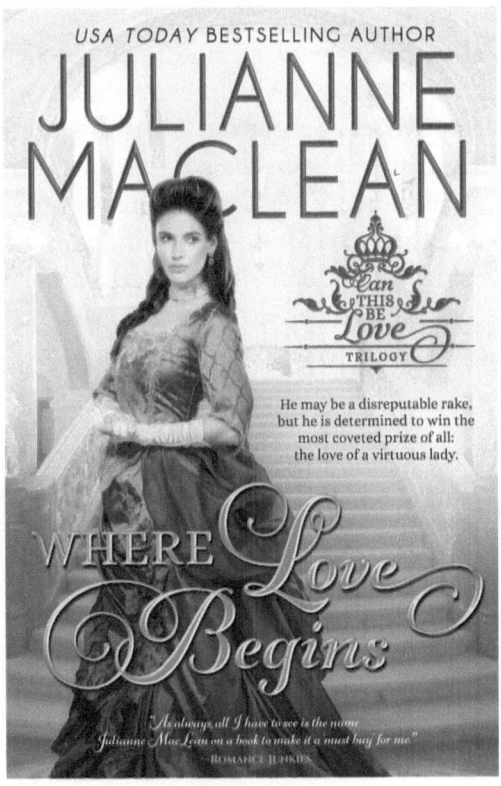

USA TODAY BESTSELLING AUTHOR

JULIANNE MACLEAN

Can THIS BE *Love* TRILOGY

He may be a disreputable rake,
but he is determined to win the
most coveted prize of all:
the love of a virtuous lady.

WHERE *Love Begins*

*"As always, all I have to see is the name
Julianne MacLean on a book to make it a must buy for me."*
—ROMANCE JUNKIES

Lord Martin Langdon has been deeply wounded
by love in the past, so he takes pride in his scandalous reputation where the art of seduction is a most

rewarding—and emotionally painless—pastime. When he sails off to the Isle of Wight to race his champion yacht in the English Channel, he learns of a particularly beautiful woman who is "impossible to flirt with," and grows determined to prove that not even the prim and proper Evelyn Wheaton can resist his charms.

Evelyn knows all about the reckless rogue's shocking reputation and she wants nothing to do with him. She may be looking for a husband, but Lord Martin is certainly not a candidate. The smoldering looks he sends her way, however, are a different matter entirely. She suspects there is great passion to be had if she could throw caution to the wind and surrender to his charms . . . but dare she risk her heart? And will Martin, who hides a most tormented past, be able to surrender to true love at last?

"Spectacular historical romance!"
—*The Romance Reviews*

Excerpt from
Where Love Begins

Teaser Excerpt
Copyright Julianne MacLean Publishing Inc. 2020

*Twenty years from now, you will be more dis-
appointed by the things you didn't do than by the
ones you did do. So throw off the bowlines. Sail
away from the safe harbor. Catch the trade winds
in your sails. Explore. Dream. Discover.*

—*MARK TWAIN (1835-1910)*

Chapter 1

April 1881

FOR THE FIRST TIME IN Evelyn Foster's very proper and correct sixteen years of life, she was about to do something horrendously and unspeakably naughty. And contrary to what one might think—that she was young and impulsive, and therefore experiencing a thrill from the wickedness—she was not the slightest bit thrilled. In fact, she would even go so far as to say she was vexed, irritated, and most decidedly angry, for she would never have entertained such a notion herself—that it might be "amusing" for her and her best friend Penelope to sneak into the boys' dormitory at Eton while everyone was at supper.

Perhaps the most distressing part of it all was that they were sneaking in because of *him*. Lord Martin Langdon, the Duke of Wentworth's younger brother, the mischievous boy who was always getting into trouble for wild antics—like engineering a teetering bucket of water over his precept's door, or sending a raft down the Thames fashioned with exploding fireworks, directly below Windsor Castle when the Queen herself was in residence.

On top of all that, Lord Martin was, at seventeen, already known to be a self-proclaimed womanizer. He was an objectionable, disreputable young man, and Evelyn knew it in the clearest realms of her intellect.

So why was she having any part of this? she asked herself for the hundredth time, shaking her head as she crossed a moonlit field with Penelope.

She was there because her beautiful blond friend fancied herself in love with the rascal and could not be talked out of it. And Evelyn could hardly sit home wondering what would transpire—because, though she hated to admit it, she had her own strange and confusing fascination with him.

"Hurry up, Evelyn," Penelope whispered, as they scuttled through the dark side streets toward the campus, dressed in boys' clothing they had borrowed from Penelope's younger brother. "We don't have much time, and I don't want to get caught on the way out."

"I'm coming." And I must be mad, Evelyn thought, feeling the chilly night air on her cheeks as she quickened her pace to keep up.

At that moment, Penelope began to jog, and they hurried across the street, keeping their heads down beneath the brims of their tweed caps. At long last, they reached the iron gate outside the chapel, and Penelope pushed it open. Evelyn winced at the piercing screech of the hinges. "Doesn't anyone own an oil can?"

"Don't worry yourself," Penelope said. "Follow me."

They crossed the tiny cemetery but stopped suddenly when a beagle barked at them from the other side of the fence.

Evelyn jumped with fright. "Goodness, what next?"

Penelope grabbed her arm and pulled her toward the back of the chapel. "Ignore him. We're almost there. I know a place where we can squeeze through the fence and get into the courtyard."

Evelyn was breathing hard now, not enjoying this at all. "I think we should turn around. We're going to get caught. And if my father finds out...."

Penelope didn't stop to discuss it. She merely spoke over her shoulder. "I've come all this way. I'm not turning back now. I want to see where he sleeps."

Evelyn halted on the gravel path. "Where he sleeps? Penny! I thought you were just going to slip the note under his door."

"Yes, unless I can get it open with one of my hairpins."

Unable to believe what she was hearing, Evelyn huffed in frustration. "You have gone positively mad."

Penelope stopped and turned, and though Evelyn couldn't see her friend's expression in the moonlight, she could hear the bright, beaming smile in her voice. "Yes, I have gone mad. Mad with *love*."

Evelyn felt a jolt of irritation.

Or was it jealousy?

No. Not that. She could not let herself entertain

such foolishness. She shook her head and stepped forward to make one more plea. "You know the stories about him, Penelope. He's not worth it. He will break your heart. If only you would listen to reason."

Penelope reached the back corner of the cemetery near the chapel wall and wrapped her hands around the bars. "That's your problem, Evelyn. You're always logical, when sometimes you just have to trust your heart. Break the rules and defy reason if you must."

Evelyn continued to stand on the path, watching Penelope squeeze through the fence. Defy reason? For what purpose? To have her heart crushed into pieces and trod upon like her mother's had been for as long as she could remember?

Penelope grunted as she continued. "And I don't understand why you can't see that he's wonderful, especially after what he did for you. You should think of him as your hero, Evelyn. He saved your life! How can you think badly of him?"

Evelyn recalled that day on the lake six years ago, when she had fallen through the ice, and he had pulled her to safety.

"We were children," she said with a shiver. "Of course I will always be grateful for what he did. He was my hero that day, but I cannot overlook the fact that he is no longer that boy. He has grown into a scoundrel, and everyone knows it. I do not see him with starry eyes like you do."

What would be the point? She was an awkward, unattractive girl with spectacles who was too brainy for her own good and possessed an unconventional passion for science and physics. She was skinny as a

bean pole, with dull brown hair and a nose that was
simply too long. Never in a thousand years could she
attract the attention of a boy like Martin, and the few
times she had encountered him in town whenever she
and her mother were visiting Penelope's family, he
didn't even seem to know who she was or remember
that he had once saved her life—even after Penelope
introduced them and told him her name. He'd been
too distracted by his flirtations with Penelope. Playful, blond, pretty, bouncy Penelope.

Evelyn doubted he even remembered that harrow-
ing day on the lake. He had never mentioned it or
revealed the smallest hint of recognition.

Penelope sounded irritable all of a sudden. "He is
not a scoundrel, and I wish you would stop saying
that, because I love him." She turned, preparing to
climb down into the courtyard. "Look, you don't
have to come if you don't want to. You can wait here.
I will be faster on my own anyway."

Evelyn paused a moment, considering it. She could
wait there, couldn't she? She could avoid watching
her beautiful friend wallow in the romance of her first
love affair, sighing and boasting about how much her
handsome prince loved her in return and how happy
they were.

Blast it, why did Penelope have to choose *him* to
chase after? Couldn't she have picked someone else?
Why Lord Martin?

Evelyn watched her friend climb down the wall
and disappear from view, then heard her shoes hit the
ground on the courtyard below.

"Are you coming or not?" Penelope whispered

heatedly.

Evelyn felt the knot in her belly tighten and knew she could not possibly stay behind. She had to go because Martin was in a strange way *hers,* even if she knew she could never have him.

"All right, I'm coming," she said grudgingly, marching to the fence.

A few minutes later, Evelyn and Penelope were standing on the grass outside Martin's dormitory, under Penelope's cousin's open window on the ground floor.

"Hoist me up," she said, raising a booted foot.

Evelyn huffed with frustration and bent forward to form a stirrup with her hands, a maneuver they were adept at, as they had been climbing the same rocky outcropping behind Penelope's house for years as a shortcut to town.

An instant later, Penelope was climbing into Gregory's room, then turning and offering her hands out the window. "There's no one here. Take hold."

Evelyn locked wrists with Penelope and climbed the wall. It was another maneuver they knew well, and it was unimaginably easier without corsets. Though climbing through the window itself held some challenges.

As soon as she was safely inside, Evelyn, who was an only child, wiped her hands on her breeches and glanced around. The room was very plain, with dark blue bed linens and a single framed picture on the wall. "I have never seen a boy's room before."

Penelope, who had four brothers, merely shrugged. "Let's go. Lord Martin's room is only three doors down, but we need to hurry. I doubt we'll have much more than fifteen minutes before a few of them start coming back."

"Do you have the note?" Evelyn asked, focusing on the practicalities in order to distract herself from the sheer panic she was feeling, having snuck into a boy's dormitory. Not to mention that it was Martin's.

Penelope tapped her jacket pocket. "Right here."

Evelyn had read the note earlier. It was full of flowery, romantic outpourings of love. With Martin's reputation with the girls, he would probably read it and head for the Highlands. Evelyn tried to warn Penelope about that, but she just wouldn't listen. She wouldn't listen to anything Evelyn said.

They opened the door a crack and peered into the quiet corridor. Ascertaining there was no one about, they tiptoed down the hall to Martin's door.

"This is it," Penelope whispered, her eyes bright. "This is where he lays his beautiful head each night. What do you think he dreams about? Me? Could I dare to hope? He did tell me I was the prettiest girl in Windsor. Remember?"

Evelyn stared speechless at Penelope, wondering if this could possibly get any worse. "All right, we're here. Slip the note under the door, and let's go before we get caught."

Penelope nodded and reached into her pocket but paused before she bent to slip it under. Her eyes shifted to the doorknob.

No, Penelope, don't....

But Evelyn didn't say those words because she knew it would make no difference. Penelope was desperate for Martin in every way, and she was not going to leave without attempting to see his bed, and heaven help them, sniff his pillow.

"I just want one little glimpse," Penelope whispered, wrapping her hand around the knob.

"Please, make it quick." Evelyn glanced over her shoulder to ensure no one was coming, then struggled with her confusing mix of emotions—the anger toward Penelope for dragging her into this and the strange exhilaration flooding her veins for what they were about to see. Lord Martin's bed. She supposed she should admit that to herself. She wanted to see it, quite shamefully in fact. So she prepared herself to follow her friend inside.

Penelope lifted a finger to say *"shh,"* then slowly turned the knob. Thankfully, the door didn't creak, and they were very quiet as they tiptoed into the dark room. But when the light from the corridor spilled across the floor, there was a sudden movement to the left. The bed linens flipped over, the mattress squeaked and bounced, and Evelyn and Penelope found themselves gaping with open mouths at a young man's naked chest—Martin's chest!—as he sat upright and squinted into the light.

"Bloody hell," he said, holding up a hand to shade his eyes.

Neither Evelyn nor Penelope could speak. Nor could Evelyn tear her eyes away from that bare, muscled chest and his tousled black hair as he ran a hand through it in exasperation. She was stunned, paralyzed by the shocking display of skin before her eyes.

He was so handsome, she couldn't breathe.

Her mental prowess returned however, when someone else's head popped up from under the covers—a
young woman's head. Her frizzy red hair was matted
and tangled, and she was clutching the covers up to
her neck.

Evelyn could see her naked arms and shoulders and
knew enough about sin and wickedness to understand
what monkey business they'd been up to. She felt suddenly nauseous.

"Blimey, don't you know how to knock?" the girl in
the bed shouted, then she reached behind her head
and biffed a pillow, knocking over a half-empty bottle of rum, which smashed on the floor. The pillow
hit Penelope square in the face, knocking her cap off.
"Get out, ya' bloomin' idiots!"

Penelope's wavy hair came loose from the pins and
fell down upon her shoulders.

Martin sat up straighter. "You're girls."

He looked carefully at Penelope. "I know you.
What's your name again?"

She let out a sob and fled from the room. Evelyn
quickly followed, shutting the door behind her. She
did not allow herself to think about what she had just
witnessed.

Another door opened around the corner, down the
hall, and fast footsteps approached. She bolted in the
other direction, following Penelope into her cousin's
room. Penelope was already scrambling out the window, sobbing uncontrollably.

Evelyn darted to the window. "Be quiet, Penny!
Someone heard us! We have to get out of here!"

She tossed herself out and hit the ground beside

Penelope, then took off in a sprint, grabbing her friend's arm to drag her faster across the dark field, but Penelope was crying so hard, she could barely keep up.

"Don't think!" Evelyn said, without looking back. "Just run as fast as you can!"

They scrambled down a drainage ditch at the edge of the field, then back up the other side to reach the shelter of some buildings. Evelyn looked back at the dormitory and saw lights illuminating the windows. There seemed to be frantic activity in the building.

No doubt, Martin had been caught with the girl in his bed and probably wouldn't be flirting with Penelope any time in the near future. Not after this. He would be furious with her, to say the least.

A few minutes later, they were free of the campus lights and making their way to Penelope's house, walking quickly along the river.

Stopping to catch her breath, Evelyn checked over her shoulder and was panting when she spoke. "I think we're safe now. Let's just hope Lord Martin doesn't tell anyone it was us."

Penelope stopped and sank to her knees on the grass. "Oh, Evelyn! Did you see her? How *could* he?"

Evelyn swallowed hard over her own shock and disbelief, and the strange, intense twinge of possessiveness she was feeling. Who was that girl and what precisely had she been doing to him under the covers...? Evelyn didn't really want to know. It made her sick just to think about it. Sick!

She knelt beside her friend. "I'm so sorry, Penny."

Penelope continued to weep inconsolably, while

Evelyn fought to bury her own distress and pat the dirt down hard on top of it. She would not let herself give in to the idea that she was hurt by any of this. What just happened was no surprise. She knew what kind of boy he was and she had warned Penelope about it beforehand. Martin was wild and dangerous. He was not worthy of anyone's adulation.

She laid a comforting hand on Penelope's shoulder.

"You tried to tell me," Penelope sobbed, "but I wouldn't listen. I just wouldn't hear it, but you were right all along. He *is* a scoundrel. A despicable, vile, loathsome cad! I hate him!"

She broke into another fit of sobs.

"You'll be all right," Evelyn said gently. "You'll get over this."

"Will I? How? I loved him, Evelyn! Loved him! He was the only man in the world for me, and now I'll be brokenhearted for the rest of my life! Oh, I don't want to live! I should drown myself in the river tonight! Then maybe he'll regret what he did to me."

"You're not going to drown yourself," Evelyn said firmly. "He's not worth it."

Penelope hiccuped. "You've said that before, but you don't understand, Evelyn. You don't know what it feels like to be madly in love! You're far too sensible. You have no idea what I am going through!"

Evelyn gazed intently into her friend's weepy eyes, saw the unabashed despair in them, and wanted to shout back at her with fury and inform her that yes, she did understand. More than Penelope could ever know.

But she did not shout those words because she

knew that Penelope was right on one level. Evelyn
was indeed sensible. Too sensible to ignore her firm
resolve and allow herself to surrender completely to
her emotions. And thank God for that. After tonight,
she would work even harder to be prudent, because
she could never again put herself in the path of such
peril. She did not want to end up like Penelope,
weeping her heart out over a rake like Martin who
didn't deserve her tears.

"No one could possibly know how devastated I
am," Penelope sobbed. "He doesn't love me! Oh, why
didn't he love me? What's wrong with me?"

Evelyn shook her head. "Nothing's wrong with
you. You're a beautiful girl, and someone else will
sweep you off your feet again before you know it."

"No, I will never love again. I'll enter a convent."

Evelyn sighed and stood up, helping Penelope to her
feet. "Come on, let's get you home. You'll feel better
after a good night's sleep."

"I will never feel better. My life is over."

But Evelyn knew her friend. She would get over
this, and she would fall in love again, too, probably
with the very next young man who flattered her. That
was Penelope. She was openly passionate, she enjoyed
attention, and the young men certainly enjoyed giving it to her.

Thankfully, Penelope found the strength to stand
and walk, and Evelyn put an arm around her to lead
her home.

Chapter 2

*D*URING THE WEEK THAT FOLLOWED, Evelyn and Penelope waited anxiously for a shrill whistle to blow in their direction or for some official representative of the school to demand an appointment with their parents. But no such whistle blew, nor did they hear a word about a bedroom scandal at Eton. Though they supposed such scandalous happenings were quietly swept under the school carpets, especially when they involved the younger brother of a duke.

Hence, they spent the week doing nothing out of the ordinary, wandering in and out of local shops with their mothers, who had been friends since childhood. They sipped tea and ate scones in Penelope's garden, read and went for leisurely walks along the riverbank before dinner.

Thankfully Penelope's tears flowed less dramatically as the week pressed on, and by the end of it, she was regarding Lord Martin Langdon as the most despicable boy in Windsor, claiming she had no idea how *any* girl could consider him handsome, for his hair was always in disarray, and he was a rake of the highest order, destined for failure in every regard, not to mention that he had a most unattractive smile.

Evelyn knew very well that his smile was by far his best feature, nothing short of disarming to any female within a ten-yard radius, but naturally she did not argue the point with Penelope. She instead agreed wholeheartedly and assured her friend that she was quite right on every front. It seemed as if the whole scandalous affair had indeed blown over.

At the end of the week, however, when it came time for Evelyn and her mother to go home, she discovered with some alarm that the storm had not passed at all—for there she was, standing on the platform at the train station, barely five feet from Lord Martin Langdon himself.

Ten days had passed since she had seen him in his bed, bare chested and cursing at her, having just sat up beside a naked girl. Evelyn bit down on her lower lip and swallowed with difficulty.

"The train is late as usual," her mother said, checking the timepiece on her chatelaine and taking a step forward to peer down the tracks. "Perhaps we should have had your father send the coach."

Evelyn could not reply. She was too unnerved by the presence of Lord Martin not far from where she stood. Did he even know she was one of the intruders that night? Good heavens, was he staring at her? Or was she imagining it because she was completely obsessed with being caught?

She continued to stand on the platform, looking straight ahead while her heart hammered noisily in her chest, until she couldn't take the stress of it any longer. She had to know if he was looking at her, so she discreetly turned her eyes in his direction.

To her utter horror, he *was* staring at her, squinting irritably with pure venom in his eyes.

Evelyn sucked in a quick breath and looked the other way. Heaven help her, he *did* know.

"This is becoming ridiculous," her mother said, checking her timepiece again. "Stay here with the bags, dear. I'm going to ask the guard how much longer it will be."

Before Evelyn could voice a protest, her mother headed back into the station, leaving her completely alone on the platform.

Well, not completely alone. She was standing next to Lord Martin.

Evelyn wet her lips. Her heart raced madly as she struggled to act casual. Could he see her chest heaving?

Then he did the unthinkable. He spoke.

"Well, well, well," he slowly said, rocking back on his heels. "If it isn't Miss Evelyn Foster."

She felt her eyebrows fly up in shock. She hadn't thought he'd known her name—because he never seemed to remember it—and he had certainly never addressed her before or acknowledged an acquaintance, much less given her the slightest notion that he even knew she existed.

"Do you have any idea what havoc you caused?" he asked, glancing over his shoulder toward the station door, watching for her mother.

Evelyn fought to hide her unease and somehow managed to return his dry but heated gaze. "Havoc *I* caused? It is my fault, is it, that you had a woman in your bed? Pardon me, but I beg to differ."

She could hardly believe she was engaging in such an improper conversation. And with Lord Martin, no less.

His blue eyes—with their impossibly long, black lashes—narrowed. "It's your fault I was *caught,* Miss Foster."

All at once, the anxiety she was feeling turned to anger, because she hadn't wanted to be sneaking into his dormitory in the first place, and everything else was his fault for being such a habitual flirt and leading Penelope Steeves to believe he was in love with her!

Evelyn couldn't contain herself. With all her many frustrations boiling up to the surface, she faced Lord Martin and narrowed her eyes from under her thick spectacles. "I do beg your pardon, sir, but when a gentleman like you behaves inappropriately—leading an impressionable young lady to believe there is some genuine affection between you—that gentleman must accept the consequences of his actions."

Martin gazed at her for a long, heated moment, then appeared almost amused, but not quite, for there was a perceptible bitterness about him when he scoffed.

"I beg *your* pardon, Miss Foster, but your friend has a head on her shoulders that is in working order, does she not? You and she both should have known it was unwise to sneak into a male dormitory, where women are strictly prohibited."

Evelyn glared at him. "And what of the woman in your bed, sir? Where was *her* head?"

His mouth curled up in a patronizing grin. *"I don't think you'd want to know."*

Evelyn sucked in a breath. She didn't know what he was implying exactly, but she was quite sure it was beyond scandalous.

But heaven forbid he should think her frazzled by the remark, so she raised her chin, squared her shoulders, and pretended she was unruffled. Though she had no idea what to say.

Martin clenched his jaw and faced forward again, evidently also at a loss for words.

They stood in silence for a few seconds, while Evelyn wallowed in her anger, for what right did he have to blame her for *his* indiscretion? He'd had a woman and a bottle of rum in his room during supper hour!

Evelyn checked over her shoulder to see if her mother would soon be returning, but she was still inside the station, chatting leisurely with a woman in a large hat.

As the seconds ticked by, the tension on the platform seemed to grow heavier than lead. She felt it throbbing all around her, and soon found herself breaking the silence again and asking a question rather hesitantly. "What havoc was there, exactly, after you were caught?"

She shouldn't have asked it, but she wanted to know if he had revealed her and Penelope's involvement. Because heaven forbid her father should get wind of it. She was enough of a nuisance to him as it was.

Lord Martin looked at her and spoke with scorn.

"I had to explain myself to the headmaster, who was unimpressed with me, to say the least, but that is nothing new. Today I am officially suspended from school and will be forced to go and stay with my aunt in Exeter, and every day she will remind me that I am doomed to a life of complete and utter failure." He squinted contemptuously down the tracks. "I will be counting the days until the school will take me back. *If* they take me back."

"You're not going home?" Evelyn asked. "To your brother? The duke?"

Lord Martin gave her a snide look and shook his head. "My brother prefers to let other people put me on the straight and narrow."

Evelyn felt a stab of pity for him suddenly, for he appeared without support of any kind, and she had heard some rumors about his home, Wentworth Castle, being a rather dark and dismal place. But then she reminded herself that he had brought all this on himself. He made his own decisions to misbehave.

"Maybe you're the one who needs to put yourself on the straight and narrow," she told him flatly.

Lord Martin grimaced, as if he couldn't believe his ears. "You are very self-righteous, aren't you, Miss Foster?"

"And you, sir, are very rude." She had never been so outspoken in her life.

He looked in the other direction, shaking his head dismissively, as if Evelyn were a complete dunderhead who knew nothing about the ways of the world.

She squeezed her reticule. It always hurt to feel completely unappealing to young men, to say nothing of how it felt when the young man in question was Lord Martin. There were moments when she remembered how grateful she had been to him six years ago when he pulled her out of the freezing water and onto the ice. He had been only eleven years old, and she had thought him the greatest hero in the world. But now....

He was hardly a hero today. He was bitter and rebellious and didn't seem to care about anything but his own selfish and irresponsible pleasures. He had sunk very low, and it was, in a word, heartbreaking to see the hero of her childhood dreams waste the courage and gallantry she had seen in him that day on the lake.

He turned to her for one final word. "Don't worry, Miss Foster, I didn't expose you or your friend. I told the headmaster I had no idea who you were, and he seemed to believe me. He thinks he's looking for a couple of boys."

Evelyn squeezed her reticule in her hands again and felt rather sheepish all of a sudden. "Well, I suppose I should thank you for that, at least."

He spoke with a cool reserve. "No need."

Just then, Evelyn heard her mother's heels clicking across the platform. "We shouldn't have to wait much longer," she said, then pointed down the tracks. "Oh look, here it comes now."

Evelyn leaned forward to see the steam train approaching from a distance. Martin did not look her way again. He bent and picked up his bag, then strolled in the other direction.

A short time later, they boarded the first-class carriages, of which there were two, thankfully. Evelyn was not surprised when Martin chose the one behind hers.

As soon as they were seated, her mother leaned close and said, "Wasn't that Lord Martin Langdon, the Duke of Wentworth's younger brother?"

Evelyn gazed out the window and tried to sound blasé. "Was it? I didn't notice."

"You didn't notice, Evelyn?" her mother replied. "Surely you recognized him. He saved your life once, darling."

Evelyn suspected her mother could see straight through her mask of indifference, but she retained it, nonetheless. "Well, if it was him, he didn't recognize me. It was a long time ago. I doubt he even remembers it."

"Honestly, Evelyn. How could anyone forget pulling a little girl out of a frozen lake?"

Evelyn shrugged. "Well, maybe he does remember it. He just doesn't know it was *me*."

And something about that made her feel strangely lonesome.

Meanwhile, in the first-class carriage directly behind Evelyn's, Martin closed his eyes and tipped his head back on the upholstered seat, wondering if that fall through the ice years ago was the reason Miss Foster had ice water in her veins.

Honestly, she was the most uptight, frosty, prudish girl he had ever met, always acting as if she didn't know him, when she must remember that he had saved her life. How could she forget? Bloody hell, he hated the way she always looked down her nose at him, if she even bothered to meet his gaze at all. It didn't matter what he said or did, she never said hello to him or gave him the slightest smile.

Not that it mattered, he told himself. Miss Foster could go strolling on a dozen more frozen lakes with thin ice if she was so inclined. He certainly wouldn't try to stop her, because thanks to her and her foolish friend—what was her name? Penelope something?—he was going to have to spend the rest of the month bored out of his skull in Exeter, with an aunt who would constantly remind him that he was doomed to a life of failure.

Chapter 3

Ten years later

 $\mathcal{W}$ ITH THE BRIGHT, SUMMER SUNSHINE at his
back and a fresh wind in his face, Lord Martin Langdon stood at the helm on the sloping deck of
his champion racing yacht, *Orpheus.* He glanced up at
the grand sweep of the mainsail and felt the incompa-
rable exhilaration of the wheel tugging in his hands. A
salty spray flew upward from the windward rails, and
Orpheus's bow plunged forward with a thunderous roar
into the waves.

"Ready to tack!" he called out to his crew, feeling
grateful for this welcome sense of purpose at the helm
and the rare satisfaction that came from knowing he
was in absolute control. He felt confident, at ease, and
his blood was racing with anticipation for the coming
week.

The crew moved into position, and he turned the

wheel hard over to leeward and ducked as the boom swung across. "Coming about! Release the jib!"

He held the wheel hard over until they were sailing on the edge of the wind again, then glanced up to check the trim of the sails on the new tack. He settled in on a close-hauled course, smiling at the speed of the maneuver.

"Well done!" he shouted with a smile. "The trophy will be ours again by the end of the week." The men cheered. "Oh, but wait," he added with a warning tone. "Do not be too pleased with yourselves just yet, gentlemen. Our greatest challenge is still ahead of us—and that is to navigate safely through the unfathomable sea of champagne corks that will be before us by nightfall."

His crew—four of the best yachtsmen in England— laughed and shoved each other around.

Though he himself did not share in their laughter, Martin relished the sound of theirs, then closed his eyes for a moment, basking in all the tremendous power of the *Orpheus*'s streamlined hull and the overwhelming might of the canvas straining aloft. She was superior to all the other English racing yachts in form and workmanship, and she had set the fashion for the new decade. And because of her, Martin, who had contributed to the genius behind her design, had become the famed racing champion of Britain for two years running.

This week, he would make it three. He was determined.

"There's the *Britannia!*" his first mate shouted, as they sliced through the choppy waters, heading for

Cowes on the Isle of Wight.

Martin had come early to study the winds and currents and commit everything to memory. Apparently, the Prince of Wales had come early as well, most likely to show off his impressive new cutter, which he had commissioned just this year.

"She's a beauty," he replied.

Martin's first mate and closest friend, Lord Spencer Fleming, stepped past the windward shrouds and came to stand at Martin's side. He pointed toward the royal mansion on the hill.

"How much shall we wager Her Majesty is sitting on the terrace of Osborne House this very minute with a telescope and a frown, watching all the attractive young ladies stepping on and off her son's yacht?"

Martin glanced up at the house. "I'll wager you wish you had a telescope to watch them, too."

"Must you rub salt in the wound?" Spence asked.

"What in the blazes do you mean?"

"I mean that as soon as you set foot on the Royal Yacht Squadron landing stage, every young lady in Cowes will be flocking to your side, and I might as well be a codfish."

Martin chuckled, hoping that would indeed be the case, because he had been feeling on edge lately and desired the particular distractions that only a week in Cowes could provide. The kinds of distractions that made him laugh and smile and forget certain less agreeable aspects of his life.

"And I'll be greeting them with open arms," he assured his first mate, feeling more than certain that a few pretty ladies would cure everything. For the duration of the week anyway, which was all he could ask for.

He turned his head slightly to feel a shift in the wind, noted the closing distance to the Squadron, and knew it was time to decrease speed. Anticipation coursed through him for all the pleasures and amusements about to come his way at last, and for the great sense of accomplishment he would feel when he crossed the finish line on race day. God knew he sorely needed it.

"Let's drop the jib," he said.

"Right then." Spence relayed the message to the crew, and Martin kept the boat steady while the men lowered the sail.

He held their course, sailing toward Cowes, where the waters were calmer and dotted with a colorful fleet of yachts, all here not only for the race, but for the garden parties and balls and champagne, and the delicious gossip exchanged on the exclusive back lawn of the Royal Yacht Squadron. For Cowes week was, without question, one of the most fashionable social occasions of the year, and he was more than ready to settle in and have a devil of a good time.

Moments before the *Orpheus* changed tack near the *Britannia,* Evelyn Wheaton—the wealthiest widow in England after inheriting her father's millions—stood on the public parade just below the Royal Yacht Squadron, gazing across the Solent and enjoying the salty fragrance of the sea. Her skirts whipped noisily in the brisk wind, and she had to hold on to her hat to keep it from flying off.

Beside her stood Henry Kipper, Lord Radley, a baron who had been a social mentor to her father—God rest his soul. Lord Radley was one of the oldest members of the exclusive yacht club and took great pleasure in that fact. Today, he wore a white sailor's hat, white flannel trousers, the traditional blue jacket of the yachting fraternity, and he carried a shiny black walking stick.

"I believe that might be the *Orpheus* on her way in," he said, raising an out-of-fashion quizzing glass to his eyes and squinting into the distance.

Evelyn gazed across the water and spotted the champion sloop skimming toward the royal *Britannia* at an alarming speed.

Of course, she was not surprised. She knew the identity of the skipper. Who didn't? He was the country's most celebrated sportsman. He was charming in public, a hero to the children, and he set the standard for excellence among sailors and shipwrights all over the world. On top of that, the more voracious gossips in London enjoyed delicious tittle-tattle about him behind closed doors: They said the only thing their champion racer liked better than a fast boat was a fast woman.

Evelyn knew that better than anyone, didn't she? She had seen it firsthand ten years ago. She had witnessed the evidence in the flesh, and she also knew that he was not *always* the smiling charmer he pretended to be.

All at once, a flock of butterflies invaded her belly. She hadn't seen Lord Martin in a very long time, and it was unsettling, to say the least, to think that she might actually speak to him during Cowes Week.

Would he remember her? Probably not, thank goodness. She didn't want him to. She wouldn't know what to say. It would be very awkward, and she would feel so foolish for harboring that strange infatuation all those years ago. She did not even want to remember their acquaintance, if one could call it that.

Still, she hadn't felt butterflies like these in years, and the sensation was most unnerving. She wished they would stop.

"Does he not worry he might cause a mishap?" she asked with concern as the *Orpheus* heeled over at an impossible angle. "There are hundreds of boats in his path."

Lord Radley lowered his quizzing glass and smirked. "I don't suppose that young man worries about much of anything. That's his third racing yacht after all."

Two young children in white sailor suits and hats went dashing by, their mother following quickly behind, pushing a baby in a pram. Evelyn gazed longingly at the pram for a few seconds, then forced herself to return her attention to the exploits on the water.

"What happened to the first two?" she asked, locating the *Orpheus*. Her heart skipped a beat as the keelboat changed direction again, narrowly missing another yacht.

Oh, he had not changed. Not one bit.

Lord Radley raised his quizzing glass again. "Wrecked them both, I daresay. Ran the first one aground after a month and the next a year later. Quite a shame, really. They were magnificent boats, though perhaps a little too slow for his taste. But at least he seems to have learned something. He exercises more caution now that he's got a champion yacht."

Evelyn pursed her lips and shook her head. Caution, indeed.

"Some say he's been spoiled by his wealthy brother," Lord Radley said. "The duke replaced both yachts without blinking an eye, almost immediately after Lord Martin wrecked them."

By the looks of things, he'll have to replace this one before long, too, Evelyn thought.

"Shall we walk up to the lawn?" Lord Radley suggested, offering his arm. "We shall indulge ourselves in the puff pastries and ask which ladies are having tea on Bertie's yacht today and then we shall speculate about their manners and morals like a couple of carrion crows."

Evelyn laughed, thankful that the butterflies in her belly had finally stopped fluttering. "Lord Radley, you are positively wicked," she said, knowing, of course, that he jested.

"And perhaps we shall see if my nephew has arrived yet," he added. "I shall be most pleased to introduce you."

It was the second time that afternoon her escort had mentioned his nephew George, who had just inherited his title as Earl Breckinridge. He was here to sail his yacht in the race as well, and from what Evelyn had heard, the earl had a spotless reputation and was known to be a gracious and courteous gentleman—quite the opposite of Lord Martin Langdon.

Evelyn suspected Lord Radley would be pleased to see a match between her and his nephew. He did, after all, consider himself her unofficial guardian, and had acted as such ever since her father passed away a year ago, six years after Evelyn lost her mother. Lord Radley wished to see her safely and happily married again, this time with children, because she was now completely alone in the world.

She had indeed been very lonely since her mother's passing. She'd even been lonely during her brief marriage to the vicar. Especially then, she supposed, for she had married him only to remove herself from her father's home, so as not to burden him with her undesirable presence any longer. She still remembered the day he told her the vicar had asked for her hand in marriage....

"You had better accept," he said in his cool, stern voice, without even bothering to lift his gaze from the papers on his desk, "because you won't get another offer. Not with your looks. Now get out of here. I'm busy."

Of course, when it came to Lord Radley and his nephew, the proposed alliance had little to do with her looks. There was the more important matter of her inheritance, which made her an attractive prize for any man, and she was not blind to the fact that Lord Radley would derive great pleasure from seeing it settled upon his nephew. She was not offended by this, mind you. Quite to the contrary, she was thankful for it, for at twenty-six, she was not as young as the other ladies who were in Cowes seeking husbands. And she was completely aware of the fact that she had never been pretty.

She realized with rather perverse amusement that

no one could ever accuse her of not being a realist. How could she be anything but? She had always gotten the cold, hard truth from her father, who would have preferred she'd never been born.

Filling her lungs with the fresh, salty sea air, she decided to dispense with those memories and anything that resembled a complaint. She was thrilled to be here for this exciting week at Cowes. Absolutely thrilled. She wanted to marry again because she desired the life she never knew—one filled with children and the laughter they would bring into a home of her own. She had been in mourning for the past two years, starting with her husband's death and followed immediately thereafter by her father's, and before that, she had already been living without laughter in her life, simply keeping quiet. It was well past time for a change.

In that regard, she was glad she had her wealth to attract a husband. At least she had *something,* and she would not be reluctant to use it to find a husband she could love and respect.

Thus, she linked her arm through Lord Radley's and accompanied him up the drive to the back lawn of the yacht club, where there was sure to be much laughter and conversation, and perhaps even a potential fiancé among the crowd.

Where Love Begins – Available Now

Books by
Julianne MacLean

HISTORICAL ROMANCE

The American Heiress Trilogy:
To Marry the Duke
Falling for the Marquess
In Love with the Viscount

Can This Be Love Trilogy
(American Heiress Spinoff):
Love According to Lily
To Annabelle, With Love
Where Love Begins

Love at Pembroke Palace Series:
In My Wildest Fantasies
The Mistress Diaries
When a Stranger Loves Me
Married By Midnight
A Kiss Before the Wedding–
A Pembroke Palace Short Story
Seduced at Sunset

The Highlander Series:
Captured by the Highlander
Claimed by the Highlander
Seduced by the Highlander
The Rebel – A Highland Short Story
Return of the Highlander
Taken by the Highlander

ABOUT THE AUTHOR

Julianne MacLean is a *USA Today* bestselling author of more than thirty novels, including the contemporary women's fiction *Color of Heaven Series*. Readers have described her books as "breathtaking," "soulful" and "uplifting." MacLean is a four-time Romance Writers of America RITA® finalist and has won numerous awards, including the *Booksellers' Best Award* and a *Reviewers' Choice Award* from *Romantic Times*. Her novels have sold millions of copies worldwide and have been published in over a dozen languages.

MacLean has a degree in English literature from the University of King's College in Halifax, Nova Scotia, and a degree in business administration from Acadia University in Wolfville, Nova Scotia. She loves to travel and has lived in New Zealand, Canada, and England. MacLean currently resides on the east coast of Canada in a lakeside home with her husband, daughter, and mother. She invites readers to visit her website for more information about her books and writing life, and to subscribe to her mailing list for all the latest news: www.JulianneMacLean.com